A CATERED CHRISTMAS COOKIE EXCHANGE

Books by Isis Crawford

A CATERED MURDER

A CATERED WEDDING

A CATERED CHRISTMAS

A CATERED VALENTINE'S DAY

A CATERED HALLOWEEN

A CATERED BIRTHDAY PARTY

A CATERED THANKSGIVING

A CATERED ST. PATRICK'S DAY

A CATERED CHRISTMAS COOKIE EXCHANGE

Published by Kensington Publishing Corporation

A Mystery with Recipes

A CATERED CHRISTMAS COOKIE EXCHANGE

ISIS CRAWFORD

KENSINGTON BOOKS
www.kensingtonbooks.com

Longely is an imaginary community, as are all its inhabitants. Any resemblance to people either living or dead is pure coincidence.

KENSINGTON BOOKS are published by

Kensington Publishing Corp.
119 West 40th Street
New York, NY 10018

All Kensington titles, imprints and distributed lines are available at special quantity discounts for bulk purchases for sales promotion, premiums, fund-raising, educational or institutional use. Special book excerpts or customized printings can also be created to fit specific needs. For details, write or phone the office of the Kensington Special Sales Manager. Kensington Publishing Corp., 119 West 40th Street, New York, NY 10018. Attn. Special Sales Department. Phone: 1-800-221-2647.

Kensington and the K logo Reg. U.S. Pat. & TM Off.

Library of Congress Control Number: 2013940651

ISBN-13: 978-0-7582-7489-2
ISBN-10: 0-7582-7489-0
First Kensington Hardcover Printing: November 2013

eISBN-13: 978-0-7582-9157-8
eISBN-10: 0-7582-9157-4
First Kensington Electronic Edition: November 2013

10 9 8 7 6 5 4 3 2 1

Printed in the United States of America

*For Anna Jae, Mila, and Cora,
my delights*

Acknowledgments

I'd like to thank Lexi Baker for her proofreading skills and Betsy Shue for her good humor and organizational abilities.

Prologue

Millie Piedmont carefully transferred the batch of cookies she'd just made from the cooling rack to one of the wax paper–lined square metal cookie tins lined up on the counter. She always used this tin to take her cookies to the Christmas Cookie Exchange Club. She noted with satisfaction that the tin was still pristine. She'd gotten it almost fifty years ago when she was twenty-two, and it looked the same now as it did then. Well, not completely—there *were* a few nicks and scratches, but given the amount of time she was talking about, it looked pretty darn good, if she did say so herself.

Before closing the lid, Millie stood there and admired her creations. The cookies were beautiful and tasted even better. She was thrilled. She was more than thrilled. She was elated. She had spent weeks perfecting the recipe. She just knew she was going to win the *Baking for Life* contest with Millie's Majestic Meltaways. She couldn't believe the TV show was coming to Longely. Longely!

She couldn't have imagined she was going to be on TV. She couldn't have imagined she was going to meet Carl Baxter. He was so cute, with those dimples, and the way he had of calling everyone "dear," and the cowlick that stood up on the back of his head. Just the thought of seeing him up close and personal made her blush. And she could hardly wait to watch Bernie's and Libby's faces when they tasted the Meltaways and tried to guess the secret ingredient. Millie smiled as she imagined the expressions on the faces of the other Christmas Cookie Exchange Club members when the winner was announced and it was her. Alma would pitch a fit, Sheila would make her sour pickle face, and Lillian would claim she was coming down with a migraine and would have to leave immediately.

Millie laughed out loud with delight as she imagined the resulting hullabaloo. But it was about time she was officially recognized as the best baker in Longely—long past time—because she was. There was no doubt about *that.* Ask anyone. In fact, she'd go further. She was one of the best bakers in all of Westchester County. No. Why be modest? She *was* the best. And now that fact was going to be recognized on national TV.

After all, Famous Amos had his day, so why shouldn't she have hers? Better late than never was what she said. So what if she was eighty-two? Her age might even work to her advantage once she had done a little freshening up. Look at Betty White. She was certainly doing pretty well and she was older than that.

Millie decided that maybe she'd get the bags under her eyes removed, along with some of the flab under her jaw, which she could do if she had the money. And then she'd put the rest of the money in the bank, except for about ten thousand. She'd use that to buy her niece Amber a car—a nice used car. Heaven only knew, Amber deserved it, even if she did get herself up in those strange outfits she insisted on wearing. But Millie was willing to overlook that, because she was the only one of all her relatives who was nice to her.

Yes, indeedy. It was going to be a very good week. Millie was sure of it. She tested the lid to make certain it was on securely, then put the tin with the Millie's Majestic Meltaways—MMMs, for short—on top of the tin with her cashew nut bars, which were also wonderful. They always disappeared immediately at any social gathering she took them to. Whenever people tasted them, they begged for the recipe, and she always gave it to them, with a few minor omissions.

That was because she didn't want anyone making them while she was still alive. That wasn't unreasonable, was it? Who knew? She might have to sell them to support herself someday. And speaking of keeping body and soul together, she just hoped she'd get to the run-through. She'd already told Amber she was nervous about getting there in one piece. She'd hoped her niece would take the hint and offer to drive her there. Unfortunately, Amber was holding down the fort at A Little Taste of Heaven while Bernie and Libby were helping set things up for the TV show at the Longely Community Center.

"You should have called me sooner," Amber had chided when Millie had broached the subject. "Maybe I could have worked something out."

And Millie would have if she'd gotten the call earlier instead of three hours ago. She told herself she was being silly, but the truth was the call had made her angry—furious, really—when she'd gotten it. It was only after she'd hung up that she'd gotten the heebie-jeebies.

The caller had tried to disguise her voice, but Millie had known who she was immediately. She should have given Millie more credit than that! How stupid did she think Millie was? And Millie had told her so in no certain terms, which was when she'd hung up. But Millie had called her back and given her another piece of her mind anyway. Pretending that she didn't know what Millie was talking about! Really. Millie sniffed at the idea. Well, she'd show her a thing or two. Yes she would. Especially when she won the contest. If she thought she could discourage her and deprive her of her rightful due, she had another think coming.

Millie tapped her fingers on the table while she replayed the conversation in her mind. Maybe she *should* have told Amber about the phone call. No. She'd been right not to. She didn't want Amber to worry. She also didn't want Amber to think she was just some crazy old lady imagining things, which she wasn't. She was as sharp now as she had been at eighteen. It's just that the conversation was improbable if considered from the outside—especially if you were Amber's age.

The problem was that Amber was too young to understand the lengths to which some people would go to get what they wanted. Amber thought she was sophisticated and wise in the ways of the world just because she dyed her hair those funny colors, but the truth of the matter was that she knew very little and could imagine even less. Millie looked at the clock on the kitchen wall. Time to get going. She went to the hall to get her coat. On the way, Millie passed the hall mirror and stopped to study her reflection.

Even if she said so herself, she had to admit that despite the sag under her chin and the bags under her eyes, she didn't look half bad. For openers, her hair looked good— she'd just had it cut and colored yesterday. Unlike Pearl, she saw no reason to be gray if you didn't have to be. And she was wearing her good black, flared knit skirt, the one that took ten pounds off her hips and thighs, and her paisley print blouse, which she'd gotten at Neiman Marcus when she'd been in Dallas for her cousin's wedding ten years ago. You buy good and it stays good. That was the trick with shopping, Millie thought as the phone rang.

"Yes, I'm on my way," she said into the receiver. Then she hung up.

Really, she thought as she gathered up her cookies, her handbag, her cell phone, and her keys. She didn't need reminding about the time she had to be at the Longely Community Center. She was always on time, unlike some other members of the Christmas Cookie Exchange Club whom she could name. Mainly Pearl and Barbara and Teresa, who were always running at least half an hour late. It would be interesting to see if they showed up on time for the run-through.

Millie sniffed again as she thought about the earlier phone call she'd received. She had to admit it had certainly riled her up, which she guessed was the whole point. But now that she'd had three hours to think about it, she was just annoyed. Some people never learn, she decided as she locked the front door to her house, walked to the garage, and got into her 2009 black Buick Lucerne. She took a few minutes to settle herself in and move the pillow she sat on to the correct position.

Then she turned the ignition key. The vehicle started up with a satisfying roar, and she slowly and carefully began backing the large car out of her driveway. Her son couldn't understand why she had needed a new car. In fact, he couldn't understand why she had to drive at all. But what was she supposed to do? Stay cooped up in the house all day? Or move to one of those assisted-living communities?

Her son thought that was a great idea, and so did her daughter, for that matter. But she had told both of them that hell would freeze over before that happened. She had lived in her house for almost thirty-five years, and as far as she was concerned, she was planning on dying in it.

If her son and daughter wanted a house, let them buy one of their own, not go after hers. Millie's breast heaved with indignation at the very idea. Not that they had asked. Oh, no. They'd just told her she should put the money from the sale in trust. But Millie knew that, despite what they said about having her best interests at heart, getting their hands on her house was what was behind their suggestion.

Okay. It was true. She *was* slowing down a bit. And her reflexes weren't as fast as they used to be; neither was her night vision. But she compensated for that. She drove slowly and stuck to the roads she knew. In fact, she had driven them so often she could probably drive them blindfolded. And as for driving at night, she usually had one of her younger friends pick her up.

Millie thought about the drive back from the Longely Community Center as she coasted to a stop at Winton Street and Angora Avenue. Of course, it would be dark when she got out, since it was dusk now. Maybe she could ask Bernie and Libby to drive back to her house so that she could follow them. Millie was sure they wouldn't mind. Despite their mother's worries, they had grown up to become nice young ladies. Millie smiled as she concentrated on the road.

There was no traffic on it, which was why she always took it. The traffic patterns on the other roads were a little more complicated, but this was a straight shot to the Longely Community Center. There were only two lights and two steep blind curves, and she could slow down for those. With no one behind her, she didn't have to worry about irritating anyone.

Much better to be safe. Slow and steady wins the race. Amber was always complaining about her maxims, but they were true, Millie thought as she reached up and adjusted the rearview mirror. People were in such a rush nowadays. Always trying to do five things at once, which meant they all turned out badly. It certainly wasn't like that when she was young. People had time for things then, time to do them right.

Millie slowed down a little more and gripped the wheel more firmly while she checked the speedometer. After all, as she had told her son, she'd never been in an accident in her life, and she didn't intend to start now.

Millie patted the cookie tins beside her and told them they were about to make her famous. Maybe she would take Carl Baxter a pie tomorrow after the taping. An apple pie. She made excellent ones, if she did say so herself. Or maybe one of her pumpkin pies, the one with the ginger snap crust. She slowed down a little more because the curve coming up could be tricky.

It was darker than Millie had anticipated, and she had to lean forward and squint in order to see where the road ended and the dirt began. It was tough for her because there were no streetlights and no moon to light her way. But after a moment she remembered to put her brights on. That helped, and she relaxed her grip on the steering wheel a little as she sped up. While her foot was on the gas pedal, she gave herself a pep talk, telling herself that she'd driven this route hundreds of times and it would never do for her to be late for the run-through.

Millie was thinking about what she was going to say to Carl Baxter when she spotted something big in the middle of the road. She squinted. She wasn't certain, but it looked like a deer. Where had it come from? It certainly hadn't been there two seconds ago. She honked. It didn't move. Why wouldn't it move? Millie wondered as her heart started thumping in her chest and she slammed on her brakes. The tires screeched, and while the Buick slowed down, it wasn't slowing down fast enough.

It occurred to Millie that at this rate she was going to plow right into the dratted thing, so she did the only other thing she could do. She swerved to avoid it. As she turned the wheel, she could feel the car pulling to the left. She tried to straighten it out and failed. Then she heard a crunch as the tires left the tarmac and hit the dirt and gravel. She turned the wheel again, but it was too late. She was heading straight for the oak tree that had killed

Sheila's husband five years ago in that terrible automobile accident.

Millie felt a jarring sensation as the Buick hit the tree. The seat belt bit into her chest while the air bag inflated, hitting her in the jaw. She heard a hissing noise and felt a burning sensation, and then everything was quiet. The deer wasn't in the road anymore. She thought she'd hit it, but maybe she hadn't. If that was the case, she wondered where it had gone. Then she decided it had probably gone back into the woods as she glanced down at the seat beside her. Miraculously, the cookies were still in the tins. They'd slid off the seat, but hopefully they'd be okay. They had to be. Simply had to be, after all the work she'd put into them. She tried to unbuckle her seat belt, but she couldn't.

The darn thing must have gotten stuck. She tried again. Nothing. Her heart raced even faster. She could feel it beating against her chest. *Okay, Millie, calm down,* she told herself. *Everything is going to be fine.* She took a deep breath. Then another one. When her breathing had returned to normal, she reached for her bag. A searing pain shot up her side.

I must have broken some ribs, Millie thought as she gasped. "I can do this," she said out loud as she reached out again. "I can and I will." This time she managed to reach the bag with her fingertips and drag it toward her. The movement cost her, and she sat perfectly still for a moment until the pain receded. Then she dug around in her purse until she found her phone. The effort produced a cold sweat, and she had to sit still for another minute before she could proceed. Thank heavens for speed dial, Millie thought as she called Amber. She couldn't believe that moving her fingers could cause such pain.

"Are you okay?" Amber asked, answering on the third ring.

"You have to get the cookies," Millie managed to croak out.

"What?" Amber said. It was busy at the shop, making it difficult to hear above the din.

Even though it hurt to talk, let alone breathe, Millie managed to repeat what she'd just said. Then she added, "Amber, come get them now and take them to the show. I'm where Sheila's husband had his accident."

"Aunt Millie, what's the matter?" Amber asked as she boxed up four chocolate and three vanilla cupcakes for Mrs. Morris. "Are you all right?"

"I knew I should have listened to my gut," Aunt Millie moaned, those words costing her her last bit of energy. "But I didn't and she got me."

"Who finally got you, Aunt Millie?"

"Are you talking to me?" Mrs. Morris asked Amber.

Amber shook her head. "No. My aunt."

"Millie?" Mrs. Morris asked.

Amber nodded.

"What happened?"

"That's what I'm trying to find out," Amber replied.

She asked again, but Millie didn't answer.

She couldn't. She was trying to form the words, but nothing came out. For some reason, she couldn't get her tongue to move. Instead, she thought she heard a car going by. They're going to stop, she told herself, feeling a burst of relief.

She tried to keep herself together while she waited for them, but she couldn't focus. Her next-to-last thought before slipping into a coma was, *My God. I didn't tell Amber whom I was talking about.* Her last thought was, *Thank heavens I didn't wear my stockings with the hole near the elastic. That would have been beyond mortifying.*

Chapter 1

Bernie was lifting a folding chair off the pile of chairs in front of her when Libby came running into the auditorium of the Longely Community Center.

"You've come to help me set up the chairs, how sweet," Bernie told her sister, who was supposed to have been there twenty minutes ago.

"Forget the chairs," Libby replied. "We have to go."

"Why?" Bernie asked. She and Libby were supposed to be setting up the extra chairs for tomorrow's airing of *Baking for Life,* although why they weren't taping the show from the Longely High School auditorium was something Bernie couldn't begin to fathom. "Go where? What's the matter?"

"Amber's Aunt Millie was just in a car accident."

"Jeez." Bernie put down the chair she was holding. "Was it bad?"

"Evidently bad enough," Libby told her. "She's in the hospital."

"So we have to go back to A Little Taste of Heaven?"

"No. We have to go to the scene of the accident."

"Then who's at the shop, if Amber isn't?" Bernie asked,

thoughts of customers not being waited on dancing in her head. "Besides Googie, that is?"

Libby smiled apologetically. "George."

"George who?"

"The George who is one of Googie's friends."

Bernie raised her eyes to the ceiling. "Oh God. Shoot me now." While Googie was a fairly responsible individual, having worked for them behind the counter for the last five years, his skateboarder friends were not.

"It'll be fine," Libby told her.

"You've got to be kidding me. It will not be fine."

"It could be worse, Bernie."

"Worse?" Bernie repeated "How?"

"We could have Selma," Libby pointed out.

Bernie groaned. Selma had tried to steal eight hundred dollars from them in addition to breaking their mixer and hiding dirty pans in the cabinet.

"After all," Libby continued, "let's not forget that George worked down at The Little Red Hen in Brooklyn last year, so he does have some idea of how to work in a bakeshop. You liked him, remember?"

"I did?" Bernie asked.

"Yeah. He filled in for Googie for a couple of days last year when Googie had the flu."

Bernie snapped her fingers. She was beginning to re-member who Libby was talking about. "He's the one with the stretchers in his ears and the shaved head, right?"

Libby nodded.

Bernie felt slightly relieved. At least George could work the register and knew a croissant from a French maca-roon. She sighed. "Libby, why do things like this always come at the worst possible time?"

Libby didn't argue. It was three weeks until Christmas, one of their busiest times of the year, and being guest judges on the baking show had put them squarely in the weeds, as her sister liked to say.

Bernie reached up, took the elastic out of her hair, and redid her ponytail. "Not to be mean or anything," she said when she was done, "but why do we have to go to the accident site? Isn't this a police matter?"

"Because Amber wants us to. She says the cookies are missing, and she thinks maybe someone caused Millie's accident."

Bernie frowned. "What you said makes absolutely no sense. Could you be a little clearer?"

Libby unbuttoned her sweater because it was hot inside the Longely Community Center. And then because it was her firm belief that she thought better after she'd eaten some chocolate, she reached into her jeans pocket, drew out two Hershey's kisses, and unwrapped and ate them while she organized her thoughts. "Evidently," she began when she was done, "Millie was coming here to the run-through with her cookies when she got into the accident."

"I knew that," Bernie said. "All the members of the Christmas Cookie Exchange Club are coming."

"Yes, indeedy. Anyway," Libby continued, "she called Amber before she passed out and told her to come get the cookies."

"The cookies she was taking to the show for judging? The ones she baked from the dough we were storing under lock and key until yesterday?"

Libby nodded. "Exactly. But when Amber got there and saw her aunt passed out she called 911. Then, after they came and took her aunt away, Amber remembered about the cookies and went back to look for them. But they weren't in Millie's Buick."

"Maybe Millie forgot them at home," Bernie suggested. "Maybe she was confused. After all, she'd just been in an accident."

"That's what I said to Amber," Libby agreed. "But here's the thing. When Amber got to the hospital, Millie had regained consciousness. Amber said it was like Millie was waiting for her."

"And . . . ," Bernie said, making a rolling motion with her hand to indicate that Libby should move the story along.

"And she told Amber to avenge her. And then she blacked out again."

"Avenge her?" said Bernie.

"That's what Amber said she heard," replied Libby.

"The poor woman was probably in shock," Bernie observed. "Or maybe Amber heard wrong."

"Maybe, but now Amber is insisting that someone caused her aunt's accident and stole the cookies."

"Correct me if I'm wrong, but are you saying that someone engineered Aunt Millie's accident with the specific intent of stealing her cookies?" Bernie asked.

"Amber's saying it, not me," replied Libby.

Bernie lifted up her arms, then let them drop. "That's ridiculous."

"Agreed," said Libby.

"I mean who would steal Amber's Aunt Millie's cookies? What would be the point?"

"So they won't be in the contest." Libby shrugged. "I know it's absurd, but there it is."

"And Amber wants us to do what?" asked Bernie.

"What do you think? She wants us to investigate," said Libby.

"Great. Simply great," Bernie groused. "Come on. Like we don't have enough to do?"

"Do you want me to say no to her?" Libby demanded.

Bernie was silent for a moment. Then she said, "Yes. I do."

Libby scowled. "Seriously? You may want to rethink that answer."

Bernie nibbled on her lower lip for a moment. "I guess we can't, can we?"

"No, Bernie. We can't," Libby replied even though she would have liked to tell Amber they couldn't go.

Bernie clicked her tongue against her teeth. "So tell me exactly what, according to Amber, we are supposed to do."

"She wants us to look at the scene of the accident before the cops come and take the car away. I figured we'll do that, and then we can tell Amber that everything is okay and that will be that. We'll be off the hook."

Bernie thought for a moment. "That should work."

"I thought it would be the easiest thing to do."

Then Bernie had another thought, a more discomforting one. "You know," she continued, "not to play devil's advocate or anything . . ."

Libby rolled her eyes. "Something you enjoy doing . . ."

Bernie raised her hand. "Just hear me out. Much as I don't like to say this, suppose Millie is right? Suppose someone did want to hurt her and steal her cookies? After all, the Christmas Cookie Exchange Club members *do* take their baking very seriously."

Libby snorted. "I refuse to believe that. Who are we talking about? A bunch of middle-class old ladies who have known each other for thirty or forty years. Not possible," Libby declared.

"Everything is possible," Bernie asserted.

"Not this," Libby shot back.

"The world is a strange and wondrous place," Bernie retorted.

Libby started toward the door. "I wouldn't know. I don't have time to look. I'm in the kitchen all day long."

Bernie tsked. "So young and yet so bitter."

"No. Just tired. I've got to say, though, that if I never see another bûche de Noël it won't be too soon for me. Of course, I'd miss the chocolate buttercream," Libby reflected. "And the ganache. And the meringue mushrooms."

She stopped as another thought occurred to her. "What about the show? What if Millie doesn't make it?"

"I guess they'll have to do it with seven bakers instead of eight," Bernie answered as she reached for her coat. "Unless, of course, Millie makes a spectacular recovery."

"I hope she does," Libby said, but given what Amber had said, she had her doubts.

She and Bernie stopped on their way out of the Longely Community Center and told the producer, Penelope Lively, what had happened.

"Friggin' great," Penelope muttered. "Just what I don't need. Terri," she yelled, calling for her assistant, "get over here."

"Not a happy camper," Libby noted as she watched Penelope reach for her cell phone.

"I wouldn't be either," Bernie replied as they stepped outside.

Once they were in their van, Libby called Amber and told her they were en route. They arrived at the scene of the accident fifteen minutes later.

Chapter 2

The van's brakes squealed as Bernie came around the curve. She stopped two inches in front of the orange traffic cones that were ringing the scene of Millie's accident.

"That was close," Libby observed. "Too close. Mathilda would not be happy if she'd gone into the Buick."

"No, she wouldn't," Bernie agreed of their van.

"And we don't have money for a new van, and I'm not sure it would be worth fixing this one. The insurance company would probably just total her out."

"Libby, don't talk like that," Bernie chided. "You'll upset Mathilda." Bernie caressed the van's dashboard. "Don't worry," she crooned to it. "I won't let anything happen to you." She took a deep breath and let it out. "Sorry," she said to it. "The curve came up faster than I expected."

"It always does," Libby commented.

Bernie glanced over at her sister, trying to decide whether she was being sarcastic and decided she wasn't. As Bernie pulled the van over to the side of the road, she reflected that even in the daylight she would have had trouble avoiding the Buick, but at night, in the dark, it would be nearly impossible. The front half of the Buick was smashed up against the tree, and the back part was sticking out into the road.

And you wouldn't see it until it was too late. Especially if you were flying along. Which was why this particular stretch of road had such a bad reputation. Between the curve and the tree, it was impossible to see around the bend. If she remembered correctly, three people had died here over the last ten years.

"I'd forgotten how bad this curve is," Libby observed.

"Me too," Bernie said as she parked. Although she really hadn't.

She was thinking about how she and her friends used to race along here when she'd been seventeen and stupid, and how lucky they'd been not to end up dead or in a wheelchair. She remembered that the road surface got slippery when wet, so it was easy to slide off onto the gravel, especially if you were going fast. And oh boy, were they ever. At least once or twice a week. She recalled one memorable evening she'd gotten her dad's car up to eighty miles an hour on this stretch of road. It had been raining and she'd fishtailed like crazy. Luckily, she'd managed to regain control and not kill the other kids in the car. In fact, she hadn't even gotten a dent in her dad's vehicle. He'd never known what had happened. Thank heavens. Otherwise she would have been under house arrest for at least five years.

But that was then, and this was now. For openers, it was dry tonight, and while it was cold, chances were there weren't any icy patches on the road. In addition, Bernie was willing to bet four pecan pies that Millie wasn't going even thirty miles an hour when the accident had happened. In fact, if she was going more than twenty miles an hour Bernie would have been surprised. But given the fact that the front end of Millie's Buick looked like one of Bernie's pleated skirts, twenty miles an hour had been enough.

"Ready?" Libby asked Bernie.

Bernie startled. "Absolutely," she said, coming back to the present.

A little ways up, she saw Matt, one of Longely's finest, sitting in his patrol car. He was waiting, Bernie assumed, for the tow truck to come and cart Millie's Buick away. Then she spotted Amber's car parked behind the police car. When Amber saw Bernie and Libby, she got out of her car and ran toward them, purple and pink braids flying. Somehow they didn't clash with her orange jumpsuit, a fact Bernie found intriguing.

"The cookies aren't here," she told Bernie and Libby before they'd even had a chance to get out of their van. "I looked all over the place."

"Well, let's take another look and see," Bernie said as she turned the van off and got out. "Maybe we'll have better luck."

Matt lifted his head when he saw Libby, Bernie, and Amber approaching. "Hey, ladies," he called out. "My favorite people."

Bernie laughed. "That's because we give you extra muffins."

Matt grinned. "Which is why you're so well protected. How's your dad doing?" he asked.

"Crabby," Libby said.

"It's when he's nice that you have to watch him," Matt observed.

Bernie laughed again. "Exactly. Hey, Matt, is it okay if we look inside the Buick? Millie thinks she left something in the car and she sent us to get it."

Matt raised an eyebrow. "So you left the store and came running over to find it? It must be quite an important something."

"Actually, we left the Longely Community Center to come running over and find it," Libby said.

"Would you mind telling me exactly what it is that you're supposed to recover?" Matt asked.

"Cookies," Bernie said.

"Cookies?" Matt echoed.

"Yeah, cookies," Libby said. "They're Millie's submission for the *Baking for Life* contest."

Amber leaned forward. "When I saw her at the hospital, she asked me to get them, so I came out here to look, but I couldn't find them, which was when I called Bernie and Libby. They're very important to her."

"The cookies?" Matt asked, clarifying.

"Millie's Meltaways," Amber said. "Millie's Majestic Meltaways, to be precise. Of course, she had her cashew bars in another tin, but I don't think she cares about them as much."

Matt clicked his tongue against the roof of his mouth while he thought. "Well, I guess, given the circumstances, the fact that she can ask for them is a good thing."

"That's what I'm thinking," Amber answered. "Being in the show was, is, very important to her."

Matt shook his head. "Hope she makes it."

"Me too," Bernie said. "So are we good to poke around?"

"Sure," Matt said. "Look away. But do it fast because the tow truck is coming soon."

Libby moved a little closer to the patrol car. "Matt, were you the first person on the scene?"

"No. The person who called in the accident was. She took off after I arrived. Lucky for Millie she'd gotten lost coming back from a visit to Selma Mince and her husband." He went on to give more details.

"I don't suppose you noticed any cookies in the front seat," Libby asked when Matt was done speaking.

"No. But then that wasn't my first priority." He looked at Amber. "Your aunt was in pretty bad shape, and I was more concerned with getting the ambulance here as quickly as possible."

"So what do you think happened?" Bernie asked him.

Matt put down his cell phone and took a sip of his coffee. "Simple. I think Millie lost control of her car and plowed into the tree."

"Is that the way you're writing it up?"

"You betcha," Matt said, doing his best cowboy imitation.

"Was she going fast?" Libby inquired.

Matt snorted. "What do you think?"

"I'm taking that as a no," Bernie said.

"You would be correct," Matt told her. "In fact, quite the opposite. I'm guessing her speed was most likely between fifteen and twenty miles an hour. But that can do it. I mean, if she wasn't wearing her seat belt she'd have been dead."

"So why do you think she went into the tree?" Libby asked him.

Matt scratched his head. "It could be any number of reasons. Maybe her night vision is really poor and she had trouble seeing the road. Maybe there was something in the road. Maybe she had some kind of attack."

"Maybe," agreed Bernie, who thought that the latter was the most likely possibility.

"I guess that's for the docs to decide." Matt fished around in the front seat and came up with a flashlight. "Here," he said, handing it to Bernie. "This might make things a little easier. If you have any other questions, just ask," and he went back to the Scrabble game he'd been playing on his phone before Bernie, Libby, and Amber had arrived.

As the three women approached the Buick, Bernie looked up at the oak tree Millie had crashed into and thought about how large it was and how it was impossible to see around the bend in the curve because of it. Then she wondered which was older: the tree or the road?

"I looked for the cookie tins," Amber said, breaking Bernie's train of thought.

"So you said," Bernie replied. "But you told Libby you wanted us to look too. If you don't, we'll be glad to leave."

Amber rubbed her hands together. "No. No. Stay."

"Did your aunt tell you why she plowed into the tree?" Bernie asked Amber as she clicked on the flashlight.

Amber shook her head. "She doesn't remember. She doesn't remember anything."

"Probably a concussion," Libby surmised.

"So, Amber, what did she say?" Bernie asked.

Amber kicked a pebble on the ground. "Nutty things."

"Like what kind of nutty things?" Libby asked.

Amber took a deep breath and let it out. "She told me at the hospital that someone was trying to kill her. But, I mean, who would want to kill Aunt Millie?"

Libby lifted an eyebrow. "She really said that?"

Amber nodded. "Twice. The accident must have gone to her head. I mean no one would want to do something like that. Absolutely no one. She could be crabby and annoying, but you don't kill people for that."

Bernie smiled. "Hopefully not. Otherwise our town would be a lot smaller."

Amber favored her with a small smile before going on. "I should have driven her to the Longely Community Center. She asked me to but we were really, really busy at the shop, so I told her I couldn't. But I should have gotten one of my friends to drive her. I could have done that. Then none of this would have happened."

Libby went over and gave Amber a hug. "This isn't your fault. It truly isn't. She had an accident." Libby emphasized the word *accident*. "This is a bad stretch of road."

Amber nodded. "You're probably right."

"As for the someone-is-trying-to-kill-her thing," Libby continued, "you know how paranoid she can get. Remember when she thought someone stole her ring?"

Amber let out a strangled laugh. "And it was in the medicine cabinet behind the toothpaste tube?"

Libby nodded. "Exactly." She rubbed her hands to warm them up, then pointed to the Buick. It was time to get down to business. "Okay, Amber. Was the passenger side door closed or opened when you got here?"

"Closed."

"So how did you check for the cookies?" Bernie asked.

"I climbed into the driver's seat," Amber replied.

"All the other doors were closed?" Libby inquired.

"Yes, they were," Amber told her.

Bernie nodded. That should make things simple enough, she thought, because it meant that the cookies hadn't gone flying out of the car and into the woods, which would have been difficult to search in the dark. This was a prospect she had not been looking forward to, especially since she was wearing her good pink cowboy boots, the ones with the crystals on them. She walked around the Buick, opened the passenger-side door, and played the light over and under the seat.

She saw that Amber had been correct—not that she had doubted her. There were no cookies on the seat. Then Bernie crouched down and looked under the seat. There was nothing there either, except for one black woolen glove. She left it where it was, straightened up, and backed out of the Buick.

"See, I told you," Amber said as Bernie put her hands on the small of her back and stretched.

"Yes, you did," Bernie said when she straightened up. She had to start doing Pilates again, because her lower back was starting to give her trouble. "But it's easy to overlook things when you're upset." Bernie opened the passenger-side rear door and played the light along the backseat and the floor.

"Anything?" Libby asked as she stamped her feet and

rubbed her arms to keep warm. It was colder out here than she had anticipated it would be, and she wished she'd worn her parka instead of the fleece she had on.

"Nothing," Bernie replied, her voice muffled by the inside of the car.

"Maybe Millie put the cookies in the trunk?" Libby suggested once Bernie straightened up.

"Maybe," Bernie agreed, and she went around to the driver's side, reached back in, and grabbed the keys out of the ignition.

"I don't think they're in there," Amber said as Bernie tried to open the trunk.

Bernie grunted as she twisted the key.

"She'd never transport her cookies in the trunk," Amber said. "They were too valuable. She liked to have them where she could see them at all times."

"Well, it won't hurt to check," Bernie said. "That's if I can get the dratted thing open. I may need a crowbar," she said as she banged on the trunk with her fist. A moment later she heard a pop and the door flew open. "Nothing that a little force can't fix," she noted, looking inside.

Libby and Amber joined her. The three of them stared down at the trunk. It was pristine. There was absolutely nothing in it. It looked as if it had been freshly cleaned.

"My aunt is a very neat lady," Amber commented.

"Scarily so," Bernie replied, thinking of the mess that existed in the back of their van. In fact, Millie made their mother look like a slob.

Amber grabbed her pigtail and started twirling it around her finger. "So my aunt was right. Someone did steal the cookies. Someone was out to get her."

Bernie held up her hand. "Let's not jump to any conclusions before we look in her house."

"Look in her house?" Amber parroted, giving Bernie a quizzical look. "Why?"

"Maybe she forgot the cookies in her house," Bernie said. "Maybe she got discombobulated. It happens."

"Not to my Aunt Millie it doesn't," Amber said. "I think what happened was that someone came along, saw my Aunt Millie lying there, and stole the cookies."

"Why?" Bernie asked.

"Because they wanted to eat them," Amber replied. "Everyone knows what those tins mean."

"Not everyone," Bernie said.

"Most people," Amber said.

"I guess it's possible," Libby agreed. "Nevertheless, we should still go check out her house on the off chance they're there."

Amber let go of her pigtail and started playing with the buttons of her jumpsuit. "I guess."

"Do you have any other suggestions?" Bernie asked Amber.

Amber shook her head. "Not really."

"Then let's go," Bernie said. She glanced at her watch. It was a little after eight. If they hurried, they might be able to wrap this up by nine and still salvage the evening.

Chapter 3

"So the cookies weren't in Millie's house?" Sean asked Bernie as he and his daughters tucked into slices of chocolate truffle cake and sipped their coffee.

Even though it was eleven o'clock at night, Sean wasn't about to let that stop him from enjoying his daughters' baking or their coffee. Fortunately, he'd been blessed with an iron-clad digestive system and sleeping after drinking coffee had never been a problem. If it had been, he never would have been a policeman for all those years.

"No, they weren't," Libby said as she sampled the icing on the cake.

It was made with butter, egg yolks, sugar syrup, 70 percent dark chocolate, and a little bit of coffee, plus a teaspoon of vanilla. In other words, the buttercream was perfect. It was ambrosial. In her opinion, people who made frosting out of flavorings, powdered sugar, and butter shouldn't call their product buttercream frosting. Because it wasn't. It was some pale imitation. This, the stuff that she and Bernie made, was the real deal. And even though it was technically tricky to make—you had to be careful not to scramble the eggs when you heated them up or when you added the hot sugar syrup—the end result was worth the trouble.

Libby was thinking that it was more than worth the trouble when she picked up the truffle that was sitting on top of her slice of cake and bit into it. She'd made the truffles two days ago and stored them in the fridge because they didn't have a long shelf life—maybe a week at the most—due to the fact that she'd used heavy cream in them.

They were good too. Really good. Better than the ones Harrods made, in her humble opinion. They literally melted in your mouth. Maybe, Libby thought, we can sell them in A Little Taste of Heaven as a holiday gift or for Valentine's Day. Get some nice boxes. Maybe something pale green and silver or a rosy pink and gold. Do a variety of flavors. Modern ones. Like lavender and honey. Or lime and chili. Or almonds and sea salt. She was trying to come up with other combinations when she became aware that Bernie was talking and turned her attention to her.

"And we looked," Bernie was saying to her dad as she added a little more cream to her coffee. This morning she'd decided she had to go on a diet because her jeans were getting tight around the waist, but not tonight. Tonight she needed cream in her coffee and chocolate cake in her stomach. After all, what was an extra five hundred calories, give or take a few? Tomorrow was another day. "We looked all over the place."

"What do you mean by 'all over the place'?" asked Sean, seeking clarification.

"I mean," Bernie replied, "that we looked in the kitchen, the living room, and the dining room."

Sean took a sip of coffee, then put the cup down. "How about upstairs?"

"That too," Bernie replied. She paused for a moment to stretch. She'd had a kink in her back ever since she'd offloaded three fifty-pound bags of flour from the van this morning. "We looked in the bedrooms, and we even checked the basement and the garage in case Millie had taken them out there and forgotten to put them in her car. The cookies weren't there. They weren't in Millie's house."

Libby weighed in next. "Dad, it's the neatest house I've ever been in," she told him. "There is nothing—and I mean nothing—out of place. It's even neater than Bree's. If the cookies were there, believe me, we would have found them."

Sean took another forkful of cake and let it dissolve in his mouth while he thought over what Libby and Bernie had just said. He was glad that Mr. Evans, whoever he was, hadn't picked up this cake—thereby leaving it for the family to enjoy.

Sean frowned and put his fork down. "So what I hear you saying is that someone actually took the cookies." He didn't try to hide the skepticism in his voice.

"I know it's hard to believe, but it certainly looks that way," Bernie replied. "I mean they weren't in the house. To top it off, all the doors and windows were locked. We checked," Bernie said, forestalling her dad's next question.

"So someone really did take them out of the car," Sean mused. "Either that or Millie just imagined making them."

Libby gave her dad the look.

He raised his hand. "I was just covering all the possibilities."

"A highly dubious possibility because she's been talking to us about the cookies she was going to submit for judging for months now," Libby said. "Isn't that right, Bernie?" she asked, turning to her sister.

"For at least three weeks," Bernie replied. "And Millie might be annoying, but she's definitely not crazy, Dad."

"I didn't say she was," Sean answered.

"And anyway," Bernie added. "We found the cookie

pans soaking in the sink, so there's no doubt she'd used them.".

"You didn't tell me that," Sean said. He ate another sliver of cake, then went on to a different topic. "Libby, correct me if I'm wrong, but what I'm also hearing from you and Bernie is that everyone knew about her cookies, right?"

"Everyone in the Christmas Cookie Exchange Club did," Libby answered. "No doubt about that. No doubt at all."

"Those people would be?" Sean asked. "Refresh my memory."

Bernie rattled their names off. "Barbara Lazarus, Lillian Stein, Teresa Ruffino, Alma Hall, Sheila Goody, Pearl Pepperpot, and Rose Olsen. And of course Millie Piedmont."

Sean took a deep breath and let it out. "Ah yes. How could I have forgotten. Down at the station we liked to call them the busybody brigade."

Libby laughed. "Or worse."

"That too," Sean said, thinking of the time last week when Alma Hall and Sheila Goody had almost caught him smoking outside the shop.

"Do I smell tobacco?" Alma had asked, wrinkling up her nose as she'd passed by him while he'd been standing in the alley by the shop.

Sean had pretended to smell the air. "I don't," he'd lied as he moved his foot over the butt he'd just disposed of. At the time he remembered thinking that she reminded him of a bloodhound, with that droopy face and big nose of hers.

Then Sheila had squinted at him. "There must be something wrong with your nose because I can smell the tobacco from here. Are you smoking?" she asked him, making it sound as if he were engaged in some unspeakable rite.

"Me?" Sean had said. "Never. It must have been from some passerby," he'd told Sheila, favoring her with his most convincing, boyish smile. "Smoking is a filthy habit. I think people that do that should be tied to the mast and flogged to within an inch of their lives."

"You are not as funny as you think you are," Alma had told him.

"And you're not as clever," Sean had shot back.

Alma had sniffed, and she and Sheila had walked off. Thank heavens. Because the last thing he needed was for them to tell Libby and Bernie that he was smoking.

Alma and Sheila liked causing trouble—they lived for it, actually—and since his daughters didn't know he'd gone back to smoking, the two older ladies would have hit the jackpot. At the time, he'd considered doing a preemptive strike and telling Bernie and Libby, but after further consideration, he'd decided against it.

Why disturb the balance? Because if he was being honest with himself, he knew that they knew. His daughters weren't stupid, after all. Far from it. Furthermore, they knew that he knew that they knew. No, on reflection it was better to keep things status quo. That way they didn't have to have the "Dad, You Have to Quit for Our Sakes" talk. On that note, he turned his attention to the matter at hand.

"Who else knows about the contest?" Sean asked his daughters.

"We know," Libby answered. "The TV crew knows. Amber. There was a small article in the local paper."

"I didn't see it," Sean said.

"That's because it was about four lines," Libby told him. "When you come right down to it, it's really not such a big deal except to the Christmas Cookie Exchange Club members, of course. The show doesn't have a big following."

"It's not exactly as if they're wrestling alligators." Sean smiled at the thought. Now that would be a sight to see. He took another sip of coffee. "Okay," he said after a moment. "Moving on, all of these women are in their late sixties and early seventies, correct?"

Libby nodded. "Yes."

"So what you're positing," Sean continued, "is that one of our female senior citizens came along right after Millie's accident, opened the door, took the cookies, closed the door, and went on her way, leaving Millie seriously injured."

"Or caused the accident in order to steal the cookies," Bernie said.

Sean ate the last mouthful of cake on his plate. "Don't you think that, given the age, the gender, and the social class of the people we're talking about, that seems even more unlikely than the first scenario you proposed?" he asked after he'd finished swallowing. "And that's saying a lot. Elderly middle-class women don't do the kind of things you're proposing."

"Not as a rule," Bernie agreed.

"But then how do you explain the cookies disappearing and Millie's comments?" Libby demanded.

"Millie had an attack and hit the tree and the cookies went flying out the window," Sean said promptly.

"The Buick's windows were closed," Libby reminded him. "At least, that's what Matt said."

"He was the first responder?" Sean asked.

Libby nodded.

"He's pretty reliable," Sean conceded as he studied the Christmas lights on Mrs. Sullivan's notions store across the street. Each year they got more and more elaborate. At this point, the shop looked like a gingerbread house. "Always has been."

Everyone was silent for a moment.

Then Sean asked, "Who called the accident in?"

"A passerby," Bernie answered.

"A local?" her dad inquired.

Bernie shook her head. "A visitor to the Minces."

Sean raised an eyebrow. "He . . ."

"She," Bernie corrected.

"Fine. She. Was a little out of the way."

"She got lost," Libby explained. "She took a left at Route 21 instead of a right."

Sean nodded. It was an easy enough mistake to make. "She stayed at the accident scene?"

"Until Matt arrived," Bernie replied. "But," she continued, anticipating her dad's next question, "she didn't touch anything or move Millie except to open the door and check and make sure she was breathing. She told Matt that she was afraid to do anything else. She was afraid she'd make matters worse."

"Wise choice," Sean said. Unless it was absolutely necessary, it was always better to wait until the EMTs arrived. Sean thought for a while. Then he said, "You know what I would do if I were you? I'd go back to the scene when it's light out and look around and see what I can find."

Libby drained the last drop of coffee from her cup. "Any particular thing you'd be looking for?"

"Obviously, the cookie tins," Sean replied promptly. "I mean they can't just have disappeared. Either someone took them or they're lying on the ground. Besides, then you can tell Amber you've covered all the possibilities. You owe her that much."

"True," Bernie said.

"We owe Millie as well," Libby added. "Even if she does always make snide comments about our cinnamon rolls."

"That's because she thinks hers are better," Bernie replied. "Which they are so not."

"Agreed," Sean said. "They're like hockey pucks."

"Plus she uses cheap cinnamon," Libby said.

"The cheapest," Bernie agreed.

"You mean there are different kinds?" Sean asked.

"Four," Libby told him. "Three of them are cassia

root." She stifled a yawn. She was too tired to get into it now. "I guess we should get to bed if we're going to be mucking around in the woods tomorrow," she said, changing the subject.

"And doing all those snowflake cookies," Bernie added.

"Whose idea were those anyway?" she asked. They were extremely time-consuming, what with making the dough, rolling it out, cutting out the cookies, and then baking and icing them. In addition, the pans took up every inch of oven space, effectively ruling out the oven for other uses.

"Yours," Libby said.

Bernie was taken aback. "Are you sure?"

"Positive." Libby remembered the conversation well. "I tried to tell you not to do them, but you kept telling me they'd go really fast."

Bernie didn't reply. She decided she had to be exhausted because she couldn't think of a snappy comeback.

Chapter 4

It was gray and overcast the next morning as Libby and Bernie left A Little Taste of Heaven and walked outside to the van. They each held cups of French roast coffee, heavy on the cream and light on the sugar, and a petite pain left over from the day before.

"It's going to snow," Libby predicted as she took a bite of her roll and savored the crunch of the crust, the softness of the dough, and the sweet taste of the butter she'd slathered on it. "God, I love these rolls," she added as she got into the van and turned it on. In this kind of weather the van had to be warmed up before it would run well. "It's one of the pleasures of winter."

Bernie grunted her agreement as she took a swallow of her coffee. She definitely was a dark-roast person, she decided. She'd heard the blather about the higher temperature roasting killing the finer notes of the coffee beans, but the light brews just didn't do it for her, and she wasn't a big fan of the pour-over either, while she was on the subject. Maybe her palate wasn't sufficiently sophisticated. Yes. That must be it, she decided as she finished her roll, closed her eyes, and leaned her head back against the seat.

She was tired, and it was only eight-thirty in the morning, but then she and her sister had been up baking since five.

"I spoke to Amber while you were taking a shower," Libby said.

"And?" Bernie replied. She kept her eyes closed.

"Millie isn't any better. They moved her to the ICU early this morning." Libby looked at her watch. "Amber told me she was going over there to check on her."

Bernie opened her eyes, sat up, and took a swig of her coffee. "So she won't be in this morning?"

"No. She will be. But she'll be late. I already called and asked George to fill in till she shows up at the shop. He wasn't so bad," Libby added in response to the expression on her sister's face.

"Except for the fiasco with Mrs. Wills's cookies," Bernie said, brushing a bread crumb off her lap. She'd gotten an early-morning phone call from Mrs. Wills, who'd told her what had happened. At length.

Libby took a sip of her coffee. She'd melted a small square of 72 percent chocolate in it and the result had exceeded her expectations. "Well, Mrs. Wills does mumble."

"Agreed. But how do you get almond shortbread and French macaroons mixed up? Then there was turning on the coffee machine and forgetting to add the water. Now that's bad."

"It could have been," Libby conceded, visualizing having to buy a new coffee-making system. Not cheap. "At least Googie caught it in time," Libby said as she put the van in reverse. "Good Mathilda," Libby crooned to it as she gently pressed the gas pedal. A moment later they were off and running. "All I can say is thank God for small mercies."

"It's definitely going to snow," Bernie commented, changing the subject as she looked at the sky while they drove through Longely.

As the town spooled by, Bernie decided she liked the

way it looked at this time of year. She liked the wreaths with their big red bows on the doors and the candles in the windows. She liked the Christmas lights wound around the eaves of the houses and twisted about the street lamps and the trees.

She even liked the inflatable snowmen and the lighted wire deer that moved their heads from side to side and up and down. However, she could do without the snow. It was one thing when she was skiing in Aspen, but quite another when she was shoveling sidewalks in Longely. Bernie was thinking about how long it had been since she'd been on the slopes when they arrived at the site of the accident.

Between last night and this morning, the traffic cones and the debris had been cleared away. The only reminder of what had happened was the gash in the tree trunk that Millie had hit. Libby drove by it and parked on a straight part of the road so that anyone coming around the bend could see the van. Their vehicle wasn't much, but it was all they had, and she had no intention of losing it to a freak car accident.

Everything was silent when Libby turned off the van and pocketed the key. Then she and Bernie got out. The sound of the van doors shutting cut through the quiet.

"Pretty deserted," Bernie commented. "There aren't even any crows." Which was saying a lot because these days there were crows everywhere in Longely. They'd become the new geese.

"So I noticed," Libby agreed, looking around. "No one ever uses this road. I mean it's not exactly a direct route to anything. It meanders all over the place. Dad said it used to be a plank road before they had cars." She indicated the landscape with a sweep of her hand. "This all used to be farmland."

Bernie reached into her jacket pocket for her gloves and slipped them on. "Maybe that's why Millie took it."

"Because it used to be a plank road?"

Bernie laughed. "No, although given the way she drives everyone might have been happier if she did use a horse and carriage. I'm just saying that Millie might have chosen to use this road because there isn't any traffic on it and it was easier for her to drive on. Except, of course, at night because there are no lights on it."

"It was dusk when Millie crashed," Libby pointed out.

"Sometimes dusk is even harder to see in than the dark," Bernie said. "Everything is gray. At least in the dark people are using their lights."

"I wonder if Millie was using her high beams," mused Libby.

Bernie shifted her weight from one foot to another. Then she bent down and pulled up her socks. "Another question to ask Matt," she said when she was done.

"If this turns into a real investigation," Libby said.

"Which we hope it doesn't, right?"

"Right," Libby said, nodding her head. "But Dad is correct about one thing."

"What's that, Libby?"

"This thing . . ."

"Thing?"

"Situation. Is weird. There is definitely something off about it."

"I'm sure there's a simple explanation," Libby said.

"Me too," Bernie replied. "I'd just like to find out what it is."

"I don't think that's too much to ask," Libby replied.

"Neither do I," Bernie agreed.

The sisters fell silent as they walked along the side of the road to the scene of the accident. They kept their eyes down, looking for the cookie tins, but they didn't see them or anything that remotely looked like them lying among the gravel that lined the road's shoulder.

"God, it's quiet," Libby said uneasily for the second

time after another minute had gone by. "I mean you can't even hear the traffic out here."

"That's because there isn't any, and there isn't any because there are no houses out here," Bernie said.

"It's kind of spooky," said Libby.

"Some people would say it's peaceful," Bernie replied.

"Not me," Libby answered. "I like neighbors. Sleeping out here would give me the willies." She shivered and jammed her hands more firmly in the pockets of her down parka. Even though she had gloves on, her hands were still cold. "Now what are we looking for again?" she asked.

Bernie shrugged and zipped up the collar of her sheepskin jacket, the one she'd bought for 60 percent off at this little shop in Brighton Beach late last winter when they spent the day in Brooklyn. "Besides the cookie tins?"

"Yes. Besides the cookie tins."

"I'm not sure. I guess this is going to be one of those 'we'll know it when we see it' deals."

"If we see it, Bernie."

"Exactly, Libby. *If* being the operative word."

The sisters looked at each other.

"This is going to be a wild goose chase, isn't it?" Libby said to her sister.

"Possibly," Bernie said.

Libby cocked her head and looked at her sister.

"Okay, Libby. Probably. Because even if we don't find the tins, that doesn't mean someone who was driving by didn't see them and stop and pick them up."

"At night? On this stretch of road? I don't think so."

"You're right," Bernie admitted as she flipped up the hood on her coat.

Libby sighed and stifled a cough. She just knew she was going to get sick. "We should be back at the shop working."

They had six orders to get out, as well as nine tortes, the snowflake cookies, and twenty assorted cheesecakes in addition to their regular menu, and as if that weren't enough, they had to be at the Longely Community Center at six-thirty tonight for the judging.

"I know. But you said it yourself. We're doing this to make Amber feel better," Bernie reminded her. "I mean she's always been there for us. We can't ignore this, especially since she asked for our help."

"You're right. You're right," Libby said, looking abashed. "I'm just crabby . . ."

"And tired . . ."

"And overworked."

"Exactly," Libby said.

"Welcome to retail at Christmas," Bernie said.

Libby laughed. Then she got serious. "Poor Millie. Christmas is a rotten time to be in a hospital."

"Maybe she'll be out by then."

"Hopefully."

"What does Amber say the docs are telling her?"

"They don't know. It's a wait-and-see situation."

"That sucks," Bernie said.

The sisters stopped in front of the tree Millie had crashed into. Bernie put her hand up and touched the gash in the trunk that Millie's Buick had made and shook her head. "I hate to think what would have happened to Millie if she'd been going faster."

"She'd be dead," Libby said matter-of-factly. "No doubt about that." She looked into the woods. "Now how are we going to do this?"

"I was figuring we'd split up and walk around and see if we can spot the cookie tins."

"Do you know what the tins look like?"

"No," Bernie said. Talk about stupid questions. "But how many other tins could there be lying around on the forest floor? None. That's how many."

Libby studied the ground for a moment before saying, "They could be hidden behind a branch or under a rock."

Bernie let out an exasperated sigh. "Then we won't find them. Obviously."

"Obviously." Libby frowned. "You know what we should have brought along? What would have helped?"

"A flask of hot chocolate?"

"A metal detector."

Bernie rolled her eyes and hugged her collar to her to stop the wind from going down her jacket. "Such a practical suggestion. You mean the one we don't have in the storage closet."

Libby put her hands on her hips. "Ha. Ha. I think the suggestion has merit."

"You would."

"Meaning..." Bernie started to speak, then changed her mind. "Anyway, metal detectors don't pick up tin."

"Of course they do."

"No. They don't."

"They pick up pennies, don't they?" demanded Libby.

"I guess they do," Bernie conceded.

"So why not tin? After all, it is a metal alloy."

"Fine. You're right." Bernie brushed a wisp of hair off her forehead. She was too tired to argue anymore. "Unfortunately, we don't have a metal detector lying around."

"I know."

"So why did you bring it up?"

"I was talking theoretically."

These were the times when Bernie wanted to strangle her sister. Instead she took a deep breath and said, "Okay, now that we have that settled, why don't we just do a quick walk through the woods. At least," Bernie added, trying to inject a more positive note into the proceedings, "the ground is relatively bare. Not like it would be in the summer or the fall. It'll make things easier to see."

"Not by much," Libby muttered.

Lord grant me strength, Bernie thought as she stepped into the woods. Libby followed.

"How about you go to the right and I'll go to the left?" Bernie said.

Libby nodded her agreement. She looked at her watch. "How long do you think we should do this for?"

"Half an hour?" Bernie suggested, thinking of the tortes waiting to be made and the fact that they had to pick up more sugar before they went back to the shop.

"Works for me," Libby said as she set off. She'd taken five steps when an idea occurred to her. "There aren't any snakes here, are there?" she asked her sister. She hated snakes. She hated them almost as much as she hated spiders.

"None. They hibernate in the winter."

"You're positive?"

"Absolutely. Except for the big Burmese pythons. I understand one of them ate a deer recently. Just kidding," Bernie said when Libby came to a dead stop. "Really." Bernie raised her right hand. "I sister swear."

"That's not funny," Libby huffed.

"You're right," Bernie said, endeavoring to look contrite and failing. "It's not." Somehow she managed to stifle her laughter.

Libby gave her a dirty look before going back to searching. Sticks cracked under her and her sister's feet.

"Having trouble?" Libby asked as Bernie stumbled and cursed.

"Not at all," Bernie said. She wasn't about to admit that wearing boots with four-inch heels while walking around in the undergrowth probably hadn't been the best idea.

"I just don't want you to twist your ankle or anything," Libby said in her most sickly sweet tone, "and not be able to wear stilettos. That would be a tragedy."

Bernie decided not to bother answering. After all, they were supposed to be looking for something, not sniping at one another. She and her sister both kept their eyes down.

They saw rocks and fallen branches and empty beer bottles and fast-food wrappers, but no cookie tins.

"Think we've gone far enough?" Libby asked Bernie after five minutes had elapsed.

"I think maybe we should give it another twenty feet or so. I mean, if the tins are going to be here, they'll be near the road."

Bernie looked at her watch. Another twenty-five minutes to go. In different circumstances, she would have found this a pleasant outing. As in if it were warmer and if they didn't have so much work to do. Then she felt a freezing drizzle falling on her face. Lovely. Enough was enough. She was just about to tell Libby she would wait for her in the van when she spotted something about twenty yards away in the underbrush. She squinted, trying to make it out. It was brownish. And had some sort of shape. It definitely wasn't a tree.

She took another couple of steps. Once she got away from the bushes she had a clear, unobstructed view. She walked up to it slowly. She expected it to take off at any second. Instead it stood and regarded her with unblinking eyes. When she was about ten feet away, Bernie stopped. She suddenly realized why it wasn't running.

"Libby," she called out. "Come over here and have a look at this."

"Did you find the tins?" Libby called back.

"No. But I think I might have found the reason why Millie went off the road. I think we'd better call Matt."

Libby joined her sister a moment later and listened while her sister explained her idea. "That's a big jump you're making," she told Bernie when she was done.

Bernie regarded the figure for a moment before replying. "Well, the cookie tins aren't here, but this is. To me that's not a good mix."

Chapter 5

Matt shook his head as he stared at the spot where the life-sized plastic buck, complete with antlers, was standing. "You got me back here for this?" he demanded of Bernie.

Bernie put her hands on her hips. "Yes, I did," she declared.

"It's a hunting target," he observed. He was coming off a twelve-hour shift in another half hour and desperately wanted nothing more than to go home, take a shower, and fall into bed. Why Bernie had called him here was something he couldn't begin to fathom.

"It could also be a murder weapon," Bernie said.

Matt readjusted his hat and half turned to keep the sleet off his face. Was he missing something here? "Excuse me. Whose murder are we talking about?"

"Millie's," Libby promptly answered.

"Has she died?" Matt asked her.

"No. Not yet," Bernie admitted. "Okay. Attempted murder. But she hasn't come out of her coma yet, either, so she could be a murder victim."

Matt folded his arms across his chest and looked from

one sister to another while he struggled to maintain his professional facade. And failed. "No possible way."

"Why?" Bernie demanded.

"What do you mean 'why'? You have no evidence." He pointed at the deer target. "This could be here for any number of reasons." He took a deep breath. "You are really stretching this whole thing pretty thin. You want my advice? Go back to the shop."

Bernie stuck her chin out. "I'm talking about possible scenarios," Bernie replied, trying to keep the anger out of her voice. "You should listen."

"Bernie, let me repeat." Matt pointed at the deer. "This is a hunting target, a bow-hunting target to be specific." Then he indicated the heart painted on it. "See the target? Someone dragged it out here to practice on. It's as simple as that."

"I don't think so, Matt," Bernie said, determined to get her point across. "I think that someone put it in the road so that Millie would see it and crash into that tree, someone who knows how Millie drives and how easily she panics."

Matt scowled. He didn't want to talk about this anymore, and he certainly did not want to talk about it standing outside in icy drizzle. All he wanted to do was get in his squad car, go back to the station, and clock out.

"Talk about wild conjectures," Matt shot back. "You have no evidence. No evidence whatsoever. If your dad was here, he'd say the same thing."

Bernie ignored the last comment and pointed at the target instead. "Then why is the deer . . ."

"Buck," Matt corrected.

Bernie waved her hand in the air. "Whatever."

"You should at least use the correct terminology."

Bernie took a deep breath and let it out. "Fine. Then why is that buck there?"

Matt realigned the brim of his hat again and hunched

over slightly to protect himself from the icy rain. "I already told you. Someone was practicing his bow skills on it. This is a perfect spot. No one's around. Or maybe someone's wife decided to throw it out."

Bernie pointed. "And leave it there instead of putting it in the trash?"

"Sure," Matt answered. "Makes sense to me. This way the husband wouldn't see it and dig it out of the trash. Or going back to the hunting scenario, maybe someone brought the target out here to practice on and hurt his hand doing something stupid or twisted his ankle falling over a tree root, and he had to go back home. So he left the target here. They're not that expensive. You can get them at any sporting goods store. Maybe he's planning on coming back for it later."

"You should impound it," Libby said.

"And do what with it?" Matt asked, thinking of the ribbing he'd take if he brought that thing back to the station house. He could hear it now: "Nice goin', Matt. Good collar." Besides, he didn't think it would fit in his squad car. No, scratch that. He *knew* it wouldn't fit in his squad car.

"I don't know," Libby told him. "Dust it for fingerprints."

Matt snorted. "Okay. Aside from the whole fingerprint deal, which is definitely not as easy as they make it look on TV, I can't impound anything. This is not a crime scene." Matt indicated the tree that Millie had crashed into with a nod of his head. "That is an accident scene." Then he indicated where the three of them were standing. "This is nothing, because nothing has happened here."

"You don't know that," Bernie told him.

"I most certainly do," Matt replied through gritted teeth. He loved Libby and Bernie, but not when they got like this.

"This could become part of a crime scene if it turns out that Millie's accident was engineered," Bernie said.

"Wouldn't you then feel foolish letting this opportunity go to waste?"

"I can live with that," Matt said. He was about to explain to Bernie and Libby about the amount of paperwork their suggestion would entail when he heard his radio crackle into life. Thank God, he thought. Finally. A graceful way to get out of here. "Gotta go, ladies," he said to Bernie and Libby. With that he turned and started back to his patrol car. On the way, he snagged his pants leg on a fallen tree branch. Great, he thought. The perfect end to the perfect day.

Libby and Bernie watched him trudge toward the road.

"I must say he wasn't very open-minded," Libby said to Bernie.

"He certainly wasn't," Bernie replied as she watched Matt's patrol car take off down the road. "The question is: what are we going to do with this thing?" she asked, referring to the buck.

"We could take it with us," Libby said. "On the other hand, if Matt is right, that means we'll be stealing someone's property."

"Not to mention messing up a crime scene." Bernie reached for her phone. "I'm going to take a couple of pictures to show Dad."

"Good idea," Libby said. "As Dad always says, 'When in doubt, document.' "

Then she took a chocolate kiss out of her jacket pocket, unwrapped it, and popped it in her mouth. Was Matt right, after all? The more she thought about it, the more she felt he might be. She had a hunch her dad would think so too.

Not that she'd say anything about her qualms to Bernie, she decided, as she watched her sister snap a couple of pictures of the target. If she did that, given the mood they were both in, Bernie would just call her a flip-flopper and she'd call Bernie pig-headed, and they'd be off and running, and she didn't want that to happen. Things were stressful enough as they were. A couple of minutes later, Libby watched Bernie tuck her phone back in her bag, bend over, and start studying the ground.

"What are you doing?" Libby called out. She checked her watch. Time was a-wasting. "We have to get back to the shop."

"I'm looking for drag marks," Bernie told her. "Someone had to have dragged this thing out here."

Libby laughed. "So now you're a Boy Scout? Weren't you the one who got thrown out of the Brownies?"

"That was for bad behavior," Bernie said.

"Anyway," Libby went on. "What difference does it make? Of course this thing was dragged out here. How else did it get here, fly? The question is: was it in the road?"

Bernie straightened up. She chewed on the inside of her cheek for a moment and reached for her cell phone.

"Who are you calling?" Libby asked.

"Brandon."

"Why? He probably just fell asleep."

"I know, but he used to hunt and I want him to see this."

"Bernie, we need to go."

"He'll be here in five minutes," Bernie told her. "Five minutes! What's the rush?"

Libby just shook her head and walked back to the van. There was no point in arguing with her sister when she got this way. But at least it was warm in the van. She had a chocolate bar stashed in the glove compartment for emergencies, and if this didn't constitute an emergency, she didn't know what did. As she climbed inside Mathilda, she decided to call Googie and get him to get George to start prepping things in the kitchen. At least that way the morning wouldn't be a total loss.

* * *

Fifteen minutes later an extremely grumpy, pajama-clad Brandon arrived at the scene. Bernie ran over and kissed him as soon as he got out of his Jeep.

"Thank you," she cried.

"This better be good," Brandon said as he zipped up his parka. He'd gotten to bed just three hours ago. "I closed last night."

"I didn't know anyone else to call," Bernie said. "And you do know about this stuff."

"That was ten years ago."

Bernie gave him her most charming smile. "But you still know more than I do."

Brandon looked at her for a moment and said, "Sometimes being your boyfriend really is a pain in the butt."

"That's so mean, Brandon."

"But so true, Bernie. Show me what your problem is so that I can take care of it and go back to bed."

"You heard about Millie, right?"

"I heard that she was in a car accident."

"We think that accident might have been caused," Bernie said. And then she went into her explanation.

Libby decided, judging from Brandon's facial expression as Bernie talked, that he seemed as impressed by Bernie's theory as Matt had been. Libby watched from the warmth of the van as he and Bernie tramped into the woods to look at the deer target. Then he came out and carefully began walking along the road. Bernie walked with him.

"What are we looking for?" she asked.

"Something to tie the target in place or give it some stability. Maybe a rope or a wooden platform with wheels. Ordinarily, you wouldn't need something like that because these things come with a base, but it was really windy last night and there's a good chance the target would have tipped over," Brandon said. He kept his eyes down on the road as he spoke.

Bernie did likewise. The two of them walked in silence down the stretch of road that encompassed the area between where Millie had hit the tree and the telephone pole several yards away.

"Even if we don't find anything, that doesn't prove I'm wrong," Bernie said to Brandon. "A negative doesn't prove a positive."

"But it doesn't disprove it either," Brandon said. "Can we please just concentrate on the road?"

"We are concentrating on the road," Bernie said.

"Not if we're talking we're not," Brandon told her.

"So you're saying you want me to shut up?" Bernie asked.

"Well, I wouldn't have put it that way, but yes I do."

"Fine," Bernie huffed. "All you had to do was ask."

"I am asking," Brandon said.

Bernie pressed her lips together, made an imaginary locking motion with her thumb and forefinger, and threw the key away.

"You don't have to be that dramatic," Brandon said.

"Shush," Bernie said, pressing her forefinger to her lips again and making a big show of staring at the ground.

Five minutes later, Bernie and Brandon saw what they were searching for.

"Look," Bernie said, pointing at a large rock outcropping that had a length of twine tied around its base.

"I see it," Brandon said as he moved toward it.

Once he was in front of it, he squatted down for a better look. Bernie joined him.

"Millie would have seen the target, not the rope that was securing it," she mused.

Brandon grunted, picked up the rope, and pointed to the end. "Somebody cut this with a knife."

"Meaning?" Bernie asked.

"Meaning," he said, "that whoever set the target up didn't want to take the time to undo his knots."

Bernie grinned. "So that means that I'm right," she said triumphantly.

"No," Brandon said. "But it doesn't mean you're wrong either." Then Brandon got up and walked over to the other side of the road.

"What are you doing?" Bernie asked.

"Looking for another rope anchored to another rock on this side. Now, that would lend more weight to what you're suggesting."

Bernie got up and joined Brandon, but neither she nor he saw anything, and after five minutes they abandoned the attempt.

"Whoever did this could have just used one rope," Bernie said as she took out her phone and snapped a picture of the rope they'd found.

"I'm not disagreeing with you," Brandon said as he squatted down and took another look at the rope. "I'm guessing from the rope's color and condition that it hasn't been here that long. In fact, the rope looks pretty new." He got up and brushed a few pieces of gravel off the knees of his pants. "But I think you're still skating on pretty thin ice. This whole scenario you've conjured up . . ."

"Conjured?" Bernie squawked.

"As in dreamed up."

"I know what 'conjured' means, thank you very much, and I haven't dreamed up anything," Bernie replied indignantly.

"I'll be interested to hear what your dad has to say when he hears about this," Brandon said to Bernie.

"He'll agree with me." Bernie was about to explain why when Libby beeped the van's horn.

Bernie and Brandon both jumped at the sound.

"We have to go," Libby yelled to Bernie as she rolled down the van's window. "Amber just called. Millie's, and she wants to talk to us."

"About what?" Bernie called back.

"I don't know," Libby replied. "Amber didn't say."

"Good," Brandon said. He began walking to his car. "Now maybe I can go back to sleep."

"Is Marvin around?" Bernie asked Libby after she'd climbed back into their van and brushed the particles of sleet off her bangs. Brandon's last comment had given her an idea.

"Yeah. Why?"

"I figure if he isn't busy, he and Dad can drive over and see the target and the rope. Four eyes . . ."

"In this case eight . . ."

"Whatever . . . being better than two, or four."

Libby nodded. She had to admit it was a good idea. "I'll call and ask."

"Good." Bernie rubbed her arms with her hands in an effort to take off the chill. "Can't you get the heat in this thing up any higher? My comforter is warmer than this."

"Then maybe you should have brought it along," Libby told her as she punched in Marvin's number on her speed dial.

At least, Bernie thought as she settled back in her seat, the hospital would be warm.

Chapter 6

The rain was falling harder now, coating the roadway and the trees with ice, so it took Bernie and Libby longer than usual to get to Longely General Hospital.

"You know you can go over twenty miles an hour," Bernie said to Libby as they turned onto Route 42.

"I would if our tires were in better shape," Libby shot back. Her hands clenched the steering wheel. She hated driving under circumstances like these, but she was damned if she was going to admit that to Bernie.

"They're not that bad," Bernie said.

"They're not that good either," Libby countered through gritted teeth. If they'd left a half hour ago, as she had wanted to, they wouldn't be driving through this mess now.

"Do you want me to drive?" Bernie asked Libby.

Libby shook her head. "I'm fine," she lied.

"You are so not, Libby."

"I would be if you would stop asking me how I was every five minutes, Bernie."

Bernie grimaced. "You blame me for this, don't you?"

"What's this?" Libby asked, feigning innocence.

"This being the fact that we're on the road now."

"Not at all," Libby told her, lying again.

Bernie shrugged. "If that's the way you want it."

"It is."

"Fine. Just remember I offered to drive."

"Thanks, but I prefer to get there in one piece."

"What's that supposed to mean, Libby?"

"Exactly what you think it does, Bernie,"

"Let's take a time out from each other," Bernie suggested.

"Works for me," Libby answered.

Bernie turned her head and gazed out at the passing scene, while Libby leaned over and clicked on the radio. The sound of Aretha filled the air. The sisters didn't talk until ten minutes later when they hit Park Street, at which point Libby extended an olive branch.

"I hope this stops soon," she said, pointing to an overhead power line that was bowed under the weight of the ice.

"But it is beautiful," Bernie commented. "You have to admit that. The ice makes everything look magical."

Libby snorted. "Yeah, but that's not going to help if the power goes out. I think we need a backup generator in the shop," Libby said, continuing with her original train of thought.

"Agreed," Bernie told her. Libby was right. A power outage at the shop would be a disaster. They'd lose thousands of dollars' worth of ingredients. Better not to think about it, Bernie decided, so she changed the subject. "I wonder what Millie wants to talk to us about?"

"She probably wants to know about her cookies," Libby said, her eyes glued to the road as she slowly glided through a stop sign because it was safer than stopping. At this point she felt as if she were driving a large, lumbering beast.

Bernie brushed a lock of hair that had come loose from her ponytail off her forehead. "What are we going to tell her?"

Libby sighed. "Good question."

"She's going to be very upset when we tell her we can't find them."

"That is an understatement," Libby observed. She was definitely not looking forward to this.

Neither sister spoke again until they'd pulled into the hospital parking lot.

"We're here," Libby announced as she shoehorned Mathilda into the parking space that was the nearest vacant one to the door and turned off the van. It shuddered to a stop after making an awful grinding noise. "I guess she doesn't like this weather either," Libby observed.

"Who does?" Bernie replied.

As she looked at the building, she thought about the fact that neither she nor Libby had been here since their mother had broken her arm—that is, unless she counted the time the three-year-old she had been babysitting for had squeezed half a tube of toothpaste into her ear. God, what a nightmare that had been. Who would have thought that anyone could even do something like that? She certainly hadn't. It had been the last time she'd babysat. Not that anyone had asked her since then.

"At least it's not sleeting anymore," Libby said.

"I'm not sure this is much better," Bernie said as the wind blew the rain sideways. She watched as a gust of wind plastered a newspaper against the hospital's foundation plantings. "Maybe we shouldn't have asked Marvin and Dad to run out."

"They'll be fine," Libby assured her. "Marvin told me he's taking the hearse."

Bernie laughed. "Dad will be so pleased." She flipped up her hood. "We have to go."

"Absolutely," Libby agreed, putting her hood up as well. "Amber's waiting."

But the two women continued to sit there. They'd hit a

wall. They were cold and wet and tired and finding it difficult to move.

"On the count of three," Bernie said.

"Make that five," Libby said. "Or better yet, ten."

"Five," Bernie said.

"Okay. Five," Libby grudgingly conceded.

Bernie began counting down. "One. Two. Three. Four.
Five."

At which point Libby and Bernie threw open their re-
spective doors and ran into the hospital lobby.

"It really is awful out there," Bernie said as she pushed
her hood back and followed Libby to the elevator. "Do we
know where we're going?"

"We do." Libby showed her the text Amber had sent
her while they were in transit.

Amber was pacing up and down outside the ICU when
Libby and Bernie walked up the corridor. One look at
Amber's face and Bernie knew.

"I think we're too late," she whispered to Libby.

"I think so too," Libby whispered back as Amber came
rushing up to them.

"Millie's gone," Amber told them, tears pouring down
her face.

Bernie and Libby reached over and hugged Amber to
them.

"She made me promise you would find her murderer,"
Amber said.

"Murderer?" Libby asked. "Is that what she said?"

"More or less," Amber replied. She blinked her eyes
and looked down at the floor.

Libby was about to ask her what she meant by that, but
before she could, Bernie glared at her and Libby bit her
tongue. Her sister was right, she decided. This was not the
time to cross-examine Amber.

"You will, won't you?" Amber begged, lifting her head

and looking from Libby to Bernie and back again. A tear trickled down her cheek. "Promise me that you will."

"Of course we will," Bernie said, looking at Libby. "Won't we? Won't we?" she repeated when Libby didn't answer.

"Absolutely," Libby said. "But Amber," she continued in a gentle voice. "Maybe the police are better suited to investigate your aunt's death."

Amber sniffled. "They're not going to."

"Why not?" Bernie asked.

"Because they're saying Millie's death was an accident. They're saying she shouldn't have been driving." Amber started crying again.

"I'm so sorry," Bernie said as she and Libby hugged Amber to them again.

"Me too," Amber managed to get out while Bernie stroked her hair and told her that things would be all right and that she and Libby would do whatever was necessary.

The three of them stood in the hallway while people eddied around them, giving them a wide berth. *As if grief is contagious,* Libby thought.

Finally, Amber stopped crying and disengaged herself from Bernie and Libby. "One other thing. Millie wanted you to get her recipes and give them to me."

"Okay," Bernie said. "We can do that."

"As soon as possible," Amber said. "Like today."

"Why the rush?" Bernie asked.

Amber sighed. "She didn't say, but I think she was afraid that someone was going to try to steal them."

"What do you think?" Bernie responded, deciding that this was more of Millie's paranoia.

"I don't know." Amber pulled at her braids. "She was sounding crazy, but, after all, look what happened."

"Did she say who she thought would steal the recipes?" Bernie asked.

Amber swallowed and shook her head.

"Are you sure?" Bernie gently inquired.

Amber blinked back tears. "I don't know. Maybe she did. But in the end I couldn't understand what it was she was trying to say. She just kept squeezing my hand and mumbling things. I should have tried harder. I should have listened more closely."

"You were doing the best you could," Libby reassured her. "Did she say anything else? Anything at all?"

"She just talked about people being out to make sure she didn't win the bake-off." Amber looked down at the floor and then up at the sisters again. Bernie decided that without her makeup Amber looked about ten. "She made me promise to take her place in the contest."

Bernie raised an eyebrow. Somehow she didn't think the other members of the Christmas Cookie Exchange Club would be pleased.

But if Amber noticed Bernie's expression, she ignored it and plowed ahead. "She also told me that she'd hidden her recipe for Millie's Majestic Meltaways in the composting bin, so in case you guys didn't find the cookies, I could make a new batch. You didn't find them, did you?" Amber asked in a pleading tone.

"No, Amber," Libby answered. "I'm sorry, but we didn't. I think they're gone."

Bernie shifted her weight from one foot to the other. Her right knee was starting to bother her again. She should really go back to doing her exercises. Of course, she could always give up wearing heels, but that wasn't going to happen.

"Did Millie say anything about a deer?" Bernie asked Amber.

Amber looked at Bernie as if she was crazy. "A deer?"

"Yes. A deer," Bernie repeated. "A buck, to be specific."

Amber wrinkled her nose. "A buck?"

"That's a male deer," Bernie explained. "The kind with antlers."

"Like what?" Amber asked.

"Like seeing one in the road," Bernie answered.

"Do you think that's what made her go into the tree?"

"I don't know, Amber," Bernie told her. "It's certainly possible."

Amber shook her head. "No. She didn't say anything like that. At least not that I understood."

"Exactly what did she say?" asked Libby for the second time.

She'd found that if you asked a question enough times, the odds were you'd get some kind of answer. Her dad claimed that it took people a while to remember things, especially if they were under stress, and over the years Libby had learned that he was correct.

Amber nibbled on her fingernails while she thought. "She was rambling on about things."

"What things?" Bernie asked, picking up on Libby's lead.

"Things like how Lillian needed to lose weight, and how Barbara's hairdo was horrible, and how they wouldn't photograph well on the TV show, and that they should do something about that. Then Millie started talking about how she was going to get her hair done and get a nose job when she was rich and famous and maybe buy a place down in Florida and invite me to it for the holidays."

"So she was mostly talking about the Christmas Cookie Exchange Club members and the TV show?" Libby asked.

"Completely. Except she told me she wants you to have her cinnamon bun recipe. She thought maybe it would help you increase sales because her recipe is so much better than yours. She said even you and your sister know that."

Libby and Bernie couldn't help laughing. Millie always had to have the last word. Especially when it came to baking. In this case she had.

"We'll name them Millie's buns," Bernie said, giving a warning glance to Libby to stop her from objecting. Even though Libby was the kindest person imaginable, she took her food extremely seriously.

Amber grinned. "She would like that."

"Good," Bernie said. "Then it's settled."

After all, Bernie thought, what was the harm? It would make Amber happy. She'd just make a few additions and deletions before she sold them at the shop. Maybe change the proportion of flour and butter and eggs. Add a little more cinnamon, a little less sugar. Little things like that. Not that she'd tell Amber what she was going to do. Sometimes, honesty really wasn't the best policy. Or, at least, it wasn't the kindest policy.

Chapter 7

The wind had died down and the rain had stopped by the time Marvin and Sean arrived at the scene of Millie's accident. Marvin carefully parked the hearse on the side of the road, well away from the blind curve, and turned off the ignition.

The last thing he needed was an accident with the company car, even if it was his company. Well, his and his dad's company. Mostly his dad's, if you wanted to be accurate, although one day it was going to be his. And an accident would be particularly bad today, not that it was good any day, but in a little while he had to drop Mr. Simmons back at his house and pick up a client, as his father liked to put it, from the hospital morgue.

"Well," Marvin said to Sean, after he'd checked the time on his phone. He was still golden.

"Well what?" Sean replied as he looked out at the stretch of woods in front of him.

Listening to Bernie and Libby, he hadn't been able to decide whether the scenario they were proposing was valid or not, but now that he was here, he was beginning to form an opinion. There was definitely no substitute for seeing something yourself instead of relying on other people's descriptions, he decided. He'd thought so when he'd been the Longely chief of police, and he thought so now.

"Well, what do you think?" said Marvin.

"I think it's a strange place to set up a deer target," Sean replied as he buttoned up his jacket and put on his gloves. "And a strange time too, as long as we're on the subject."

"Why a strange place?" Marvin asked. He'd never done any hunting and had absolutely no idea what a deer target looked like, much less that something like that even existed.

"Because," Sean explained, pointing to a sign lying face-down on the ground that neither Bernie nor Libby had seen, "this land is posted. You can't hunt here, for openers, let alone go tromping through it. So that's a biggie."

"Do you think someone took the sign down?" Marvin asked.

"Well, they could have, but it would be kind of a silly thing to do." Sean paused for a moment to take a last sip of the coffee he'd taken from the shop. Then he recapped the thermos, took a bite of his apple-walnut muffin, and continued. "That's the kind of behavior that could get you shot. No. The sign probably just fell down. Another thing," he said, setting the thermos on the floor. "Usually—in fact, almost always—when you set up a deer-hunting target you do it in a field, you don't do it in the woods. That way, if you don't hit the target, you can find your arrow, a thing you want to do since arrows are expensive. You really don't want to lose them."

"People really hunt deer with bows?" Marvin asked.

Sean confined his comment to a "Yes, Marvin, they do."

"Isn't that kind of mean?"

"You think shooting them is any better?" asked Sean.

"I hadn't really thought about it much," Marvin confessed.

"Then how about we concentrate on the matter at hand?"

"I am."

"No. You're not. You keep interrupting."

"Sorry," Marvin said.

"Okay, then." Sean broke off another piece of muffin and popped it into his mouth. "On the other hand," he went on, after he'd swallowed, "if you are a member of a bow-hunting club you'd go to the club to practice, and those places do set up multiple deer targets in the woods, but they mark off how many yards away the target is." Sean took a third bite of his muffin and put the rest back in the paper bag. "So the problem, as I see it, is that neither of those two scenarios can explain what Libby and Bernie found—a single deer target twenty feet away from the road. That makes no sense, unless it was used for the purpose that Libby and Bernie think it was."

Marvin gave him a strange look.

"Why are you looking at me like that?" Sean demanded.

"No reason, really. I'm just surprised. You sound as if you know a lot about this."

Sean laughed. "I do. I used to hunt. I belonged to a bow club when I was a kid."

"Really, Mr. Simmons?" Marvin said as he eyed Sean's muffin.

"Yes, really, Marvin."

Seeing Sean eat had reminded Marvin that he hadn't had any breakfast that morning. "I don't suppose you have any more of those?" Marvin asked wistfully.

"As it so happens, I do." Sean reached in the paper bag and brought out another muffin. "Here. Have this."

"Thanks, Mr. Simmons." Marvin took a bite of the muffin and sighed in pleasure. He could eat Libby's muffins all day long. Of course, he could eat her pies and cookies and biscuits all day long too. Which was why he'd gained twenty pounds in the last year. "I didn't know that you hunted."

"Neither do my daughters," Sean told him. "There's no

reason you should tell them." He could just hear Libby now—"Dad, how could you have hunted poor, innocent Bambi?" She'd gotten upset when he'd used traps to catch mice.

Marvin grinned. "I haven't told them about your smoking, have I, Mr. Simmons?"

"That's because you want to keep going out with my daughter," Sean told him.

"This is true," Marvin replied.

Sean folded his arms across his chest. "However, you did tell them about my driving your dad's Taurus." He still hadn't quite forgiven Marvin for that one. The girls had gotten quite a bit more upset than his actions had warranted, in his opinion.

"That wasn't my fault," Marvin protested.

"Then whose was it?" Sean demanded. "Curious George's?"

"Yours," Marvin stammered. "You didn't bring the car back when you said you would and I got scared. I thought something had happened to you."

"Marvin, you worry too much," Sean told him.

"I know," Marvin said, hanging his head and making Sean feel guilty about what he'd said.

"Although," Sean said, "I suppose there are worse faults to have." Then he opened his door, took his cane, and stepped outside.

It was chilly and damp, and he was glad he'd zipped up his coat. He scanned the gravel and the ground in front of him. It was uneven and full of tree roots and rocks, and for a moment he regretted saying yes to Libby about doing this, because walking on the forest floor could be a problem for him, even with the cane. Not that he'd ever have said that to his children. Hell, he would have said, "No problem," if they'd asked him to walk over hot coals or go through a swamp filled with water moccasins.

"How far in did Libby say the target was?" Sean asked Marvin.

"Twenty feet or so," Marvin replied.

He wasn't looking forward to walking through the woods either, though for different reasons than Sean. He had on his good suit and shoes, because after he did the morgue pickup, he had to officiate at the Russell funeral, and it would never do to have dirt on his shoes or on his pants. It would be seen as a sign of disrespect. Unfortunately, he didn't have time to change.

"Let's get started, then," Sean said, and he took a step into the forest.

Marvin quickly came up beside him. Although Marvin tried not to make it obvious, he was ready to catch Sean in case he tripped or fell. He knew that Sean knew what he was doing, and Marvin also knew that on one level Sean appreciated the possible help, while on another level it made him angry that he needed it, so it was better to pretend it wasn't happening. They were just two guys walking around in the woods together.

Marvin stifled a cough. "Millie's daughter called."

"And?" Sean asked, his eyes on the ground.

"She and her brother have decided to do the funeral at our place."

Sean waited.

"They want her cremated. No viewing. No memorial service. No nothing."

"No autopsy either?" Sean asked.

"Nope. The daughter doesn't want one, and since cause of death is going down as a car accident, it's not necessary."

"I guess we can construe from what you just said that Millie didn't enjoy good relations with her son or daughter," Sean commented as he stepped over a tree root.

"I think that would be a fairly accurate statement."

Marvin bent down and flicked a wet leaf from his trouser cuff. "But then I don't think anyone liked Millie very much. She was a very grumpy person."

"She wasn't to Amber," Sean pointed out.

"That's what Libby tells me," Marvin said.

"I think everyone else was afraid of her," Sean mused.

"You're kidding," Marvin said, picturing Millie in her print dress and orthopedic shoes. This was not someone who engendered fear in his mind.

Sean shook his head. "No, I'm not. She was the J. Edgar Hoover of the Christmas Cookie Exchange Club. She had the goods on everyone, and she wasn't afraid to use her information to get what she wanted."

Marvin snorted. "What could she have possibly wanted?" he asked. "This was a woman who didn't dress particularly well, or have a fancy house or car, or take big vacations. From what I could see, her biggest deal was Christmas and making cookies for everyone."

Sean stopped and looked at him. "I think she wanted power. As with a capital P. Some people just like to have power over everyone else. They just like the idea that they can make people squirm," Sean said, thinking back to an incident several years ago when she had tried to have her neighbors arrested because their two-year-old used to cry in the middle of the night and Millie claimed the baby was doing it on purpose to keep her up.

Sean looked around. All he saw were tree trunks and gray sky. So where was this deer target Libby and Bernie were going on about? He was positive they'd gone in about twenty feet, just as Bernie and Libby had said they should.

"Are you sure this is where the deer target was?" Sean asked, turning to Marvin.

"That's what Libby said," Marvin replied.

"That's what I heard too. Why don't you call and ask her to make sure," Sean ordered.

The last thing he wanted to do was spend any more time than he had to tromping around in the woods. Even though he was pleased to see that he hadn't slipped and that his footing was stable, he still wasn't entirely comfortable.

"I can do that," Marvin told him.

"Then do it," Sean snapped.

Marvin opened his mouth to say something, thought better of it, and punched in the numbers instead. "Yup. This is the place," Marvin said when he got off the phone.

Sean looked around. "Well, I don't see it." Of course, he wasn't entirely surprised. Measurements and directions weren't his daughters' strong suits.

"Neither do I," Marvin agreed. "It looks like a deer, right?"

"Correct. After all, it is a deer target, right?"

"Right," Marvin muttered.

"What did you think it was going to look like?"

"I didn't really think much about it," Marvin confessed. Actually, he'd thought they were looking for a target tacked to a tree, but he would rather have died than confess that to Libby's dad.

"Well," said Sean. "These things look exactly like a deer, and they are usually made of plastic, so they're hard to miss."

"I knew that," Marvin told him.

Sean smiled. "Sure you did," he replied, giving his possible future son-in-law a pass, as he watched Marvin dig into the pocket of his coat and take out his phone again.

"We have to get going soon," he announced after he'd checked the time.

"Give me ten more minutes," Sean told him, and then he said, "Why don't you wear a watch? It would be simpler to glance at your wrist than have to dig your phone out of your pocket every time you want to know what time it is."

Marvin shrugged. "I just got out of the habit of wearing one, I guess."

Sean sighed. He would never understand this generation. Ever. They kept on saying they were making things easier, but really they were making them more complicated. Oh, well. He stood there for a moment, looking around the forest. He didn't have a clue which direction to take. The best thing to do, he decided, was to walk in ever-widening circles. That way they would cover as much territory as possible in the time they had.

He and Marvin started walking once again, keeping their eyes on the ground and the brush around them. They saw tree roots, dead leaves, and rocks. Occasionally, they came upon discarded beer and soda bottles and fast-food wrappers, but not that many of them, Sean observed. But why should there be? These were definitely the woods less traveled. They weren't near anything. In truth, these woods weren't particularly attractive as far as woods went.

They were on their last circle when Sean thought he spotted something lying next to a rock that didn't look as if it belonged there. He went over and prodded it with his cane.

Marvin came up behind him. "What is it?" he asked.

"Don't know," Sean said. "Pick it up and let's find out."

Marvin looked at it. It was covered with dirt, and he would rather not have touched it. However, since he realized that this was not an option, he bent from the waist and gingerly picked it up with his fingertips, making sure to hold it away from his suit. It was surprisingly heavy, he thought, as he handed it to Sean. Sean weighed it in his hand.

"It's a hoof," he said. "A plastic hoof."

"From the deer target?" Marvin asked.

"I'd think so," Sean said. "What else would it be from?"

"So that means someone took the target," Marvin said.

"Well, it didn't just disappear into space," Sean said, who was busy calculating the time between when Libby and Bernie saw it and now. "Of course," he added, "it is possible that the owner came back and got it." Although privately he doubted that was the case. That would have been too big a coincidence, and he didn't believe in coincidence.

"Are you going to call and tell Bernie and Libby?" Marvin asked.

"In a couple of minutes," Sean said. "Right now I want to go back and see if the rope is still there." He handed the hoof to Marvin. "Here. You carry this," he told him. "I have my cane to deal with."

Marvin cleaned off the leaves and dirt as best he could, but there was still a layer of grime attached to the thing, so he held it as far away as possible from himself so that he wouldn't get his suit dirty. He followed Sean through the forest until they were back out on the road. Sean looked around until he found the rock that matched the description Bernie had given him and walked over to it. The rope was gone. Marvin came up beside him a moment later.

"Does this mean what I think it means?" Marvin asked as he stared at the place where the rope had been.

"Yes," Sean leaned on his cane. The walk through the woods had tired him out. "It means that someone caused Millie to crash into the tree."

"Are you going to call the police?" Marvin asked.

Sean shook his head. "No. There's no point. This whole thing is circumstantial. We'd need more evidence than this to get the police involved."

"Then what are you going to do?" Marvin asked.

"That's easy. I'm going to call Bernie and Libby and let them know what's what, and then I'm going to go home and do some thinking."

Chapter 8

Libby looked at the three charter members of the Christ-mas Cookie Exchange Club standing in the shop and sighed. She should be in the kitchen working on the tortes instead of out here calming the ruffled waters. She shook her head. The expression was "smoothing ruffled feathers." The day must have taken more out of her than she thought it had.

She'd bet herself that Barbara Lazarus, Lillian Stein, and Teresa Ruffino would be the first to show up to talk to her about Millie, or Millie's tragic accident, as Teresa had taken to calling it—emphasis on *tragic*—and she'd been right. She just hadn't expected the three ladies to show up quite this soon.

As she watched them, she was struck once again by how different the women of the Christmas Cookie Exchange Club were from each other, a fact they were proud of. In fact, Pearl Pepperpot was constantly saying that the UN could take a lesson from how well the group got along. Libby wasn't so sure that applied to the three that were here now, however, or really to any of them. The words that came to her mind when she thought of the Christmas Cookie Exchange Club were *backbiting* and *gossipy*, but maybe she was wrong. Maybe Pearl Pepperpot was right. After all, none of the women looked or dressed the same, Libby reflected.

For example, Barbara Lazarus sported dyed black hair, rhinestone cat's-eye glasses that were so old they were about to become fashionable again, and bright red lipstick. She was given to tight skirts, high heels, and low-cut tops, while Lillian Stein, the flower child of the group, had long, gray hair that she wore in a braid down her back and favored jeans, flannel shirts, and anything that looked as if it had come from the sixties. Teresa Ruffino, on the other hand, always wore her hair pinned back in a bun, sensible shoes, and a black straight skirt and a black sweater or blouse, giving the impression she was auditioning for a part as a Sicilian widow.

The three women and Libby were standing off to the side of the shop, right by the kitchen door, effectively blocking traffic, while Bernie and Googie were waiting on customers and George was making coffee. Libby wished she was back in the kitchen doing what she had to do, but somehow or other she'd gotten stuck talking to the Christmas Cookie Exchange Club. Or the part of it that was here. She was positive she'd be seeing the rest of the group within the next hour, if not sooner, and she was determined that when they came in, Bernie was going to be the one to talk to them. Fair was fair.

The women had been here chattering on for the last fifteen minutes, and by now Libby wished they'd go away. They'd come in when Libby had been starting the ganache for the tortes, which she had put aside because she thought speaking to them was the right thing to do. Now, as the minutes ticked by, she was regretting that decision.

One thing was for sure, the news of Millie's death had spread quickly. It seemed to Libby that within a matter of minutes after coming home from the hospital, all the women that belonged to the Christmas Cookie Exchange

Club had called her and Bernie to find out, after expressing the appropriate shock at Millie's death, what was going on with the night's taping. Bernie had described it as watching the sharks circling, and she'd been right.

As if that wasn't enough, Barbara, Lillian, and Teresa had come into the store to ask the same questions they'd asked on the phone in person. Questions Libby couldn't supply an answer to. This was because she hadn't been able to get hold of the producer yet, although Libby had a pretty strong hunch that tonight's taping was going to be postponed until tomorrow. At the very least. Maybe even longer.

There was also another issue that had to be resolved. Amber was still talking about taking Millie's place on the show and submitting her aunt's recipes for the judging. Libby had already told Amber that there might be a conflict of interest involved with that, considering that Amber worked for them and she and Bernie were doing the judging, but Amber hadn't wanted to hear about that. She'd just started to sob, at which point Libby had told Amber it was fine with her if it was fine with the producer. It was days like these, Libby thought, that made her want to go into the kitchen, lock the door, and bake.

"Don't you agree, Libby?"

Libby jumped. She'd drifted off. "With what, Barbara?" she asked.

"That it's awful," Barbara Lazarus said.

"What's awful?" Libby asked.

"Millie's death, of course," Barbara said in an accusatory tone of voice. "Haven't you been listening to me?"

"Of course I have," Libby lied, wondering as she did how many times Barbara had repeated that sentiment in the time she'd been here. It had to be at least ten, maybe even more.

"Poor Millie," Barbara said once again. She put her hand over her stomach and patted it. "This whole thing has gotten me quite upset. I don't think I could eat one of your brownies now. Too heavy. Although I think I could digest a sugar cookie. Sugar is good for the system."

"Do you want one?" Libby asked her.

"No." Barbara waved her hand in the air. "It's very kind of you to offer, though."

"Fine," Libby said, smiling sweetly as she watched Barbara frown.

"You know you want one," Lillian told her. "Take it."

"You're not helping," Barbara replied.

"You don't need me to sabotage your diet," Lillian told her. "You do that all by yourself."

Teresa cleared her throat. Barbara and Lillian turned and looked at her.

"Ladies," Teresa said, "let's not bicker at a time like this."

"We're not bickering," Lillian snapped at Teresa.

"No, we're not," Barbara said to Teresa, before addressing Lillian. "You're just being extremely unsupportive," she said to her. "And at a time like this too. I must admit I expected better."

Lillian scowled. "I'm not being unsupportive. I'm just telling the truth. Which you don't want to hear."

Barbara opened her mouth to reply, but Teresa got there first.

"Do you mind?" she said to Barbara and Lillian. "Can we stick to the topic at hand and not go off on a tangent for once?"

"Works for me," Libby said quickly.

"Good. Now, as I was saying, after Millie's last accident," Teresa continued, "we told her that she shouldn't be driving. We all told her."

Lillian nodded. "That's right. We did," she said.

"But," Teresa continued, "she'd never listen to anyone. She always knew best."

"Wait a minute. Back up. What accident?" Libby asked. This was the first she'd heard of it.

Teresa righted her cardigan and rebuttoned its top button. "It happened last year, right after our meeting at Rose's house. She went over Rose's driveway and right into Alma's car. Took the bumper clean off." Teresa frowned at the memory. "Needless to say, Alma was not pleased. Especially because she lost three whole trays of black pepper chocolate cookies. They turned into a mass of crumbs.

"Alma was so mad, but Millie just laughed." Teresa tsked and shook her head at the memory. "I bet Millie wouldn't have been laughing if it had been her cashew-nut bars that had gotten ruined. But all she said was that Alma was making a big deal over nothing and that she could do something else for her holiday presents. Then she said that maybe the accident had been a blessing in disguise for the recipients of Alma's presents."

"She actually said that?" Libby asked.

"She certainly did," Lillian said. "I was there. I heard it. We all did."

"Wow," Libby commented. "Talk about rubbing salt into the wound."

"Yup," Lillian agreed. "Millie could be really mean that way," she added as she leaned against the wall. "She said she was big on truth, but not when it came to herself. That was a whole different matter." She shook her head, remembering. "Jeepers, Alma was so mad that day. I don't think I've ever seen her so upset—unless you count the time that Millie told her that she'd used a cheap brand of vanilla in her cookies. That time Alma's face actually turned red." She leaned in toward Libby. "I never saw that before. I thought that only happened in books," she confided.

"Rose wasn't too happy either, especially when she saw

that Millie had knocked out two of her lilac bushes," Barbara added. She resettled her glasses on the bridge of her nose. "It was terrible. Those lilac bushes had been in Rose's family for years. She'd grown them from cuttings taken from her mother's yard, but all Millie said was that she'd buy her some new bushes at Home Depot and that she was making a big deal about nothing. That just wasn't right."

"No, it wasn't," Teresa said.

"When did the accident happen?" Libby asked.

"Last year," Teresa replied. "But that wasn't the end of it."

"You mean she had other accidents?" asked Libby.

Teresa snickered. "Oh yes. There was the time she went through her garage."

Libby brushed a speck of sugar off her flannel shirt. "You're kidding."

"Nope," Teresa replied. "She pressed on the gas when she meant to press on the brake and drove her car through the rear wall of her garage." She let out another giggle. "I'm sorry. I know I shouldn't laugh, but I just can't help it. Especially after she told me *I* shouldn't be driving anymore."

"Don't forget the time she hit Sheila's BMW," Barbara added. "Oh my heavens." Barbara cupped her hand on her cheek. "I don't think I've ever seen Sheila speechless before. She was so upset she couldn't get the words out of her mouth. She just gasped. I actually thought she was having a heart attack."

"So why was Millie still driving?" Libby asked. "She sounds like a complete menace on the road."

"She was driving because she could," Lillian replied promptly. "Although in fairness I should add that she isn't, wasn't, that bad when she wasn't flustered."

"Unfortunately," Teresa added, "Millie flustered easily. Everything threw her. She had what my mother, may she rest in peace, used to call a nervous disposition."

"Did you try to talk to Millie?" Libby asked.

"Of course we did," Barbara answered. "She didn't want to hear it."

"Okay," Libby said. "Then didn't anyone try to talk to someone else about the situation?"

"Alma told Millie's son and daughter," Barbara volunteered.

"What happened?" Libby asked.

"Nothing. They told Millie what Alma had said, and Millie was so mad at Alma that she said she'd get her back, and she did, too. She started a rumor that Alma bought her quilts in Brooklyn instead of making them herself."

"That's it?" Libby asked. "That's not so terrible," she observed.

"It was for Alma," Lillian told Libby. "Her reputation was besmirched and she was banned from the quilting club. It was very traumatic."

"After that," Teresa confided, "we just backed off. Millie wasn't nice when she was mad, not nice at all. No one wanted to cross her."

"I'll say," Lillian agreed. "She was a regular . . ." She waved her hand in the air. "Let's just say the *b* word would be extremely appropriate."

"So then why did you guys hang out with her if she was like that?" Libby asked the three women.

They looked at each other. Barbara cleared her throat.

"She could be very nice. In fact, she was nice most of the time. We're kind of like a marriage—this group is. You know, you may not like what the other person does sometimes, but you've been together for so long that you shrug your shoulders and let it go."

"Besides," Teresa added. "She wasn't always like this. Back in the day she used to be much nicer."

"Not to me," Barbara told her.

Lillian leaned back up against the wall. "We shouldn't

be talking like this about her. We should show a little respect."

"We're not being disrespectful," Barbara said. "We're just telling the truth."

Lillian straightened up. "Truth is a relative matter," she said.

"Are you saying I'm lying?" Barbara demanded.

"Not at all," Lillian said to her. "I'm just saying that people see things differently, that's all. I suggest we get off this topic and try to stay positive."

"Well, she was a good baker," Teresa added.

"Although," Barbara responded, "despite what Millie said, she certainly wasn't the best baker in Westchester County."

Lillian turned toward her. "Barbara, she didn't mean that when she said it. She was kidding."

"No, Lillian, she wasn't kidding and she did mean it," Barbara answered. "But that, as they like to say, is neither here nor there right now."

"What does that expression mean anyway?" Teresa asked.

Lillian glared at her. "It means it doesn't matter. Now that I finally have the floor, what I want to know is what's going to happen to Millie's cookies?" she asked. "Are they still going to be in the contest?"

"Don't be ridiculous, Lillian," Teresa snapped. "How can they be in the contest when Millie isn't going to be?"

"Actually," Libby said, "Amber wants to take her place."

"That's absurd," Barbara cried. "I never heard of anything so inane."

"I'm waiting to talk to the producer about it," Libby told her. "However, I think you should know that this was Millie's dying wish."

"That's all very nice, but Amber didn't bake those cookies," Teresa protested. "Millie made them. She can't win with someone else's recipe. That's simply not fair."

"She could accept the award on Millie's behalf," Libby pointed out.

Lillian snorted. "I'm sorry, but I just don't agree with this. At all."

"In truth," Libby told her, "it might not be an issue because the cookies seem to have disappeared."

Lillian and Barbara gasped and put their hands over their hearts while Teresa leaned forward and scrunched up her face.

"Disappeared?" Barbara squeaked.

Libby nodded. For ten seconds no one said anything. Lillian and Barbara stared while Teresa blinked. Libby decided she reminded her of a female Mr. Magoo dressed in black.

"What do you mean 'disappeared'?" Teresa finally asked, breaking the silence.

"Millie's cookies are gone," Libby said, wondering as she did if Barbara's, Lillian's, and Teresa's responses were a tad too dramatic. After all, she wasn't talking about the end of the world. She was talking about the loss of a dozen of Millie's Majestic Meltaways.

"You looked?" Barbara said.

"Yes, my sister and I looked," Libby replied. "Of course we did. We looked in Millie's car, we looked along the road where she had her accident, and we looked in her house. No luck. The cookies weren't there."

"That's horrible," Lillian cried, although Libby didn't think that Lillian looked that upset. In fact, Libby thought she looked rather pleased that Millie's cookies were gone.

Barbara pushed her eyeglasses up the bridge of her nose with her thumb once again. "But how could that be? I don't understand. Do you think someone stole them?"

"What do you think?" Libby asked.

Two spots of color appeared on Barbara's cheeks. "How would I know?" she demanded.

"I didn't say you would," Libby replied.

"If I knew I wouldn't be asking you, right?" Barbara said.

"Right," Libby agreed.

"Are you suggesting that Barbara had anything to do with their disappearance?" Lillian asked.

"Of course I'm not," Libby said, even though she had been. "Anything could have happened to them," she continued, changing the direction of the conversation. "They could have fallen out of the car, they could have been picked up by someone. We simply don't know."

"Some people will stop at nothing," Teresa said. She rubbed her hands together and rocked back and forth. "It's horrible. After all Millie's work too. I hate to think that all her efforts are going to go to waste. She spent weeks developing that recipe. I don't know what the world is coming to."

"Months," Lillian corrected. "She spent months perfecting that recipe."

"She wouldn't let us in the house," Barbara volunteered.

"She was afraid we were going to steal the recipe," Teresa said. "Can you imagine that? As if any of us would do something like that." She sniffed. "It would have been insulting if it wasn't so pathetic."

Barbara pointed to her head and lowered her voice. "Millie was losing it," she confided to Libby. "I told the girls that and I'm telling that to you."

Lillian shook her head. "I'm not sure about that," she said. "In fact, I don't think that was the case at all. I think she was just obsessed with winning. Once she heard the show was coming to town that's all she ever talked about."

"She would have done anything, and I *do* mean absolutely anything, to win," Teresa stated.

"Like what?" Libby asked.

Lillian looked at Teresa for a moment and shook her head. "Let's not exaggerate."

"I'm not," Teresa said.

"Would Millie have killed someone to win?" Lillian asked Teresa.

"No. Of course not. Don't be ridiculous."

"My point exactly, Teresa," Lillian said.

Teresa put her hands together and touched her lips with them. "I suppose you're right," she said to Lillian. Then she turned to Libby. "You have to forgive me," she said. "That statement came out wrong."

Barbara snorted. "I'll say."

Teresa glared at her.

"Sorry," Barbara said. "I'll shut up."

"Thank you," Teresa said in a frosty tone. She turned back to Libby. "I tend to get carried away sometimes," she explained. "Millie was just very competitive about her baking. Actually, we all are," Teresa continued. "Some of us are just a little more so than others in that regard."

Barbara and Lillian nodded their heads in agreement.

"Millie was good," Teresa went on. "I don't know anyone who made a better bundt cake. I don't want to give you the wrong idea. Millie just wasn't the best, if you know what I mean." Teresa sighed. "She's going to be so disappointed that she won't be on *Baking for Life*. She just loved to watch that show. If she'd known how to use her VCR she would have taped it every week. This was her dream. It's too bad she had to go and mess it up."

"That's right, blame the victim," Barbara said.

"That's not what I meant, and you know it," Teresa shot back.

"She can't be disappointed, Teresa," Lillian pointed out.

"Live people are disappointed; dead people aren't anything. Or have you forgotten?"

"Ha. Ha." Teresa pointed toward the ceiling "What I meant is that I'm sure she's watching us from up there. I'm sure she'll be able to see the show."

Lillian rolled her eyes. "Spare me."

Teresa straightened up. "I know you don't believe in the hereafter, Lillian, and that's too bad. But I do."

"Then I guess you're in trouble, Teresa."

Teresa put her hands on her hips. "What does that mean, Lillian?"

"You know what I mean, Teresa. Don't pretend that you don't."

"I most certainly do not," Teresa said and she began tapping her foot. "I don't have a clue what you're talking about."

Libby put her hands up and made a time-out sign. "Ladies, peace."

"We're very peaceful, isn't that right, ladies?" Barbara asked Lillian and Teresa.

They nodded their heads in agreement.

Barbara smiled at Libby. "We just want to know what's going on. I mean we've already baked our cookies for the show. Does this mean we have to do them over again?"

"Heavens, I hope not," Teresa said. "Mine are perfect."

"You mean you managed not to burn the bottoms this time?" Lillian asked sweetly. "Because that would certainly be a first."

Jeez, Libby thought as she watched Teresa open and close her mouth.

Finally, Teresa managed to get the words out. "How can you say such a thing?" she spluttered.

"I can say it because it's true," Lillian replied. "I've been telling you for years to get your oven recalibrated and you haven't listened."

"There is absolutely nothing wrong with my oven,"

Teresa answered. "Nothing. Unlike yours. That's why your cakes come out with partially baked centers."

"First of all, the cake you're referring to was a molten chocolate cake, and its center was *supposed* to be partially cooked. How many times do I have to tell you that?"

Teresa sniffed. "You can tell me as much as you like, but I don't believe it."

"Look up the recipe on the Internet," Lillian told her.

"I have and you're wrong."

Lillian put her hands on her hips and took a step toward Teresa. "How can you lie like that? Aren't you ashamed of yourself?"

"I'm not ashamed," Teresa spat back. "I'm not the one who served a half-raw cake to her friends and exposed them to the risk of contracting salmonella from uncooked eggs. I have to say that I think that that is one of the most irresponsible things you have ever done."

"All of you stop," Libby cried as Lillian opened her mouth to reply to Teresa. Libby couldn't stand the arguing anymore.

The three women instantly looked contrite.

"I'm sorry," Teresa said.

"Me too," Lillian added.

"It's the stress," Barbara observed. "We're all just really upset because of Millie. This whole thing has been such a shock."

Libby nodded. She wondered how much more of a shock it would be if she shared her and her sister's suspicions about the accident with these three women. She almost did, but then decided it would be better not to, at least not yet. She and Bernie needed more time to piece things together.

Instead, she decided to tell everyone that they had to go home because she had work to do and that she would call them when she knew something. She had just begun when she caught sight of Bernie talking on her cell. Bernie pointed a finger at her and mouthed the word "Wait." Then, as Libby watched, Bernie hung up and worked her way around George and Googie, came out from behind the counter, and walked over.

"Ladies," she said to Teresa, Lillian, and Barbara. "I just heard from the producer."

"And?" Barbara said, leaning forward.

"Yes," Teresa chimed in. "What are we doing?"

"They're postponing the taping until next week. As a sign of respect," Bernie announced.

"Respect?" Lillian echoed.

"Yes, respect for Millie," Bernie clarified.

"Well, I didn't think it was out of respect for me. But that's ridiculous," Barbara said. "Millie would have wanted the taping to go on. She would have hated the idea of her being responsible for the delay."

"Well, be that as it may," Bernie answered, "that's what the producers have decided."

"Maybe I should talk to what's her name," Lillian said.

"Penelope. Let's all talk to her," Teresa suggested.

"Otherwise, we'll have to bake our cookies all over again," Lillian said.

"At least your cookies can last in a pinch," Barbara told Lillian. "Mine can't."

Lillian drew herself up. "They most emphatically cannot, Barbara."

Barbara smiled a tight little smile. "Of course they can. That's one of the good things about using leaf lard. It has staying power."

"I would never use lard," Lillian exploded. "I use butter, high-butterfat butter that the co-op orders specially for me. That is an awful thing to say. I am beyond upset."

"Sorry, Lillian." Barbara looked down at the floor. "I guess I was misinformed."

Lillian scowled. "I guess you were," she said. "Who told you that?"

"Millie."

"I don't believe you," Lillian said. "You're making that up."

"It's true," Barbara insisted.

"In fact," Lillian said, "I bet no one told you that. I bet you made the whole thing up all by yourself."

Bernie clapped her hands. Everyone stopped talking and looked at her.

"Ladies," she said, "I believe the producer is at the Longely Community Center. But she's only going to be there for the next half hour. If you want to speak to her, now's the time."

Teresa grabbed her coat and put it on. "Let's go," she said.

The other two women followed her out the door. They were still bickering when the door shut behind them.

"Poor producer," Bernie said.

"All I can say," Libby told her sister, "is better her than me."

"God, I'm glad they're gone," Bernie said.

"You're glad?" Libby responded. "What about me? I need an Advil after that."

"Or a shot of scotch," Bernie said.

"Or both. But I think I'll stick with the Advil. If I had anything to drink I'd pass out, and I can't afford to do that." She looked at the clock. She was way behind schedule.

"You know we have to get the recipes," Bernie told Libby. "We promised Amber."

"And we will get them," Libby promised. "We're just not going to get them right now. Where is Amber anyway?"

Bernie shook her head. "I don't know. I haven't heard from her, but I assume she's with her mother."

Libby nodded and headed for the kitchen. At the moment, the only thing she was thinking of was the tortes and how long it would take her to put them together. She was halfway through the door when she remembered something. She turned, came back out, and walked over to Bernie.

"The next batch of the Christmas Cookie Exchange Club members who come in to the shop are all yours. I'm simply not here."

With that, she marched back into the kitchen and shut the door. The ganache was waiting, and she could hardly wait to get to it. At least the butter and the sugar and the eggs weren't going to bicker with each other. She turned on her music, made herself a fresh pot of French roast, and began. Being in the kitchen always made her feel better. It was where she belonged.

Chapter 9

It was a little after seven by the time Libby and Bernie had freed themselves up enough from their obligations at the shop to drive over to Millie's house. It was dark by now, and it smelled as if it was going to snow.

"I hope those recipes are where they're supposed to be," Libby said as Bernie parked the van in the driveway.

"Why shouldn't they be?" Bernie asked her as she noted that there were no lights on in Millie's house—not that she'd expected there would be.

"Well, the cookies weren't where they were supposed to be," Libby observed.

"True. But this is different."

"Let's hope," Libby was saying when a silver car roared past them. "Everything so far has been slightly twisted," she noted as she watched the car take the curve, fishtail, and keep going. "Bad driver," Libby commented as she and Bernie exited the van.

"Or someone in a hurry," Bernie pointed out. She took the house keys that Amber had given her out of her pocket and followed the path up to the door.

Libby was right behind her. "It's funny," she said, "but I

thought that the car that just sped by us was parked on the other side of the road when we drove in."

"Maybe it was. Maybe the person driving pulled over to read a text and it was an emergency and they zoomed off," Bernie observed.

"You're probably right," Libby said. "I just thought it was weird."

"You think everything is weird."

"Because it has been," Libby said while she and her sister climbed the four steps that led to Millie's front door. Libby stood on the landing with her hands jammed in her pockets and watched Bernie put the key in the lock. That movement was enough to swing the door open.

Bernie looked at it for a moment. Then she said, "Interesting."

"We did lock the door when we left, didn't we?" Libby asked.

"Most definitely," Bernie replied.

"Maybe Amber decided to get the recipes herself and came back and forgot to lock the door," Libby hypothesized.

"She would have told us if she had," objected Bernie. But she dug her cell out of her pocket and called her to make sure anyway. "Nope," she said when she clicked off her cell. "She hasn't been here."

"Maybe someone else has," Libby said.

"Obviously," Bernie said.

"I meant someone with a legitimate reason."

"Like who?" Bernie asked.

Libby found a chocolate kiss in her parka jacket, unwrapped it, and popped it into her mouth. "Like her son or her daughter," she said when she was done savoring the last of the kiss. This one had caramel in the center, and she decided she liked the solid chocolate ones better.

Bernie shook her head. "According to Marvin, they would be the last people Millie would have given a key to, and judging from what Amber said, she was the only family member Millie talked to."

"A friend, then," Libby told her. "Or a neighbor. They came in to get something and forgot to lock the door on the way out."

"I guess that's a possibility," Bernie conceded, sounding dubious.

"You don't sound as if you think it is," Libby said.

"It could be," Bernie told her. "But from what I've heard of Millie, it seems doubtful that she would give *anyone* the key to her house."

"Except for Amber."

"Yes. Except for Amber. You told me that Millie wasn't allowing any of the Christmas Cookie Exchange Club ladies in her house because she was afraid they were going to steal her recipe for the competition."

"Maybe the police were here."

Bernie shook her head. "There's no reason why they should be. They're saying that Millie's death was accidental. They're not treating it as a criminal investigation. If they were, they would have sealed the house."

"Do you think we should call them?"

"Who?"

"The police, of course."

"Why? Do you want to?"

"Not really, Bernie. Do you?"

"No, I don't," Bernie replied. She tucked a strand of hair back behind her ear. "Most definitely not. I'm sure there's a reasonable explanation for why the door is open. We just can't think of it at the moment is all." She stifled a yawn. "Anyway, it's been a long day, and I just want to get the recipes, go to RJ's, have a beer, and go home and go to bed. I really don't want to stand around and wait for the police to arrive and take statements and all the rest of the nonsense. We'd be here for hours."

"Works for me," Libby replied. The thought of bed and

sleep sounded wonderful to her at the moment, especially since she had to get up at five the next morning.

"Okay then," Bernie said, pushing the door all the way open. "We're agreed?"

"Yes, we are." Libby almost said "for once," but decided it would be better not to.

"Let's do this," Bernie said as she took a step inside. "How bad can it be?"

"Don't say things like that," Libby cried.

"I can't believe how superstitious you are," Bernie complained as she reached over and clicked on the hall light.

Everything looked as it had when they'd been there earlier. Libby and Bernie slowly advanced through the living room and the dining room. From what they could see, nothing had been touched. The two rooms were still pristine.

"Do you notice anything out of order?" Libby asked as they started toward the kitchen.

"No," Bernie replied. "Do you?"

Libby shook her head. One of the nice things about Millie's obsessive housekeeping was that it was immediately obvious when something was out of place, unlike Libby's own bedroom, which was heaped with piles of clothes she had yet to hang up. Then they got to the kitchen. Libby reached over and clicked on the light.

"Oh my God," she gasped.

Everything had been pulled apart.

"You can say that again," Bernie replied, grimly surveying the open cabinet drawers and the canisters of flour and sugar spilled out on the countertops, as well as boxes of cereal, pancake mix, and Bisquick. She noted the open refrigerator and freezer, whose contents were slowly melting on one of the counters. "What an incredible mess, although it's interesting that none of the cleaning supplies or the pans have been touched."

"Yes, it is," Libby agreed. She stopped to eat another

chocolate kiss. "It suggests that what we have here is someone looking for the recipe for Millie's Magnificent Meltaways," Libby said after the last of the chocolate had melted in her mouth. "That's what I think."

"So do I. This was definitely not a random act." Bernie paused for a moment and then said, "I'm going to go out on a limb here and say this is not the work of family or neighbors. No. Whoever did this knew where the recipe for Millie's Meltaways was supposed to be. Hence the undisturbed cleaning supplies."

Libby frowned. "Which means that whoever did this was most likely one of the members of the Christmas Cookie Exchange Club." She shook her head. "I'm finding that hard to believe."

"Me too." Bernie said.

"They don't seem like the types to do something like this."

Bernie rubbed her hands together and cackled. "Who knows what evil lurks in the hearts of men," she said, quoting from her father's favorite old radio show. "The shadow knows. Heh. Heh. Heh."

"I don't know about the evil part, but I do know that Millie would be turning over in her grave if she could see this," Libby observed.

"The hell with turning over. She'd be spinning." Bernie took out her cell and snapped some pictures of the kitchen to show her dad. "I wonder if the recipes that Amber wanted us to get are still in the safe," Bernie mused, "because I'm willing to bet the Meltaways recipe is not here." She pointed to the empty flour canister. "At least not if that was where it was supposed to be."

"Only one way to find out," Libby said. "It occurs to me," she said after a brief pause, "that it says a lot about Millie that she kept her recipes in a safe."

"Or," Bernie rejoined, "it says something about her friends. Given this mess," she waved her hand, indicating the kitchen, "I'd say her instincts were one hundred percent correct."

"Apparently," Libby said, thinking about their recipes lying on top of their office desk or scribbled in various notebooks piled up on the shelves lining the walls. It never occurred to her to worry about them. "But then why have friends like that? Judging from what I heard from Barbara, Lillian, and Teresa, no one was exactly in love with Millie."

"Yeah, but I bet things didn't start off that way," Bernie replied. "We are talking about people who have known each other twenty . . ."

"More like thirty . . ."

"Okay. Thirty years. A lot of grudges can accumulate during that time."

"Well, she certainly wasn't very likable these days," Libby said.

"No, she wasn't," Bernie agreed. "Truth be told, you didn't like Millie all that much. I didn't like Millie all that much."

"But Amber did," Libby said. "She really loved her." Then she stopped talking and put a finger to her lips. "Did you hear that?" she whispered.

"Hear what?" Bernie whispered back.

"That noise." Libby pointed upstairs.

Bernie listened. "You're being paranoid," she said. "I don't hear anything. There's no one here. Whoever did this is long since gone."

"No, I'm not being paranoid," Libby hissed. "I know what I heard. There. There it is again."

This time Bernie heard it too. It was like a shuffle, and then she thought she heard a word, but she wasn't sure. "It could be something in the walls," she said in Libby's ear. "Maybe a squirrel or the house settling. Or maybe our ears are playing tricks on us."

"Like what kind of tricks?" Libby asked.

Bernie shook her head. Try as she might, she couldn't think of any. "Okay," she conceded, "maybe you're right. Maybe someone is up there."

"Of course, I'm right. My hearing is better than yours."

"Marginally."

"A lot better," Libby said.

"Not so. Anyway, my sense of smell is better."

"That is so not true."

"It most certainly is. You didn't smell the pie crusts burning."

"That's because I had a cold, as you well know."

"If that's how you want to remember it, it's fine with me." Then before Libby could reply, Bernie added, "Hey, how about we stop bickering and go up there," indicating the stairs with a nod of her head, "and see what's going on."

"How about we leave instead?"

"What, Libby? Are you kidding me?" Bernie said. "I want to see who's up there. I'm not leaving now. Not when we have a chance to get Millie's recipes back. Besides, the people up there are probably the other members of the Christmas Cookie Exchange Club. We're not talking motorcycle gang scary here."

"But what if they're not?" Libby asked her sister.

"Who else could they be?" Bernie asked. "Aliens from outer space? Call if you want," she told her, "but I'm not waiting for the police to come."

"Naturally," Libby muttered.

"What do you mean 'naturally'?" Bernie asked her. "We already discussed this."

"We discussed coming in the house. We didn't discuss going upstairs when someone is in the house."

Bernie snorted. "Could you get anymore nit-picky? Come on. Where are your balls?"

"In case you haven't noticed, I don't have any," Libby snapped. She hated when her sister talked this way.

"Jeez. It's just an expression," Bernie said.

"An offensive one, given what it implies."

Bernie rolled her eyes. "Please don't do your whole feminist number right now."

Libby opened her mouth.

"Seriously," Bernie told her before she could say anything.

"Fine," Libby retorted, "if that's the way you feel, but all I'm saying is that there could be someone dangerous up there. We don't really know."

Bernie pointed to the mess in the kitchen. "Somehow I think the person or people who are upstairs are the people who did this. I don't think people who are looking for recipes are usually defined as dangerous. Since we're pretty sure we know who they are, that goes double."

Libby felt a flash of anger. She took a deep breath and let it out. She refused to let Bernie push her buttons. "First of all," she told her sister, "we don't know if what you're saying is true or not; second, the people up there might have caused Millie's accident, which makes them dangerous in my book."

"To whom?" Bernie asked.

"Obviously to us," Libby replied.

"I doubt that."

"How can you say that with such assurance?" Libby demanded.

"Well, I don't see a deer target around here, do you?" Bernie asked.

"No," Libby admitted.

"We're not in a car on a dark country road, are we?"

"No," Libby repeated.

"Ergo, you don't have to worry."

Libby said, "What if they're armed?"

Bernie rolled her eyes. "Oh please."

"No. I'm serious."

"With what? Rolling pins? Pastry bags?"

"One of those women—and I'm not saying it is one of them, mind you—could have a gun. You don't know."

"Fine." Bernie went over to the rack that Millie's pans were hanging from and grabbed two cast-iron frying pans. "Now we're armed too," she said as she handed one to Libby. "There. Does that make you feel better?"

Libby looked down at the frying pan. "Not really."

"Do you want a knife? Will that do the trick? Because I see several on the counter."

For a moment Libby considered it. Then visions of bad things flashed through Libby's mind and she discarded the idea. "No. That's okay. I'll stick with the frying pan."

"I'm glad that's settled." Bernie said, and she headed for the stairs. Libby followed.

"I still think we should call the police," Libby whispered to Bernie as they started up the stairs.

"Then call them," Bernie snapped as she continued her ascent. "I told you before I'm not stopping you."

Libby sighed. She knew she could call, but she also knew that she wouldn't call. For reasons that were unclear to her, she'd been letting her younger sister get her into trouble for as long as she could remember. Her mother used to tell her that it was up to her to set a good example for Bernie, but for some reason she couldn't seem to say no to her.

When Bernie was halfway up the stairs, she halted and turned to Libby. "What room did Amber say the safe was in?" she mouthed.

"Millie's bedroom," Libby mouthed back, although she was positive that by now unless they were deaf, anyone in the house had to know that Bernie and Libby were there too.

"Which one is that?" Bernie whispered.

"I think Amber said it was the second on the left."

"You think?" Bernie hissed.

"Yeah, I think."

Bernie shook her head.

"Don't give me that look," Libby told her.

"What look is that?" Bernie asked.

"The 'how could you be so dumb?' look."

"I wasn't thinking that at all," Bernie said as she continued her climb. "It's not my fault if you suffer from low self-esteem."

"What?" Libby squeaked.

"You heard me."

"Where did you get that from?"

"Look at your clothes, for heaven's sake."

Libby glanced down at the sweatshirt, jeans, and boots she was wearing. "There's nothing wrong with these. They're appropriate. Which is more than I can say for yours," she told Bernie. "High heels? A pencil skirt? A black cashmere sweater? That's what I always wear in the kitchen."

Bernie was just about to tell Libby she saw nothing wrong with her outfit when she heard someone yell "Now!" She started to run up the stairs. She'd just made it to the landing when the door to the room on the left was flung open and Alma Hall and Pearl Pepperpot came running out and flew past her. The whole thing happened so fast that Bernie didn't have time to grab either of the women as they went by her. She just stood there, stunned.

Chapter 10

"Help," Pearl screamed as she came barreling down the stairs.

Libby jumped aside to keep from being knocked over by her. A few seconds later Alma Hall thundered down after her.

"Watch out," Alma cried.

Libby instinctively looked around. She didn't see anyone. By the time she glanced back, both women were running out the front door. As she watched, a silver car pulled up into the driveway, and Alma and Pearl jumped into it, and the car roared off. She heard the tires squeal as it cleared the corner, and then silence reigned once again. Later, when she was telling her dad what had happened, Libby estimated that from start to finish the incident had taken two minutes—at the most.

"What was that all about?" Libby cried as soon as she recovered from her shock.

"I think I can guess," Bernie said. Her tone was grim. "And I'm really less than amused," she added, continuing into the room Alma and Pearl had come out of.

Libby was right behind her. "It's Millie's bedroom," Libby noted.

"No kidding." Bernie indicated the safe standing open in the middle of the media unit. "Guess what's not there?"

"The recipes?" Libby replied.

"Good call," Bernie said. She cursed quietly. This was exactly what she hadn't wanted to happen. She took a quick look around the room. Unlike in the kitchen, nothing was out of place. Therefore, she thought that whoever had opened the safe had known exactly where the recipes were. "I wonder how they knew the combination?"

Libby shook her head. "That's an interesting question, given who we're dealing with."

"Exactly. I have to say that being on a TV show does not bring out the best in a lot of people," Bernie observed.

"You think this is about the TV show?" Libby asked.

"What else?" Bernie replied. "Up until now everyone was acting perfectly normal, or as normally as they ever do."

With that, she went over to Millie's dresser and started opening the drawers.

"What are you looking for?" Libby asked.

"I don't know," Bernie confessed as she quickly closed the first drawer and opened the second. When she was done with the dresser she went through Millie's closet. There was nothing in there except eight print dresses spaced exactly one inch apart and four pairs of black two-inch pumps in an even line. "Amazing," Bernie said. "Who has a closet like this?"

"Someone who's OCD or who's been in the military," Libby volunteered.

"I cannot conceive of wearing the same thing every day," Bernie said as she closed the closet door.

"I can," Libby said.

"I wouldn't brag about that if I were you," Bernie told her.

"So what do we tell Amber?" Libby asked, changing the topic.

Libby's disinterest in clothes was an old bone of contention between them, and she wasn't in the mood at the moment to discuss the subject with her fashionista sister.

Bernie put her hands on her hips and started tapping her foot on the floor while she considered Libby's question. As far as she could see, they had two possibilities. They could continue searching the rest of the house, which seemed pointless, or they could go get the recipes from Pearl and Alma.

"So?" Libby asked again.

"So," Bernie replied, her mind made up. "We don't tell Amber anything yet. We find Pearl and Alma and get those recipes back. They're not theirs to keep."

Libby went over and peered inside the safe. It was empty. There was nothing inside it, not even a speck of dust. "This just gets weirder and weirder," she said. "I can understand if all this fuss was about the recipe for Oreos or Sara Lee cheesecakes. But Millie's Meltaways?"

"Millie's *Majestic* Meltaways," Bernie corrected. "Let's not forget the 'Majestic'."

"Fine. Millie's Majestic Meltaways. Millie's recipe book? Please. There has to be something else going on here. But what? That's the question."

"I told you," Bernie said as she turned and marched out of the room and down the stairs. "This isn't about money. This is about being on TV. It's about ego. In this case, a cigar really is a cigar." She stopped at the door and turned to Libby. "I'll tell you something else. I'll bet you anything that the person driving the getaway car was Rose Olsen."

"It could have been Sheila," Libby suggested as she followed Bernie out of the house.

Bernie locked up. "Sheila drives a green Subaru."

"Since when?"

"Since two months ago. No. It's Rose. Has to be. She's the only one of the bunch who drives a car that color."

"I still can't believe that those women are doing this," Libby said.

Bernie opened the door to their van and jumped into the driver's seat. "It is pretty amazing, isn't it?" she replied. "One doesn't expect this kind of behavior from suburban matrons—at least not these. We're not talking *Desperate Housewives* here. We're talking women in their seventies. Which just goes to show one is never too old to make a complete idiot of oneself."

"Maybe seventy is the new forty."

"In that case," Bernie said, "you and I are in our teens."

"You mean we're not?" Libby deadpanned.

Bernie laughed. "Well, Brandon does say that sometimes I act like I'm twelve."

"I don't think I would have believed it if I hadn't seen it," Libby said, returning to the original subject as they zoomed out of the driveway.

"Me either," Bernie said.

"Where are we going?" Libby asked her.

"To Rose's house, of course. I'm going to take the shortcut over by Lakeview." Bernie looked at her watch. Rose had a ten-minute lead on them—at most. Bernie was pretty sure she could make up the difference. First of all, Rose was a slow driver, and second, the shortcut she was going to use took at least ten minutes off the drive. "If we hurry we can beat her."

"If she's not there?" Libby asked.

"Then we'll either wait in her driveway or go to Alma and Pearl's houses."

"Just as long as you don't kill us in the process," Libby said, thinking of the condition of the roads Bernie was suggesting. They were unlit country roads, little more than gravel, two-lane jobbies that were full of potholes.

Bernie just grunted and put her foot down on the gas. Mathilda began to groan and buckle. From the sound of her, Libby guessed that they were up to forty miles an hour, which was faster than the van liked to go.

"Be nice to Mathilda," Libby implored as Bernie drove out of Millie's driveway and sped down Clark. "She's the only vehicle we've got."

"I'm aware of that," Bernie snapped. She kept her eyes on the road. Four blocks later they turned onto Route 31. Darkness engulfed them.

"We know where they live. I don't see what the big hurry is," Libby told her as she clutched the edge of her seat. She could feel the van going up and down. Was that a shock that just went? She wasn't sure. But whatever it was, it felt as if it was going to be expensive to fix.

"The big hurry," Bernie told her as she steered around a large pothole by going into the opposite lane, "is that I want to catch them as they get out of the car while they still have the recipe book."

"You think they're going to just hand it over to us?"

"If I have anything to do with it they will," Bernie said through gritted teeth.

"This is insane," Libby protested. "Rose could have picked the women up and be dropping them at their places now."

"Maybe," Bernie allowed. "But I think that they left their cars at Rose's house."

"Why?"

"Because that's what makes the most sense."

"Which they would do since they're acting in such a logical manner," Libby observed.

"Maybe you're right," Bernie admitted as she took a sharp left onto Voorhees Hollow. "But I don't care. I'd just like to surprise them, if I can. I feel it's the least we can do, given what they did to us."

"I'm all for revenge, but not at the expense of Mathilda," Libby objected.

"Mathilda will be fine," Bernie assured her sister.

"I hope so," Libby said. "But I've got to say that that high-pitched whining I'm hearing at the moment doesn't sound fine to me."

"Even if worse comes to worst, and I'm not saying it's going to, you've been saying for a while now we need to get a new vehicle."

"But not like this," Libby shot back. "And not now," she said, thinking of all the catering jobs they had lined up. Christmas and New Year were their busiest times of the year, followed by Easter and Valentine's Day.

"It'll be fine," Bernie repeated. "You worry too much."

"And you don't worry enough," Libby retorted.

Bernie just grunted and kept her eyes on the road. They were reaching a tricky spot, and she needed to focus on navigating through it and not ending up in a ditch on the side of the road. Three minutes later, Bernie took a right onto McClellan, and streetlights appeared.

"See," she said to Libby, "we made it."

"This time," Libby replied as she massaged her hand. She'd been gripping the seat so tightly her fingers were cramped.

"You always have to get the last word in, don't you?" Bernie remarked.

"I try," Libby said.

Three cross streets later, they came to Meadowbrook, the enclave where Rose lived. Meadowbrook was one of the older areas in town and was being considered for a historical designation. Three-quarters of the houses there had been built by a developer called Winnifred Brown.

He was an adherent of the Arts and Crafts movement, which meant that most of the homes in the five-square-block area sported oak trim throughout the interior, beamed ceilings, and small-paned windows. The area had traditionally attracted those of the artistic persuasion, so it wasn't surprising that that's where Rose Olsen had chosen to live when she'd moved up here from New York City.

Four minutes later, Bernie and Libby were in sight of Rose's house. They watched as Rose pulled into her driveway.

"Am I good or am I good?" Bernie crowed to Libby as she came to a screeching halt behind the silver Subaru.

"You're lucky."

"I'm also good."

"Fine. If it makes you feel any better, you're good," Libby told her sister as Bernie jumped out of the van and raced toward Rose's vehicle.

"What do you think you're doing?" she asked Rose as Rose opened the car door.

"Going home," Rose said. She peered up at a glowering Bernie. "Is something wrong, my dear? You look a little upset."

"You could say that." Bernie bent down a little. She could see Alma in the front seat and Pearl in the back. "How are you ladies tonight?"

Pearl tittered. "We're fine. Thank you so much for asking."

"How's poor Amber doing?" Rose asked.

"Amber is doing fine," Bernie said, "all things considered. Of course, she'd be doing even better if she had her aunt's recipe book and the recipe for the cookie Millie was going to submit for judging."

"What difference does it make?" Alma asked, her face crinkled in genuine puzzlement. "She's not in the contest."

"She may be," Bernie told her. "She's asking the producer if she can take Millie's place."

"That's ridiculous," Rose blurted out, echoing Barbara's and Teresa's sentiments.

"Not really," Bernie said. "Not if you think of it from the producer's point of view. It would introduce a sentimental note into the proceedings. Probably boost the ratings," she added, rubbing salt in the wound, so to speak.

Before Rose or Alma could say anything else, Pearl jumped into the conversation. "Amber doesn't have the recipes?" Pearl said, shaking her head. "I could have sworn that she did."

"No. She doesn't," Bernie replied, "as you well know."

"I don't understand what you mean," Pearl said in an injured voice from the backseat of the Subaru.

Rose turned to her. "It's okay," she told her. "The jig is up."

"What jig?" Pearl asked. "What are you talking about?"

Rose turned back to Bernie. "Pearl's had a long day," she explained to Bernie. "Sometimes she tends to get a little confused."

"I do not," Pearl huffed. "That's a horrible thing to say."

Bernie ignored her. "So have Libby and I," Bernie said to Rose. "It started at five-thirty in the morning, but of course our day didn't include breaking into our friend's house."

"Oh dear." Rose turned off her car. "We didn't break in. The door was open when we got there."

"Sure it was," Bernie said.

Rose pointed to herself, Alma, and Pearl. "Look at us. Do you suppose any of us are capable of breaking into someone's house?"

"Frankly, I don't know what to think anymore," Bernie told her.

"Neither do I," Libby added, having come up behind her sister.

Rose sighed. "I suppose," she said to Bernie, "that we owe you and your sister an explanation about why we were in Millie's house."

"I'd very much like to hear it," Bernie said.

"Me too," Libby added.

"What I want to know," Alma said as she exited the car, "is how did you get here so fast?"

"We took Route 31 and Voorhees Hollow," Libby informed her.

Rose got out of her car. "Oh dear," she said. "That's such a dangerous road. You could have had an accident. Plenty of people have. It's supposed to be haunted. Did you know that?"

"No," Bernie said, "I didn't."

"Well, I'm just glad both of you are safe," Rose told her. "That's the important thing."

"I think so too," Bernie said as she studied the three women standing before her.

Alma was small and slightly stooped, with a crown of fluffy white hair that reminded Bernie of a bichon frisé she'd once had, while Pearl was heavyset, with breasts that came into the room before she did and brightly dyed red hair that always veered toward the orange. Rose looked like the ballet dancer she'd been in her younger years. Her posture was erect and her hair was, as usual, drawn back in a tight French twist. Looking at the three women, Bernie thought that what Rose had said was true. She couldn't believe any of them had broken into Millie's house. They didn't fit the profile. On the other hand, there was no denying they'd been there.

"I suppose," Rose said, reading Bernie's thoughts. "That you and your sister would like to know why we did what we did."

"We'd like that very much," Libby said.

"It's simple, really," Rose said. Then she stopped talking.

Libby and Bernie waited. They were both eager to hear how Rose was going to spin this.

After a few beats, Rose began again. "The truth is we

thought we'd get Millie's recipe book and put it away in a safe place. It seemed like the least we could do for her, considering how much she valued it."

"That was very nice of Rose, don't you think, Libby?" Bernie said to her sister.

"Definitely, Bernie."

"I thought so," Rose replied, overlooking Bernie's and Libby's sarcasm. "We decided to take my car, since I'm the best driver . . ."

"At night," Alma clarified. "I'm better during the day. She can't parallel park."

Rose gave her an annoyed glance, and Alma put her hand to her mouth and muttered, "Sorry."

"So," Rose continued, "as I was saying, I parked on the roadway and let Alma and Pearl off."

"How were they going to get in?" Libby asked.

"Well," Rose said, looking Bernie straight in the eye, "Millie had a spare key that she left under the garbage can . . ."

"Who knows about that?" Bernie asked her.

"Everyone," Rose replied.

"It just strikes me as odd that a woman who was paranoid enough to keep her recipes in a safe would leave an extra key around," Bernie observed.

Rose sighed. "You're right. It is off. But you have to understand that the safe was a recent thing. Frankly," she confided, leaning forward, "I think Millie was in the beginning stages of Alzheimer's. Naturally, when we arrived and found the door open, we thought she'd forgotten to lock it. Which was why we didn't call the police. But then when we went into the kitchen and found that mess, we realized we were wrong."

"It was horrible," Alma said, taking up the story. "Simply horrible. Who would do something like that?" she exclaimed. "It was a desecration, what with the way Millie kept her house and all."

"So why didn't you call the police then?" Libby asked.

Pearl shook her head. "I'm not sure I can explain. I guess we were just caught up in the moment."

"And then," Alma said, "we went upstairs and found the empty safe. It was shocking."

"I can only imagine," Libby said dryly.

"It was," Alma insisted. "Ask Pearl. She'll tell you."

"It absolutely was," Pearl parroted. Libby noted that she didn't look at all upset.

"Can I ask you a question?" Bernie said to Alma.

"What?" Alma said nervously.

"How did you propose to open the safe?"

"I don't understand," Alma replied.

"Well, you ladies don't look like safecrackers."

Rose giggled. "Millie had the number taped to her computer. I saw it when I dropped Millie's reading glasses off."

"That's not very secure," Libby observed.

"Maybe not," Alma said. "But at least she could remember it."

"True," Bernie said. That was the reason she didn't use a combination lock at the gym. "Go on."

Alma looked at her. "Go on with what?"

"With the rest of the story."

"Well," Alma said, "we were just debating what to do when Rose called and told us you were pulling into the driveway."

"I panicked," Rose confessed. "Totally panicked, I'm ashamed to say, and I drove away. I really don't know what came over me."

"I don't either, leaving us behind like that," Alma snapped.

"Which wasn't very nice at all," Pearl added as she glared at Rose.

"But I came back." Rose said. "I had a moment of weakness, but I redeemed myself."

"Yes, you did," Alma grudgingly admitted.

"That's when we hatched our plan," Pearl said.

"The one about running down the stairs and almost knocking us over?" Bernie asked. "You mean that plan?"

"Well, it wasn't a very good plan," Alma admitted. "I agree. But we got scared. After all, we were in a compromising position, and we couldn't think of a good place to hide. It would have been worse if you'd found us under the bed."

"Or in the closet," Pearl said.

"In either case, we thought you'd blame us for the empty safe and the mess in the kitchen," Alma said.

"Fancy that," Bernie said.

"Why would you say something like that?" Libby added.

"I would have in your position," Alma said.

"What we did looked really bad," Pearl said. "And it's not as if you didn't know who we were."

"Yes. There is that," Bernie couldn't keep herself from adding.

"Which is why," Rose told her, taking up the narrative thread, "we realized, on the way home, that we should call you and apologize for our conduct," Rose said. "It was really quite wrong of us."

"And explain," Pearl added.

"We were just about to call you when you showed up," Rose said, looking at Libby and Bernie. "I hope there are no hard feelings."

"No," Bernie answered, "there are no hard feelings, especially if you have Millie's recipes."

"Of course, we don't have them," Rose cried. "Haven't you been listening to what we've been saying?"

"I've been listening," Bernie responded. "It's the believing I'm having trouble with."

Rose gasped and took a step back. "Are you calling us liars?" she demanded.

"No," Bernie said, "I'm not. I'm calling you fabricators of an alternative reality."

Alma sniffed. "I don't have the vaguest idea what you're talking about."

Libby explained. "I think my sister is saying that your story doesn't exactly hang together."

"That's an understatement," Bernie said.

Rose looked at Alma and Pearl before turning back to Bernie. "Come, girls, I think it's time we went inside and had a spot of tea with something a little stronger in it for sustenance. It's been quite the evening." Then she turned to Bernie and Libby. "I think you owe us all an apology for your outrageous innuendos," she told them.

"Right," Bernie said.

Rose drew herself up to her full height. "Fine. I will call the producer and tell her about your conduct and have you removed as judges."

"From your mouth to God's ear," Bernie told her.

"Your mother would have been sorely disappointed in you," Rose said. With that, she marched up the stairs to her house with her two friends trailing behind her.

"Do you think Mom would be disappointed?" Libby asked Bernie after Rose had slammed her front door shut.

"No," Bernie said, "I think she'd be proud of us."

"Me too," Libby said.

"You know what I'm thinking?" Bernie said as she turned and headed for the van.

"That we should go home and go to bed?" Libby asked.

"No. I'm thinking that this has been a long, frustrating day and that we need a drink."

Libby jammed her hands in her pockets. "Like tea?"

"Like Scotch," Bernie said.

Libby groaned.

"Come on, Libby, we're almost at RJ's."

"We're fifteen minutes away. RJ's is on the other side of town."

"Fine." Bernie put up her hands. "You caught me. We are fifteen minutes away. We'll just have a drink and go."

"You swear?" Libby asked.

Bernie grinned. "Absolutely."

Libby sighed. She didn't believe her sister, but she was too tired to summon up the energy to argue.

Chapter 11

It had started snowing again as Bernie drove through town. By the time she and Libby got to RJ's the wind had picked up, whipping the flakes into a frenzy. All Libby could think of as she watched the snow covering the streets was the shoveling she and Bernie were going to have to do first thing tomorrow morning.

"Not many cars in the lot," Bernie commented as she parked the van in front of the bar.

"Naturally," Libby told her. "Anyone with any sense is home by now. Which is where we should be," she added as she thought longingly of a pot of jasmine tea and a hot bath.

"We will be very soon," Bernie assured her as she got out of the van.

"What's your definition of soon?" Libby challenged.

But Bernie didn't answer. She was too intent on getting inside. The wind was blowing the snow in her eyes and down her neck as she hurried toward the bar's entrance. Libby was right behind Bernie as she pulled open the wooden door and stepped inside. Bernie was thinking about what kind of scotch she was going to order and whether Brandon had forgiven her yet for waking him up the way she had when she spotted Penelope Lively, the producer of *Baking for Life,* and her production assistant nursing their drinks at the bar. Bernie came to a dead stop, causing Libby to plow into her.

"Damn," Bernie muttered.

"It wasn't my fault," Libby snapped. "You stopped short."

"That's not it," Bernie told her, nodding in Penelope's direction.

"I thought she was supposed to be back in the city," Libby said as she caught sight of Penelope.

"Obviously not."

"See, Bernie, I told you we shouldn't have come," Libby hissed. "Let's go home." The last thing she wanted to do right now was discuss the show.

Bernie was just about to agree when Penelope turned and waved to them. "Hi," she called out over the sound of the newscast on the TV. From the look on her face and the way she was tapping her nails on the bar, Bernie decided she wasn't a happy camper. But then, most producers Bernie had met weren't.

Bernie tried to think of an excuse not to join her, but she couldn't. If it had been the weekend, the place would have been so jammed she could have pretended she hadn't seen or heard Penelope, but this was Tuesday and that wasn't happening. Tuesdays were always slow nights at RJ's. There were ten people sitting at the bar, a handful at the tables, and another handful split between the dartboard and the pool table.

"We have to talk to her, don't we?" Libby said out of the corner of her mouth.

"I'm afraid we do," Bernie replied. "Unless you can think of a reason not to."

Libby shook her head. Much as she wanted to, she couldn't come up with anything. "Sorry," she said.

Libby took a deep breath, and she and Bernie plastered

smiles on their faces and made their way over to where
Penelope and her assistant were sitting. Discarded peanut
shells crackled beneath their feet as they walked. It was
one of the things Bernie liked about the place. That and
the popcorn machine, the bowls of shell-your-own peanuts
and pretzels on the counter, and the dusty old beer ads
mounted on the wall. Or maybe, Bernie decided, she liked
the place because she and her friends had been sneaking in
here since they were seventeen. Of course, there was the
fact that Brandon worked here—always a plus. The
biggest plus, actually.

"Fancy seeing you here," Penelope said as Bernie and
Libby took seats next to her.

"I thought you'd be back in the city by now," Bernie
said.

Penelope shook her head. "We reality TV producers
never sleep. I was just about to call you."

"Really?" Bernie said.

"Yes, really," Penelope answered. "But before I tell you
why, I'd like to thank you for siccing the ladies of the
Christmas Cookie Exchange Club on me."

"*Siccing* is a little extreme, don't you think?" Bernie
asked. "Given Millie's accident, the ladies had questions
about the taping schedule, and I told them you were the
person to answer their questions. That is your job, isn't
it?"

"One of them," Penelope allowed as she glanced down
at her buzzing cell phone. "However, the ladies are a little," Penelope stopped to choose a word, "intense."

"Agreed," Libby said, thinking about what had just
happened back at Millie's house.

"Or maybe disagreeable is a better word choice," Penelope said. "Or possibly obsessive."

"Those too," Bernie told her. "But I'm sure you've han-
dled worse."

Penelope made a face. "Not by much." She reached for

her phone. "I think I'd better answer this. Morons," she said when she was done texting. "I'm surrounded by morons and incompetents."

Bernie watched Penelope finish her margarita in three gulps and signal for Brandon to bring her another one. He nodded.

"The usual for you guys?" he asked Bernie and Libby.

"White wine for me," Libby said.

"I'll take a shot of Black Label," Bernie told him.

Brandon raised an eyebrow.

"It's been a tough day," Bernie explained.

"Evidently," Brandon said before going off and making everyone's drinks.

"It's really too bad about Millie," Bernie said.

Penelope shrugged. "Everyone has to die sometime. As for me, I'd rather go the way Millie did. Quick."

"I guess," Libby said. She was not convinced.

"Anyway, she was old," Penelope said.

"Maybe we should just shoot people when they hit eighty," Libby remonstrated.

"That's not what I meant," Penelope said.

"Then what did you mean?" Bernie asked.

"I meant that she wasn't a kid. She'd lived her life," Penelope said as her fingers beat an impatient tattoo on the bar. "Although it's too bad she couldn't have waited to have her accident until after the filming."

Libby was about to explain the situation, but before she could, Bernie said, "Yes, life is definitely unfair."

Libby lifted an eyebrow, but Bernie shook her head. This was not the time to get into the whole "accident" thing.

If Penelope caught the raised eyebrow or Bernie's sarcasm, she chose to ignore both. "On the other hand," she continued, brightening, "as the saying goes, 'There's no storm that doesn't bring someone some good.' "

"Meaning?" Bernie asked.

"Well, Amber told me that Millie wanted her to represent her in the contest. She said it was Millie's dying wish." Penelope fell silent as Brandon approached with their order.

Bernie waited to reply until after Brandon had set everyone's drinks down in front of them and she'd taken a sip. The scotch went down nice and smooth, warming her mouth, throat, and stomach.

"That's what she told me too," Bernie said.

Penelope took a gulp of her margarita and put the glass down. Somehow, Bernie hadn't expected someone who looked so angular to be drinking something so frivolous. If she had been asked, she would have pegged Penelope for a Jim Beam or Maker's Mark kind of gal.

"At first," Penelope went on, "I was inclined to say no to Amber, but after talking it over with my production people I said yes. It gives the show a nice hook."

"What would that be?" Libby asked.

Penelope looked at her in disbelief. "Come on. You gotta get it."

"No, I don't," Libby told her.

Penelope waved her hands in the air. "It's drama. This is what people watch reality TV for. We couldn't have written anything better than this if we'd tried. You've got the whole 'dying wish' thing going. You know, this kid is taking the banner from her aunt and running with it, and it also ups the tension on the show. And let's face it, tension is good."

"I just bet it is," Bernie said dryly. "So I take it you've already told the ladies of the Christmas Cookie Exchange Club what's going to happen."

"Not yet, but I did just tell Amber."

"How long ago?" Bernie asked.

"Right before you came in. You were next on my list to call."

"That means that everyone will know," Libby told

Penelope. Then she turned to her sister. "How long do you give it? Ten minutes?"

Bernie snorted. "At the most." She extracted her phone from her bag. "You know what I'm going to do? I'm going to turn my phone off. I just can't deal with anyone else tonight."

"Not a bad idea," Libby said, visions of being pursued by the ladies of the Christmas Cookie Exchange Club dancing in her head.

Penelope's phone began to ring. She looked at the caller ID. "It's Pearl Pepperpot."

"Good luck," Bernie said.

"You know what," Penelope said, "I think my phone just ran out of power." With that she powered it down.

"They are not going to be happy," Libby pointed out.

"No, they're not," Penelope agreed. "I was hoping you could help me calm the talent down."

"How would you suggest Libby and I do that?" Bernie asked.

Penelope shrugged. "I was thinking you could call the ladies tomorrow morning and reassure them you're not going to be biased on Amber's behalf."

"There's just one problem with your idea," Libby pointed out.

"What's that?" Penelope asked, looking totally uninterested in what Libby was going to say.

"The 'what's that?' " Libby answered, "is how is Amber going to bake the cookies?"

Penelope made an impatient gesture with her hand. "Anyone can follow a recipe. Even I can do that."

"True enough," Bernie said. "Unfortunately, the Meltaways seem to have disappeared, as has the recipe—a fact I'm sure Amber has mentioned."

"As a matter of fact, she has," Penelope said. She finished her drink and threw a twenty-dollar bill on the counter. "However, she did say she thought she knew where Millie might have hidden another copy of the recipe. I'm banking on that."

Bernie leaned forward. "Really?" she said. "That's news to me. Did she tell you where she thought it might be? She never said anything about that to us."

Penelope shrugged. "I don't have the foggiest idea. I didn't ask her and she didn't tell me."

Libby shook her head. "I can't believe that she didn't tell me or Bernie."

"It's very odd," Bernie agreed. "Maybe she's just playing you. Maybe she really doesn't know."

Penelope scowled. "I will tell you what I told her. I don't care. I don't care if she's found the recipe or not." She held up her hand to forestall Libby from speaking. "The truth of the matter is that it doesn't matter to me if she uses Millie's recipe or if she enters Oreo cookies into the competition. I've given her three extra days to come up with something—whatever that may be. Then we're filming the show and moving on. We have a schedule to keep." Penelope shook her head. "It's just a show, for heaven's sake. We're not doing brain surgery here. It really doesn't matter who wins or loses." With that Penelope stood up and strode toward the door with her assistant trailing behind her.

As Bernie watched them go, she couldn't help wondering whether or not the moto boots Penelope had on were the real deal or not. She'd just decided they were when Brandon ambled over.

"What do you think about the boots Penelope was wearing?" Bernie asked him as he collected the twenty-dollar bill Penelope had left behind.

"I didn't notice," Brandon told her. "Why? Was I supposed to?"

"Not really," Bernie said. "So what do you think of her?"

"She left me a thirty-five-cent tip. What do you think I think of her?"

"Not much. I'll tell you one thing, though," Bernie said, thinking of Millie's accident that wasn't. "Winning or losing matters to someone on the show. It matters a lot."

"The question is to whom," Libby noted. "The way I see it, we have seven choices." She took a sip of her wine, put the glass down, and pushed it away. She was too tired to drink.

Chapter 12

The next morning started off well for Bernie and Libby. It hadn't snowed as much as Libby had feared, so it took Libby and Bernie five minutes, if that, to shovel and salt the pavement in front of their store. In addition, the weather report was good: it was going to be in the upper thirties, with no snow predicted, so that meant more people coming into the shop.

The muffins and the breads went in and out of the oven like clockwork. The mixer they were using didn't break. The hazelnut buttercream they were using for the chocolate tortes didn't curdle, and none of the cookie bottoms burned, so they didn't have to throw them out. In addition, Libby and Bernie managed to complete the prep work for the dinner they were catering that night for the Sloans.

The dinner followed a French-bistro theme, and while onion soup wasn't hard to make, browning the onions till they were caramelized and making the beef stock was time-consuming and laborious, and even though Libby had tried various methods to speed up the process, she always came back to the one outlined by Julia Child.

Having successfully finished with the onions, Libby

went out front and unlocked the front door. She was tally-
ing up the money in the cash drawer when Googie came in
and said hello. Libby nodded hello back and went on with
her count while Googie went into the back, hung up his
jacket in the office, washed his hands, came out front, and
started the coffee.

By now it was ten after seven. As Libby closed the cash
drawer, she noted that Amber was officially ten minutes
late. *We have to have a talk,* Libby thought as she went
into the office to check on a delivery. When Libby clicked
on the OPEN sign fifteen minutes later, Amber still hadn't
shown up.

"She's half an hour late," Libby observed to Bernie.
"That's way too much. I understand that she's upset about
Millie, but she needs to call if she's not going to be here on
time. It's not fair to Googie. Or to you and me, for that
matter."

Bernie looked up from the potatoes she was peeling.
"She's probably working on her recipe and lost track of
time," Bernie said.

"According to Penelope, she already has the recipe,"
Libby pointed out.

Bernie put down her paring knife and wiped her hands
on the towel she had tied around her waist to protect the
wool-and-silk tweed pencil skirt she was wearing. "I'll call
and tell her to get over here."

But Amber didn't answer her cell.

"Maybe she's still sleeping, or maybe she's in the
shower. Or her cell could be dead," Bernie posited after
she'd left a voice mail on Amber's phone.

"Great," Libby groused as she took off her apron and
got ready to go out front and help Googie with the customers. "Things were going so well too." This was one of
their busiest times of the day, and she and Bernie prided
themselves on their quick service.

Bernie sighed. "I'll go get her. Her house is just five minutes away."

Only Amber wasn't in her house, and none of her roommates had seen or heard from her since last night. In fact, they hadn't even known Amber wasn't there until Bernie had woken them up. The three roommates worked in a hospital and had the night shift.

At this point, Bernie called George and asked him to come in and cover for Amber. Then she called Libby and updated her on what was going on, after which she drove around looking for their wayward counter girl.

Bernie kept telling herself that she was overreacting, that she should be back at the shop working instead of driving around aimlessly and that Amber was absolutely fine, but no matter what she said to herself, Bernie couldn't shake the bad feeling that had taken up residence in her gut.

Because even though Amber looked like a freak, underneath she was an extremely responsible person, and she'd never in the five years she'd been working for A Little Taste of Heaven not shown up for work without calling and letting Bernie and Libby know that she'd be late or absent. Ten minutes later, the bad feeling Bernie was carrying around got worse when she spotted Amber's car in the parking lot of a small strip mall located over the town line.

None of the stores in the mall were open yet. It was too early. Amber's car was the only one in the lot. Bernie parked beside it, got out, and tried the doors of Amber's Taurus. They were locked. She brushed the snow off the windows and peered inside. The Taurus looked the way it always did—a mess. Used coffee cups and takeout bags were piled on the passenger's seat, while newspapers were stacked up on the backseat, along with clothes that Amber was going to take to the Rescue Mission. After Bernie tried the trunk and found it locked, she called Libby and updated her on what was going on.

"What the hell was she doing there?" Libby demanded of Bernie.

"Damned if I know," Bernie told her.

"That was a rhetorical question."

"I know," Bernie said, buttoning her jacket. The wind had started picking up again.

"Come home," Libby told her.

"I thought I'd drive around some more," Bernie replied. She decided she'd come back here later on when the shops were open and see if anyone had seen Amber.

"To what end?" Libby demanded

Bernie admitted that she didn't know.

"Exactly," Libby said. "Come home," she repeated. "We need to formulate a plan of attack."

"You're right," Bernie said, and she hung up.

She hated to admit it, but for once Libby was correct. The only thing she was doing now was wasting gas. But on the way to A Little Taste of Heaven, Bernie made a detour and stopped in at the bed and breakfast Amber's mom, Linda, ran. She hadn't seen or heard from her either, but then, as Linda pointed out, that wasn't unusual. She and her daughter didn't exactly get along.

"I agree that it's worrisome," Sean's friend Clyde said, referring to Amber's disappearance as he took a small bite of parsnip pie.

Sean put his cup of coffee down on the dining room table after taking a sip. It was now three o'clock in the afternoon and no one had heard from Amber, which was why he, his two daughters, and Clyde were gathered in the apartment above the shop trying to decide what to do.

"That's why we called you," Sean said to Clyde.

"In an unofficial capacity, of course," Libby said.

Clyde nodded. "Of course. What else?" Not only was Clyde Sean's best friend, he was also a member in good standing of the Longely Police Department. "Anyway, what other choice do you have?"

"None," Bernie said.

"Exactly," Clyde responded. "The police won't do anything," he added. "Amber's over eighteen. The most they'll do is write up a report and file it."

"Who should know that better than I?" Sean retorted, thinking back to his twenty years on the force. In all that time, only two of all the people who were reported missing hadn't shown up eventually. "After all, I used to be chief of police."

"The place was a lot better off when you were," Clyde told him. Then he turned to Libby and Bernie. "By the way, I have to tell you that this pie is wonderful. When you told me it was made with parsnips I had my doubts, but I'm a firm believer now. What's in it anyway? Besides the parsnips, that is."

"Just some orange juice, orange rind, cream, butter, orange marmalade, and Grand Marnier," Libby told him. She'd discovered the recipe in an old cookbook she'd found at a garage sale last summer and had been anxious to try it ever since. So far, despite Bernie's skepticism, it was selling well.

"Ah," Clyde said, making a doleful face. "I should have known it wasn't healthy. Nothing I like is." He took another bite. "So why," he asked when he had swallowed, "did you call me here in the first place? Not," he said hastily, "that I'm not always happy to come over and visit."

"We want your opinion," Bernie said promptly, after which she proceeded to lay out the backstory to Amber's disappearance.

Clyde listened attentively to the story of Millie and the TV show and the accident without interrupting.

"Well?" Bernie asked Clyde when she was through. "What do you think?"

Clyde added a smidgen of cream to his coffee, stirred it, and took a sip before replying. "So," he said slowly, "you really believe that someone caused Millie's accident? That it wasn't an accident at all. It was just made to look like one."

"Absolutely," Sean said, answering for Bernie.

Clyde shook his head. "I don't know. I'm having trouble believing that someone would kill someone over winning first place in a bake-off."

"Maybe the intention wasn't manslaughter," Sean said to Clyde. "Maybe whoever did this just wanted to rattle Millie and put her out of commission for a while. Or maybe this was just a prank gone awry."

"True," Clyde said.

"On the other hand, as you well know, people have killed people over a cigarette," Sean pointed out.

"Indeed they have," Clyde said.

Bernie wiped a drop of cream off the table with the end of her napkin. "I agree with Dad. Maybe whoever did this really just meant to slow Millie down," she said. "Maybe they didn't mean to kill her. At least it would be nice to think so."

"Yes, it would," Sean agreed. "The thing is," he said to Clyde, "when you put all the facts together, such as the disappearing cookies and the ransacked house, it's the most logical conclusion."

"Then someone kidnaps Amber because she's going to appear on the TV show?" Clyde said skeptically. "You're making a huge jump here." He shook his head. "I'm sorry. I just don't buy it. How could one of these ladies—all of whom are in their seventies and early eighties—kidnap Amber, who is what?"

"Twenty-two," Libby answered.

"Exactly," Clyde said. "I don't think that it would be physically possible. It would make more sense if the producer of the show did it. For the publicity," Clyde explained, catching the looks on Sean's, Bernie's, and Libby's faces.

"That's ridiculous," Libby said.

Clyde leaned back in his chair and folded his hands over his stomach. "That's exactly my point," he said.

"Then where is Amber?" Libby demanded.

"How would I know," Clyde said. "Maybe she ran off with her boyfriend."

"She doesn't have a boyfriend," Bernie said.

"Maybe she does now. Or maybe she got stoned with her friends and passed out somewhere," Clyde suggested.

"She's straight as an arrow," Libby told Clyde.

"Meaning?" Clyde said.

"That she doesn't drink or do drugs," Bernie replied.

"You could have fooled me," Clyde said as he unclasped his hands, picked up his fork, and finished the last morsel of the parsnip pie on his plate. "I'm sorry," he said when he was done. "But I don't know what I can do to help you here. Millie's death has officially been ruled an accident, and Amber's only been gone for less than twenty-four hours."

Sean smiled. "That's what I figured you'd say."

"I'll snoop around, but I doubt if I'll come up with anything," Clyde said. Before Libby or Bernie could say another thing, Clyde had grabbed his parka and was out the door.

Chapter 13

"He seemed in a hurry," Bernie noted of Clyde.

Sean nodded. "Family stuff."

"Like what?" Libby asked.

Sean shrugged. "I don't know. I didn't ask."

"That's so guy," Bernie observed.

"That's because I am a guy," Sean replied.

"Do you think he'll come up with anything?" Libby asked.

Sean drained his coffee cup and put it back down before answering. "No, I don't. I think he thinks we're overreacting."

"But you don't think so, do you?" Libby asked her dad.

"Honestly, I'm not sure," Sean replied. "But I think it's always better to err on the side of caution in cases like these."

"So what should we do?" Libby asked.

"Good question." Sean pushed his chair back from the table, stood up, and made his way over to his armchair because he got stiff when he stayed in one position for too long. "I've been asking myself that," he said as he gingerly lowered himself into the chair and propped his feet up on the ottoman.

"And?" Libby inquired.

"The first thing we have to do is call the area hospitals to make sure she's not there. I'll take care of that."

Bernie and Libby both nodded. They'd been about to suggest that themselves.

Sean put a pillow between his lower back and the chair and leaned back, but, dissatisfied, took the pillow out and placed it on the floor. "Damn thing," he muttered. "It makes things worse instead of better."

"Dad," Libby said, "are you okay?"

"I'm fine. Just trying to organize my thoughts and get comfortable." Another moment went by, and he said, "Okay, correct me if I'm wrong, but we are going on the assumption that Amber called up one of the Christmas Cookie Exchange Club ladies—at least one and possibly more—and told them that she either had or knew where to get her aunt's recipe and that she was entering the contest?"

"And that one of the ladies took exception to that," Libby said.

"Exactly," Sean said.

"Especially since whoever she is has gone to considerable trouble to get Millie out of the picture," Bernie added.

"Yeah," Libby said, "I can see where Amber coming into the picture would be extremely annoying to that person. Maybe terminally annoying."

"If I were you," Sean said, thinking out loud, "I'd want to have a talk with the Christmas Cookie Exchange Club ladies."

"And ask them what?" Bernie inquired.

Sean stroked his chin. "Just see if you can get them talking. Maybe they'll let some information out. Even if you don't get anything out of them, maybe the conversations will stir the pot and get something going."

"Hopefully not like someone else disappearing," Bernie said.

"Heaven forbid." Libby pulled a chocolate kiss out of the pocket of her hoodie and popped it in her mouth. "God, I hope Amber's all right."

Bernie shook her head. "I'm still having trouble seeing one of the Christmas Cookie Exchange Club ladies mixed up in Amber's disappearance."

"I am too," Libby agreed. "It just seems wrong."

"And yet," Sean said, "we're positing that one of these ladies assembled and dragged a deer target into the middle of the road for the express purpose of running Millie off it."

"Yeah, but whoever did that didn't overpower Millie. Amber is a whole different proposition," Bernie said.

"We don't know what happened with Amber," Sean pointed out as he leaned back in his chair and steepled his fingers together. "Story: This was before you were born, but I remember this eighty-year-old man, a man who couldn't have weighed more than one-hundred-fifty pounds, bashed his two-hundred-pound grandson over the head with an ax handle. Killed him."

"That's terrible," Libby cried.

"Mr. Clark didn't seem to think so. He thought his grandson deserved it. My point," Sean went on before either of his daughters could say anything else, "is that you shouldn't write someone off because of their physical condition or their age. If someone really wants to do something, they will find a way to do it. Age doesn't necessarily make people nicer. Sometimes it has the opposite effect."

Everyone fell silent for a moment.

Then Libby said, "We've got to find Amber. We have to. I just hope nothing bad has happened to her."

"She's a very resourceful young lady," Sean reassured her. "I'm sure she'll be able to figure out what to do."

"One hopes. But in the meantime we should start looking for her," Bernie said.

"Agreed," Sean answered.

"But where?" Bernie wondered. "She could be anywhere."

"She could be," Sean replied. "But I think we have to assume she's relatively close by. Now, can I make a suggestion?"

Bernie cocked her head and waited.

"Before you tackle the ladies, why don't you talk to Amber's roommates again, maybe take a look at her room. Perhaps she left something behind that could point us in the right direction. And then, after that, talk to the clerks at the strip mall you found her car in and see if they can tell you anything. You might dig something up that will help you when you talk to the members of the Christmas Cookie Exchange Club. At the very least, it might help put a time line on Amber's disappearance."

Libby nodded. "What about talking to Amber's mom as well?" she asked her dad.

Sean shrugged. "It couldn't hurt."

"But I don't think it's going to help either, considering that she and Amber never speak," Bernie commented, remembering what Linda had said when they'd talked. She was about to explain when Libby looked at her watch.

"Bernie, it's five," she cried. "We gotta go downstairs and help behind the counter."

"That late?" Bernie said, jumping up. Between five and six PM was their second-busiest time of the day.

"Go on," Sean said. "I'm going to stay here and cogitate for a while."

Bernie smiled. "I see you've been doing the crosswords again."

Sean laughed and nodded. After Bernie left, he settled back in his chair, closed his eyes, and began to think about where he would stash Amber if he were one of the Christmas Cookie Exchange Club ladies. It had to be someplace that was extremely difficult to get out of. Someplace off the beaten path.

In the meantime, Libby and Bernie went downstairs to help out Googie and George. Even though the shop was crowded, it wasn't as crowded as usual, and by six the crowd had dissipated enough so that Bernie and Libby felt comfortable leaving their dad in charge of the register and taking off on their appointed tasks.

"Hey, good luck," Googie called out to the sisters as they went out the door.

"I have a feeling we're going to need it," Libby said.

"Me too," Bernie agreed.

As they walked to the van, Libby admired the shop's window. She'd created a holiday village out of gingerbread and marzipan. There were skaters on a sugar-glass lake, and a boy and his dog walking home along a gumdrop path to a house decorated with peppermint candy canes. In the back, a marzipan father was sawing a chocolate log in half as sugar-cookie cows looked on and a cat stalked a meringue bird near a gingerbread schoolhouse.

"We did good," Bernie said, echoing Libby's thoughts.

Libby smiled. "We did, didn't we?"

Bernie flicked a feather off her parka and inspected her sleeve for a rip. She'd gotten the jacket in Vail five years ago, and she liked it as much now as she had then. "So are we starting with the strip mall?" she asked Libby.

"Does white stick to rice?" Bernie responded.

Libby laughed. "I never understood that expression."

"Me either," Bernie confessed. "I just like the way it sounds. I figure," Bernie went on, "strip mall first, because that way we'll get to talk to everyone before the shops close. Then we'll talk to the roommates, and then we'll drop in on the members of the Christmas Cookie Exchange Club. That make sense to you?"

"Yeah," Bernie said as she pulled out onto the street. "So which of the ladies should we talk to first?"

Libby shrugged. "I vote for Alma. So far she seems to have the best motive for running Millie off the road."

"You mean Millie getting her kicked out of her quilting club?"

Libby nodded. "And bad-mouthing her cookies."

Bernie leaned back in her seat, raised her arms above her head, and stretched. "On second thought, maybe it doesn't make any difference who we start with."

"Why do you say that?"

"Because the moment we leave, whoever we've talked to is going to be on the phone. Those women have a better alert system than the Pentagon."

"I hadn't thought of that," Libby admitted. "On the other hand, this discussion may be irrelevant. Maybe they won't want to talk to us."

Bernie snorted. "Are you kidding me? They'll latch on to us like a vampire latches onto a vein."

"That might be overstating things a little," Libby observed.

"Not by much," Bernie rejoined. "Remember, you couldn't get rid of them in the shop."

"True." Libby rat-tat-tatted on the dashboard of the van with her fingers, something she did when she was thinking. "Maybe," she said after a minute had gone by, "we can make that work to our advantage."

"How?" Bernie asked.

"I don't know," Libby admitted. "Yet." And she lapsed into silence for the rest of the ride.

Chapter 14

The strip mall Bernie and Libby were headed for was home to a pizza place and a Chinese takeout joint, as well as a nail salon, a Laundromat, and a yoga studio. Located off the main drag in a poorly trafficked area right outside Longely, the strip mall housed a never-ending turnover of retail establishments. Most seemed to last about a year before they folded and morphed into yet another hopeful business.

"I haven't been here in forever," Libby said as she surveyed the parking lot. It was about a quarter full.

"That's because there's nothing here worth making a trip for, except maybe the nail place," Bernie replied as she looked for Amber's car. It wasn't there. "So where did the Taurus go?" she asked Libby.

"Maybe she came back and got it," Libby said, feeling an uncharacteristic surge of optimism.

"I wish, but it was probably towed," Bernie replied as she put the van in park and exited the vehicle.

Libby sighed. She hoped not, but she suspected that Bernie was correct.

"I'll tell you one thing," she said to Bernie as she flipped up the hood on her parka to protect her face from the wind.

"What?" Bernie asked from the depths of her collar. Her eyes started to tear from the cold.

"This weather isn't helping."

"Helping what?"

"Helping our business."

"No, it certainly isn't," Bernie agreed as she picked up her pace. "Anyone's business. I know I wouldn't be out if I didn't have to be, that's for sure."

The sisters started with the yoga studio and worked their way down the strip, going from right to left. The conversation at the yoga studio yielded some promising information, but things went downhill from there. Besides the yoga instructor, no one else had seen Amber last night. And absolutely no one had seen her this morning.

"If she was here this morning, I didn't see her," the yoga teacher said as she arranged a sprig of greenery and a stem of pink carnations in a vase. She had, Bernie decided, the look of someone who had done one too many juice fasts and cleansings. "In fact," the yoga teacher continued, "now that I think about it, I'm not even sure she's the person I saw last night."

"Why don't you just tell us what you did see?" Bernie urged.

The yoga teacher stepped back to study her arrangement and shook her head. "No harm in that, I suppose," she told the sisters as she started redoing the arrangement, even though it looked perfectly fine to Bernie. "Around nine o'clock last night I glanced out the window and saw someone parking the Taurus. The person driving it didn't get out, but I didn't think much about it. I figured whoever it was had pulled over to text or something like that, so I went back to reconciling my accounts." She made a face. "New York State is such a pain. But when I looked up again, I saw a car pull up beside the Taurus. Then a girl with really bright orange and pink dyed hair got out of the Taurus and got into the other car, and it drove off."

"That's definitely Amber," Bernie commented.

The yoga teacher moved the sprig of greenery a quarter of an inch to the left. "If you say so."

"Did Amber get in the car willingly?" Libby asked the yoga teacher.

"As far as I could see she did," she replied. "Anyway, when I came in this morning and saw that the car was still there I became concerned and called the police."

"What did they say?"

The yoga studio owner shrugged. "Nothing. They didn't care. They asked me if it was posing a public safety hazard, and when I said it wasn't, they said the vehicle was my problem."

"So where is the car now?" Libby asked her.

"Over on Dell Street. I called Frank's auto and asked them to tow it. Just like the sign outside says. We have such a small lot I can't have it taking up valuable space."

"Naturally," Libby murmured, although she couldn't see this place ever being so busy that it would matter.

"We're not a parking lot," the yoga teacher said sharply. "The rule is posted in a prominent place for everyone to see."

"I'm not saying you're wrong," Libby agreed, thinking once again that she had to practice her poker face.

"Could you identify the car that Amber got into?" Bernie asked, changing the subject to one she hoped would be more productive.

The yoga teacher shook her head. "Not really. I don't do cars. They're an emanation of a destructive world."

"Really?" Bernie said, barely managing to stop herself from rolling her eyes.

"Yes, really," the yoga teacher answered. "If it weren't

for cars we wouldn't be in the mess we're in today. Our search for oil has destabilized the world, and now we're going to pay for it."

"If you say so," Libby said, moving the conversation along. "But on a less intense note, do you remember the color of the car?"

"It was light," the yoga teacher said. "That's really the best I can do."

"Was it a Subaru, by any chance?" Bernie asked.

"Sorry," the yoga teacher said. "But I wouldn't know a Subaru from a Honda. They're really not my thing. I'm better with the natural world."

Not flower arranging, Libby thought as she watched the yoga teacher redo the flowers for the third time.

"Did you happen to get a look at the person who was driving?" she asked. So far they were batting zero for three.

The yoga teacher shook her head.

Libby persisted. "Was it a he or a she? Old? Young?"

"I told you I didn't see anything," the yoga teacher replied, her voice rising in annoyance.

"You didn't notice anything? Anything at all?" Bernie asked.

"No," the yoga teacher snapped. "If I had, I would have told you." She took a deep breath and let it out. Then she took another one and smiled. The smile traveled as far as her mouth and died. "I hope you don't think I'm being rude, but you two look as if you could use my services. You'd be surprised what yoga can do for your chakras." She handed Bernie and Libby a card.

"I think my chakras are just fine," Libby said to Bernie as they entered the Chinese takeout place.

"Actually, I've been meaning to speak to you about that. I think your fourth one could use some polishing," Bernie told her.

Libby giggled. "Which one is that?"

"I don't have the foggiest," Bernie said as they reached the counter and asked the woman manning the register if they could speak to the establishment's owner.

A moment later, a tired-looking man with a stained apron tied around his waist joined them, and Bernie asked her question.

"When I left, the Taurus was still here," the owner said. "I figured it was broken down or something and that whoever owned it would come back and get it, you know? I guess not."

"Didn't see anything," the owner of the pizza shop told them. "I was too busy filling orders to be looking at the parking lot."

The owner of the nail salon informed them that they closed at seven and if the Taurus had been there she hadn't been aware of it.

"Well, at least," Bernie said as they drove away, "we know that someone picked Amber up. So that's more than we knew before."

"But who?" Libby asked, putting on her seat belt.

"That is the question, isn't it?" Bernie replied as she stopped to get gas. The van's gas gauge was almost on empty. "If we knew that, we'd be home free."

"Or heading in the right direction."

"Maybe Amber's roommates will be able to tell us something," Bernie said.

"Maybe," Libby answered, trying to stay positive.

Chapter 15

Five minutes later, Libby and Bernie arrived at the house in which Amber was renting a room.

"Wow," said Bernie as she studied the house in front of her.

Amber had changed residences four months ago, and this place wasn't an improvement. It was ramshackle, the kind of place that students and people who are out on their own for the first time rent.

The paint was peeling on the sides, the porch was sagging, the small window in the attic had been boarded up with a piece of plywood, and one side of the roof was tarped over. Someone had tried to spruce up the place by hanging Christmas lights over the front windows, but they just called attention to the place's deficiencies.

"Her last place definitely looked better," Libby commented.

"That's an understatement. I wonder why she moved?" Bernie mused.

Libby shrugged her shoulders. "Don't know. She didn't tell me."

"There must have been a compelling reason," Bernie replied. "Because I've got to say this place is really bad."

She was silent for a moment. Then she indicated the cars in the driveway. "At least Amber's roommates are here, so that's a blessing."

Bernie parked in front of two garbage cans standing on the curb, and she and Libby walked up four stairs to the porch. One of the steps had a hole in it, and the banisters looked as if they were going to fall off any minute. The stairs groaned and buckled as the sisters stepped on them, and Libby wondered if they were going to give way. A sign pasted on the door said "bell broken," so she knocked instead. A moment later the door opened. The smell of potato-and-leek soup greeted her. Libby inhaled. She wished she was eating some. It was the perfect meal for a night like this. She decided she'd make some for tomorrow's lunch.

"Yes?" the boy standing in front of Bernie and Libby said.

He was tattooed and pierced, with long, black hair that flowed over his shoulders and a sweet face that belied the piercings and the devil tattooed on his arm. Bernie figured him for about eighteen, if that.

"We're looking for Amber," Bernie said. "We're . . ."

The boy held up his hand, interrupting her. "I know who you are. You're Amber's bosses. I already explained to you on the phone that we haven't seen her. That we didn't even know she was gone."

"I know you did," Bernie continued, "but my sister and I would like to talk to you anyway."

The boy shrugged. "I don't think I can help. We're just roomies. You know. Share a kitchen. That kind of thing."

"Maybe she said something to you," Libby observed.

"Like what?" The boy asked.

"Like about her aunt. Like about the bake-off. Like about cookies."

"Cookies?" the boy repeated.

"Meltaways," Bernie said.

The boy wrinkled his nose. "Meltaways?"

"Millie's Majestic Meltaways, to be precise," Bernie said.

The boy stepped away from the door and pivoted around. "Hey, Rudy, Marissa," he yelled. "Come here for a sec."

Bernie and Libby took the opportunity to step inside the house and close the door behind them. It was too cold to be standing outside. They were surprised to find that the hallway was immaculate. The walls were painted white, the floor gleamed, the bookcases in the hallway looked handmade. Five pairs of shoes were neatly stacked on a rubber mat. It just went to prove that her mom was right, Bernie thought. You really can't tell a book by its cover.

A moment later Marissa and Rudy joined them. They looked pretty much the way Amber did. Tats, piercings, pink hair. Marissa was eating a sandwich, while Rudy was spooning up what Libby presumed to be the potato-and-leek soup she'd smelled from a bowl. Both of them were wearing hospital workers' garb.

"They"—the boy who'd answered the door indicated Libby and Bernie with a jerk of his head—"want to know if Amber said anything to you about cookies. I thought you told me that she did."

"Well, kinda," Marissa said.

"What do you mean 'kinda'?" Libby asked.

Rudy took another spoonful of soup and said, "She was going on and on about not finding the cookies, and she said she was going to carry on her aunt's name, no matter what it took. You know, like it was some kind of holy mission or something. Very weird. She kept on calling that producer lady."

"Penelope?" Bernie asked.

"I think," Rudy said.

"Did you hear what she was saying?" Libby asked.

"Something about making the cookies. Then she went out and got all this stuff and started baking."

"And then?" Bernie prompted.

"I don't know," Rudy said, "because we had to go to work, and when we came home the place was cleaned up. So I asked her on my way to bed what had happened to the cookies. I figured maybe she'd give me a couple. But she told me she'd thrown them out. I said that was too bad, and she said she didn't want to talk about it anymore, so that was that."

"Anything else?" Bernie asked.

"She was real upset when her aunt died," Marissa said. "Real upset." She took a thoughtful nibble of her sandwich. "She was saying that she was going to get that recipe if it was the last thing she did."

Bernie leaned forward. "So she knew where it was?"

Rudy and Marissa looked at each other.

"I'm not sure if she meant *get* as in 'I get it' or *get* as in 'go and physically take possession of it,' " Rudy explained.

"Did she know where it was?" Libby repeated.

Marissa took another nibble of her sandwich. "I don't think so, because she told me she was going to talk to someone about it and see what they could tell her."

"Did she say who?" Bernie asked.

Marissa shook her head.

"Did she say anything else?" Libby demanded.

"Not to us. Of course, we haven't seen her since then," Marissa said.

"Like I told you, we're on different schedules," the boy who opened the door for Libby and Bernie said.

Bernie noted that his voice had risen an octave.

Marissa turned to him and said, "Relax, Mike. She's not blaming you."

"No, Mike, I'm not," Libby quickly assured him.

"I didn't think you were," Mike said, though his face told a different story. "I just feel bad not noticing. That's really pretty lame."

Marissa walked over, put her arm around his shoulder, and squeezed. "It's okay," she reassured him.

"It is," Bernie echoed.

"I guess," Mike said.

He doesn't look convinced, Bernie thought as he turned and walked away.

"He'll be fine," Marissa told Bernie. "He just feels responsible for everyone. Something could happen on Mars, and if he knew the guy, somehow Mike will think that he should have seen it coming and done something about it."

Bernie nodded. She got it. Her dad was like that too. She looked at Amber's remaining roommates. "So is there anything, anything at all, you can tell us that might help?"

Marissa and Rudy shook their heads.

"Sorry," Rudy murmured. "We kinda all tend to go our own way. You know how it is."

"Yeah, I do," Bernie said, thinking back to all the roommates she'd had before she'd come home to Longely. "Do you think we could take a quick look in Amber's room?" she asked.

Marissa took another nibble of her sandwich. "Do you think that will really help?" she asked. "She might not like you going through her stuff."

Libby snuck a peek at her watch. She wanted to get to Alma's before it was too late. "In answer to your question, yes, Marissa, I think it might help. I wouldn't be asking if I didn't think it would. Maybe Amber kept a journal or there's a note or a piece of paper or something that will point us in the right direction."

"Frankly, at this point," Bernie chimed in, "I don't think Amber would care if we went through her stuff or not. I'm sure that all she wants to do is come home."

Marissa didn't look convinced. "But," she said, "what

if she's with some guy and she's having a real cool time and you guys just barge right in?"

"That doesn't strike me as Amber's style," Libby observed.

"It's not," Marissa conceded. She took another bite of her sandwich. "But what if she were? She'll be really pissed at us if that's the case."

Bernie laughed. "Let's hope that's what she's doing, and if she is, we'll apologize and leave, and I swear that your name will never pass my or Libby's lips."

Libby looked at Marissa. There was something in Marissa's manner that made her wonder if Marissa was telling her everything she knew. Libby leaned forward. "So," she asked, "is Amber seeing someone?"

"Not really," Marissa replied.

Bernie's eyes narrowed. "Define *not really*."

"I think this guy's a friend."

"You think?" Bernie said.

"That's the vibe I got," Marissa told Bernie. "It's all really casual."

"Define *casual*," Libby challenged.

Marissa sighed. "I don't know. They hang out together sometimes."

"Do you know this guy's name?" Bernie asked.

Marissa shook her head and ate some more of her sandwich.

Bernie turned to Rudy. "Do you?"

Rudy shook his head. "I didn't even know that she was seeing anyone."

"She's not seeing him, Rudy. She's just hanging out with him."

"Whatever," Rudy told Marissa. He drained the last of his soup from the bowl and turned to Bernie and Libby. "And you really think you can find her?" Rudy asked. "If it's like that . . ."

"Like what?" Bernie asked.

"Like kidnapped or something like that, why aren't the police here?"

"For the police to be here," Libby explained, "someone would have to fill out a missing persons report, which we will do sometime tomorrow."

"So why didn't you do it sooner?" Rudy demanded.

"Because," Bernie continued, "the sad truth of the matter is that it's not going to make any difference. The police aren't going to actively investigate because they usually don't concern themselves with missing adults."

"That's screwed up," Marissa said.

"Yes, it is," Libby agreed. "But in their defense, most people who go missing come home again. And Rudy, to answer the second part of your question, yes, I think we can find Amber."

"Why?" Rudy asked.

"Because, Rudy," Marissa said, "that's what they do." Then Marissa turned to Bernie and Libby and said, "Amber used to say you two were like a cross between Nancy Drew and The Cupcake Lady. I thought she was kidding, but maybe not."

"I guess we are," Libby conceded, "although I wouldn't have phrased it that way."

"Cool," said Marissa.

Bernie looked at her watch. She and Libby had to get down to business. "Her room?" she said.

"She's got the third bedroom to the right on the second floor," Rudy said, pointing to the stairs. "You can't miss it."

Bernie thanked him, and she and Libby went upstairs. Looking around, she was once again struck by the overall neatness of the house. Amber's room, on the other hand, was a different story.

Chapter 16

"Wow," Bernie said as she stepped inside Amber's room.

"You're repeating yourself," Libby pointed out. "That's what you said when you saw the house."

"I'm impressed. I don't think even my room was ever this bad."

"Maybe not," Libby said, "but it's come close."

Bernie nibbled on her lower lip as she surveyed the carnage. "Amber certainly has enough clothes. I'll give her that. And coming from me, that's saying a lot." Bernie reached up and tightened the elastic around her ponytail. "Well, there's one thing we know about her," Bernie told her sister.

"And that's?"

"She likes stuff."

"To say the least," Libby said. An idea occurred to her. "I wonder if Amber's room is always like this."

"You mean you think someone's gone through it?" Bernie asked.

"It's a possibility," Libby replied. "Look at what happened in Millie's house. Look what a mess the kitchen was in."

"This is a different kind of mess," Bernie pointed out.

"It's still worth asking about," Libby said. She stepped out into the hallway and called for Marissa to come up. "Is Amber's room always like this?" she asked once Marissa was standing beside her.

Marissa giggled. "Pretty much," she said. "It's bad, isn't it?"

"Yeah. I'm surprised," Libby replied. "Amber's so neat at work."

"Obviously not in her private space," Marissa said before she left and went back downstairs.

It took Bernie and Libby the better part of an hour to go through Amber's room.

"Well, at least we don't have to go through her drawers or closets since everything is out on the floor," Bernie noted. She began picking up items of clothing, shaking them out, and going through their pockets. After she was done with each piece, she added it to a growing pile in the middle of the room.

While Bernie went through the clothes, Libby looked in Amber's closet, dresser drawers, and nightstands for something that would give an indication of what had happened to her. She found nothing. Libby sighed and started on the bed, even though she suspected it was going to be an exercise in futility.

Libby held up a stuffed Minnie Mouse that was propped up against the headrest. "Somehow I don't see Amber with Disney."

"Just shows to go you that you never know," her sister replied as she went through the pockets of a purple plaid jumpsuit.

"No, you don't," Libby said as she lifted up the mattress and ran her hand under the box spring.

There was nothing there. Next, Libby moved on to Amber's desk. The first thing she did was power up Amber's computer, but it was password-protected, and after a couple of tries Libby gave up trying to figure out the password—given Amber, it would definitely be something weird—and started on the papers strewn around it instead.

They consisted of a deck of tarot cards, an astrology magazine, a bill for her car insurance, a bill for her cell phone, and a receipt from a nail salon. The three drawers yielded receipts for her rent, a few pencils, four pairs of earbuds, an iPod, a large package of cough drops, and a twelve-inch-by-twelve-inch square of fabric with an outline of a skull and crossbones stitched on it. It took Libby a moment to recognize what it was.

Libby held it up for Bernie to see. "Is this, by any chance, a square for a patchwork quilt?"

"Let me see," said Bernie, reaching out her hand. "You know, I think it is," she said after she'd studied it.

Libby shook her head. "Amber quilting. Who would have thought?"

"Not me," Bernie answered.

"It would be interesting to see what the rest of the quilt is like," Libby mused. She couldn't imagine sleeping under a quilt like that, but then she couldn't imagine Amber quilting either.

At the end of thirty minutes, the only things that Libby and Bernie had found out about Amber that they hadn't known before, besides the quilting, was that she was a fan of Hello Kitty and Boy George, that she liked graphic novels, that she had five stuffed animals on her bed, and that she hadn't taken her toothbrush or hairbrush with her, but her mascara and eyeliner weren't there.

"Maybe she carries her makeup with her," Bernie said, thinking of all the eye stuff Amber used.

"Maybe," Libby said, "but I can't imagine her leaving her computer or her iPod behind."

"Me either," Libby said. She sighed. "We haven't found out much, except for the fact that Amber is an incredible slob."

"But we will," Bernie told Libby. "We're going to talk to those ladies and kick some ass."

Libby giggled.

"You'll see," Bernie said. "We'll get to the bottom of this one way or another." She clapped her sister on the shoulders. "Are you with me?"

"Definitely," Libby said.

"Good," Bernie said. "Then let's go to Alma's house."

Libby nodded. "Alma's house it is."

Although once she was back in the van, after she and Bernie had brushed the snow off the windshield, Libby realized she didn't have the vaguest idea how they were going to accomplish their goal, especially when Alma had every right not to speak to them.

"What if she doesn't want to talk to us?" she asked Bernie. "What if she won't come to the door?"

"Don't worry," Bernie told her as she started Mathilda up. "I have a plan."

These were not the words that Libby wanted to hear. "Like what, exactly?"

"Like this." Bernie reached in her bag and came out with Amber's skull and crossbones. "Alma's a quilter, right? We'll ask her about this."

Libby raised an eyebrow.

"Do you have a better idea?"

When Libby confessed that she didn't, Bernie smirked and pulled away from the curb. The snow was coming down lightly now, and Bernie decided it looked like a lace curtain drawn over the night.

Chapter 17

It was a little after eight by the time Bernie and Libby pulled into the driveway of Alma Hall's house.

Ten Westward Drive was a modified, white clapboard ranch, with green trim, arborvitae foundation plantings, and an attached garage that someone had added a second story to at some point. The house was completely unremarkable, and made even more so by the fact that it looked exactly the same as the ones on either side of it. Even the Christmas decorations were similiar.

All three houses had white lights strung around the windows and the front door. Bernie couldn't help thinking that Ten Westward Drive was one of those houses that went into your mind and out again without leaving a trace behind. For all intents and purposes, it was invisible.

As she and Libby walked up to the doorway, Bernie heard voices coming from the television. The curtain wasn't drawn, and Bernie could see the living room from where she was standing. It was like a stage set. The furnishings consisted of a white sofa, two beige armchairs, a glass coffee table, and a shelf full of what looked like knickknacks. A rerun of *Law and Order* was on the TV, although as far as

Bernie could tell, Alma wasn't in the living room. When she and Libby got to the door, Bernie rang the bell.

"Coming," Alma called. A moment later she opened the door.

She was wearing a three-quarter-length light blue quilted housecoat, black socks that highlighted her white skin, and fuzzy slippers on her feet. Her white hair was in curlers, except for three pin curls on her forehead.

"My goodness," she said, when she saw Bernie and Libby standing there. "What are you doing here at this time of night? Is it something about the show?"

"In a manner of speaking," Libby said.

"What manner of speaking?" Alma demanded. "Have they canceled the taping?" she asked, her voice rising in alarm.

"Not as far as I know," Bernie said. "We need to talk to you about something else."

"Can't it wait?" Alma asked. "I'm busy."

"I'm sorry, but it can't," Libby replied.

Alma made a show of looking at her watch. "It's late, and I'm not dressed to receive company. We can talk sometime tomorrow if you'd like."

"We're not company," Bernie said, stepping into the hallway. "And we need to talk now."

Libby followed her sister in. She took a quick look around. The hallway was painted a cool bluish white and lined with small display units that held Alma's collections of thimbles, teaspoons, and miniature teacups. Libby made a note to herself to stay away from them. She was such a klutz, she could just imagine herself crashing into them by accident.

Alma coughed and touched her pin curls. "There's no need to be rude," she told the sisters.

"We're not being rude," Bernie said.

Alma frowned. "I don't know what you call this, but in my day people didn't barge in on people, especially in the evening, without calling first. I'm afraid I'm going to have to ask you to leave. As I said, I'm busy."

"We will leave in just a moment," Bernie assured her. "We just want you to answer one question for Libby and myself." With that she whipped out the square of material Libby had found in Amber's room. "We just wondered what this is?" she asked as she handed the square to Alma.

Alma looked at her. "A skull and crossbones, obviously."

"We thought it was going to go on a quilt."

Alma shrugged. "I guess it could. Anything can go into a crazy quilt. It could be something for a pirate flag as well." She handed the square of material back to Bernie. "But I don't see what it has to do with me."

"We found it in Amber's desk drawer," Libby told her.

Alma sniffed. "Then I suppose your time would be better employed asking Amber about it."

"I'd love to, but I can't," Libby said.

She waited for Alma to ask why, but she didn't.

"Don't you want to know why I can't?" Bernie asked when the silence had gone on for longer than it should have.

"I assume you're going to tell me," Alma replied, looking at her watch again.

"She's missing," Libby told her.

"Missing?" Alma said, as her hands moved down to her housecoat and began to finger the top button.

"That's right," Bernie said, watching Alma closely. "We were hoping that this quilt square . . ."

"If it *is* a quilt square," Alma interjected.

". . . might help us find out where she went."

Alma blinked. "I don't see how it would," she said.

"Well, we were hoping she'd talked to you."

Alma shook her head. "Hardly. Are you sure she's missing?"

"Positive," Bernie replied.

"Maybe she just ran off with someone," Alma said. "You know how young people are these days."

"Not in this case," Libby said.

"How can you be so sure?" Alma asked. "Given her hair and those things she has in her face." Alma shuddered. "I don't know why anyone would disfigure themselves like that. Who knows what someone who looks like that will do?"

Libby pointed to herself. "I know. Think about it."

"Think about what?" Alma said. Her voice took on an indignant tone. "As far as I can see, there's nothing to think about. Certainly nothing that concerns me."

Libby leaned forward. "First Millie gets into a fatal accident, then Amber disappears. You don't find that coincidence just a little suspicious?"

Alma looked up at Bernie and Libby. Her nostrils flared. "So what are you two saying exactly?"

"We're saying," Bernie went on, "that's there's a connection between the two events."

Alma Hall's eyes got smaller, which made her nose and her jowls look bigger. "What does that have to do with me?"

"It's obvious, isn't it, Alma?" Bernie said.

Alma crossed her arms over her chest. "Not to me, Bernie."

"My sister isn't implying anything," Libby said.

"She'd better not be," Alma said.

"We're just wondering if you could help us find Amber," Libby told her.

Alma looked from one sister to another and back again. "This is why you came to my door at this time of night? This is why you disturbed my rest?"

"Don't you care about Amber?" Bernie said.

Alma's eyes were now slits. "What kind of question is that?"

"Well, you didn't seem very upset when I told you she was missing," Bernie pointed out. "And you don't seem very anxious to help us out now."

"That is because I have nothing to contribute. I don't know where Amber is, and I can't believe that you would think I would know. I also can't believe that you think I had anything to do with her disappearance—if that, indeed, is what it is. Which I highly doubt," Alma told her. She raised her hand. "How you can come to a conclusion like that is beyond me."

"I didn't say that," Bernie said.

"You didn't have to," Alma retorted. "Your face said it for you. Just because I'm seventy-three doesn't make me stupid, you know. If you want to talk to someone about Amber and Millie, you should talk to Rose and Sheila. Sheila hated Millie ever since she tried to steal her boyfriend away."

"Boyfriend?" Bernie couldn't keep the wonder out of her voice.

"What, Bernie? You think that only young people have sex lives?" Alma demanded. "You don't think us older folk are entitled to them too?"

"That's not what I said," Bernie protested.

"You didn't have to. It was in your tone of voice. As for Rose, I don't think she ever forgave Millie for the comment she made about the lilac bushes she ran over. Plus, there was the small issue of the twenty dollars she borrowed from Millie and never returned."

"Twenty dollars?" Bernie said, lifting an eyebrow.

Alma put her hands on her hips and stuck her jaw out. "You don't think twenty dollars is worth bothering about?"

"It's not that," Bernie stammered. "It's . . ."

"A penny is a penny," Alma interrupted. "If you had been through the Depression you would know that."

"But what about you, Alma?" Libby asked, figuring it was time she stepped up to the plate. "I understand that Millie got you thrown out of your quilting club."

Two red dots appeared on Alma's cheeks. "Who told you that?" she demanded of Libby.

"What difference does it make?" Libby asked.

"It was Rose, wasn't it?" Alma cried.

Bernie noticed that Alma's hands were clenched into fists. "Well, Alma, is what Rose said true?" Bernie asked.

Alma took a deep breath and exhaled. Then she uncurled her hands and let them hang loosely at her sides. "Fine. It's true. Millie did do that," she admitted.

"Were her charges true?" Libby asked.

"Of course not," Alma cried. "How can you even say such a thing?"

"So you must have been pretty pissed," Libby continued.

"Wouldn't you be?" Alma asked.

"Yes, I would," Libby replied.

"It was a horrible thing to have done. Simply horrible." Alma shook her head at the memory. "And all I was trying to do was make sure that Millie didn't kill herself or someone else on the road. If I were she, I would have thanked me instead of doing what she did. There was absolutely no call for that. None. On top of everything else, she's still on the road." She patted her curlers with her right hand to make sure they were all in place. "Or was."

"Is that why you arranged for Millie to have an accident so she wouldn't win the *Bake for Life* contest?" Libby asked Alma, carefully watching her face as she talked. "You figured it was poetic justice, and on top of everything else, you'd even the score a little. Plus, no one would suspect anything, given Millie's driving record. Unfortunately, things didn't work out as planned, but then they rarely do."

"That's a ridiculous thing to say," Alma scoffed.

"I didn't say it wasn't," Libby replied. "But that doesn't necessarily make what I said any less true."

Alma sniffed. "Do you have any proof? I thought not," she said when Libby and Bernie remained silent. "Coming to the door with accusations like this. You two should be ashamed of yourselves." She shook a finger at them. "I don't need to do anything to win that contest. I'm a way better baker than Millie ever was. Way better. Ask anyone. Millie had an inflated opinion of her abilities. All of her abilities, if we're being honest."

"Does that apply to Amber too?" Libby asked.

Alma made a dismissive motion with her hand. "Amber is a counter girl, not a baker. The whole idea of Amber taking Millie's place is absurd. I don't know what that woman . . ."

"That woman?" Libby asked.

". . . Prudence." Alma moved her hand in a circle when she caught the blank looks on Libby's and Bernie's faces. "You know. The producer."

"Penelope," Bernie said. "Her name is Penelope."

"Fine. I don't know what Penelope was thinking about when she allowed her in."

"It would definitely be better for you if Amber wasn't in the contest," Bernie observed.

Alma's nostrils quivered in indignation. She pointed to the door. "I've stood for this long enough. I want you two out, and I want you out now. I have been patient long enough."

"Or?" Bernie said.

"Or I'll call the police. If you want to bother someone, bother Rose or Sheila. Now get out or I'm calling. I need my rest." Alma put her hand to her heart. "If I have an attack I want you to know it's on you two."

Libby and Bernie left.

"Does Alma have a history of heart disease?" Libby asked once they were in the van.

Bernie snorted. "Don't be silly. She's as healthy as a horse." She turned Mathilda on. "Rose Olsen's house next," she announced.

Chapter 18

It took the sisters ten minutes to get to Rose Olsen's house.

"I think I like her house the best," Libby said when she spotted the wooden bungalow with the wraparound porch that Rose called home.

"Her garden is amazing," Bernie observed. She'd been there last spring to deliver ten cheesecakes and three trays of assorted cookies for one of Rose's open houses and had been blown away by Rose's inventive use of the wild grasses lining the path up to the house, as well as the way Rose had combined foundation plantings and a perennial garden.

"Rose really does love her plants," Bernie said as she was debating whether to park on the street or in Rose's driveway. "Someone told me she had a greenhouse built in her backyard. Maybe we should do something like that."

Libby was just about to remind her sister that she had a black thumb when she saw Rose's garage door open and Rose's vehicle come flying down the driveway in reverse. "Damn," she said as she watched Rose reach the street, take a hard right, and speed down Danbury Road.

"This definitely sucks," Bernie agreed as she tracked the

taillights on Rose's vehicle disappearing around the bend. "She's a better driver than I thought. And a faster one."

"I wonder what's going on," Libby murmured. Somehow, Rose didn't strike her as the kind of person to go running off someplace. Especially given her age and the time of night, but obviously she was wrong.

"Let's find out, shall we?" Bernie said, and with that she drove into Rose's driveway, made a right, and went after Rose.

"You know we're never going to catch her," Libby observed. Rose's vehicle could go at least eighty miles an hour easy, probably more, while Mathilda could make it to fifty at the very most. And she didn't like doing that for very long.

"Oh ye of little faith," Bernie retorted. "Even if we don't catch her, maybe we'll be able to figure out where she's going."

Libby grabbed for the strap and held on tight. "I wonder if she saw us parking. I wonder if that's why she jetted out of her house."

Bernie shook her head. "Because she didn't want to talk to us? I doubt it. She was probably in the garage by the time we pulled up."

"Although there are windows on the garage door," Libby pointed out.

"Doesn't matter," Bernie said. "The angle is wrong."

"Maybe it's some sort of domestic emergency," Libby suggested.

"Maybe," Bernie said automatically. She was concentrating on her driving and only half listening to what Libby said.

"Or maybe," Libby continued, "Alma called her and told her we were coming to talk to her."

Bernie grunted.

"Of course," Libby went on, "Alma did just point us in her direction."

"Yeah, but I bet Alma didn't tell her that," Bernie said as she got to the end of Danbury. She could see Rose's silver vehicle under the streetlights in the distance. She'd taken a left and was about half a block away. "I think she's heading for Twelve Corners, Libby."

"Maybe if we're lucky we can catch up with her there," Libby said.

Twelve Corners was a large intersection with eight lanes of traffic leading off in all directions. Depending on the lane you were in, the traffic lights could take a long time to change.

Bernie grimaced. "I don't want to catch up with her. I want to follow her and see where she's going."

"You think she's going to Amber?" Libby asked. If you thought about it in purely physical terms, Rose was the strongest member of the group and thereby the most capable of an abduction and of putting the deer target in place and taking it down.

"I think it's a possibility," Bernie said. "Anyway, we don't have anything to lose."

Bernie sped up a little. She could see Rose's vehicle was in the left lane waiting for the light to change so she could make a turn onto Riverside Street. A moment later, the light went green and Rose sped off. Bernie cursed under her breath and gave Mathilda more gas. She went across three lanes of traffic, cutting off a truck in her path, but by the time she got to the light it had turned red again.

"Drats," Bernie said. This was a long light and she was positive that by the time it turned again Rose would be gone. Which she was.

"What now?" Libby asked as Bernie made the turn onto Riverside.

Bernie didn't answer. She was too busy concentrating on the vehicles in front of her as she drove down Riverside. The traffic was relatively sparse, and she was hoping to catch a glimpse of Rose's vehicle. After fifteen blocks she was forced to admit that wasn't going to happen and she gave it up, turned Mathilda around, and headed back to Rose's place.

"Let's take a look around her house," Bernie suggested.

"And see what?" Libby asked.

Bernie shrugged her shoulders. "Probably nothing," she conceded. "But as long as we're this close, we might as well take a gander."

Libby looked at her watch. It was getting late and they were no closer to finding Amber now than they were when they'd started. "You know," Libby mused, "the yoga teacher told us that Amber willingly got into the car that pulled up next to hers in the parking lot."

Bernie looked over at her sister. "Your point is?"

Libby frowned. "Well, she could have gotten in the car with anyone. It could be the new guy she's seeing, or his sister, or some old friend that she hasn't seen since fifth grade. We don't know that it was the car of one of the Christmas Cookie Exchange Club ladies."

"No, we don't," Bernie agreed. "But the odds are, given the circumstances, that it was. That's the most logical conclusion and the one that I think it would serve us best to follow," Bernie said as she pulled into Rose's driveway.

Libby opened her mouth and closed it again. Her sister was right. There was nothing more to say on the topic. Instead, she pointed to the security company sign planted near the door. It was half obscured by the snow. "I guess we could have saved ourselves a trip."

"We're not breaking in, we're just walking around. As far as I know, that's not illegal yet," Bernie countered as she turned off Mathilda, put on her gloves, buttoned her jacket, and got out of the van.

Libby followed suit. She and Bernie were peering through the windows in the garage door when someone said, "Can I help you?"

The two sisters jumped and spun around. A man was

standing behind them. Someone Bernie and Libby hadn't seen before. He'd never been a customer of theirs, because Bernie and Libby remembered everyone who came into their shop, even if they'd just come in once or twice. Bernie decided the guy looked somewhere between sixty and seventy. He was of average height and average build, with a gray beard and mustache that could use a little shaping, and he was wearing a black watch cap pulled down over his ears, a parka buttoned up to his neck, and L.L. Bean boots on his feet.

"Sorry," he said, "I didn't mean to startle you ladies. My name is Dan, and this is Rosco," the man said, pointing to the small, furry dog in the red plaid coat at the end of a leash that was sniffing Libby's boots. "I live across the street. And you are?"

"Bernie and Libby Simmons," Libby said. "I'm Libby," she said, pointing to herself, "and she's Bernie. We own A Little Taste of Heaven."

Dan peered at them suspiciously. "What is it?"

Libby moved away from the dog. She didn't like the way he was lifting his leg. "A shop. We sell baked goods and food to take out. We also do catering. We're on Main Street. I'm surprised you haven't seen us."

"My wife does most of the shopping," he explained. "I'm more of a homebody. It's an odd name, though," he added. "Don't think I've ever heard anything like it."

"That's the idea," Libby told him.

Bernie's eyes narrowed. "My mom picked out that name."

Dan frowned. "Sorry. No offense meant. My wife says I have no verbal filter."

Bernie nodded. "No offense taken."

"Good," Dan said. He gave Roscoe a sharp tug on the lead and the dog trotted over and sat beside him. "Can I help you with anything?" Dan asked, gesturing toward Rose's house.

"Well," Bernie said, thinking fast, "we were supposed to pick up our niece, but no one seems to be home."

Dan rubbed his beard with his free hand and waited for Bernie to say something else.

"We were just wondering where she and Rose had gone off to," Libby added, filling in the silence.

"You think she's in the garage?" Dan asked.

"My sister and I were checking to make sure that Rose's car wasn't there," Bernie explained.

"I see," Dan said, although Libby reflected that he sounded as if he didn't. "We've had a lot of break-ins around here recently."

"That's terrible," Bernie said, giving Dan her most reassuring you-can-trust-me smile.

"Yes, it is," Dan replied. "That's why we formed the Neighborhood Watch."

"Of which you are a member," Bernie guessed.

"Leader," Dan volunteered.

Great, Bernie thought. Just what we need. "I probably heard the message wrong."

"Rose doesn't get a lot of visitors," Dan informed Bernie. "Except for the Christmas Cookie Exchange Club ladies. Right, Roscoe?"

Roscoe barked.

"He agrees with me," Dan said. "I think it's time we went in. Roscoe's arthritis is bothering him. The cold doesn't agree with him."

"Or me," Bernie said.

She waited for Dan and Roscoe to leave, but they didn't. Dan and Roscoe just stood there, and Bernie got the definite feeling they weren't going anywhere until she and Libby departed, which made her suspect that Dan didn't exactly believe the story she'd just told him.

"Well, if you see Rose," she said to Dan, "tell her that we were looking for Amber."

Dan nodded. "Will do."

"What was that all about?" Libby asked once they were in their van and backing out of the driveway.

"What was what all about?" Bernie asked as she watched Dan and Roscoe finally cross the street and go into their house.

"The whole 'tell her we were looking for Amber' thing."

Bernie shrugged. "Just giving Rose a little push."

She looked at her watch. On the one hand, it was late to try and talk to anyone else. On the other, Sheila Goody was a well-known insomniac.

Chapter 19

Sheila Goody was probably the richest of the Christmas Cookie Exchange Club ladies. She lived up on Babcock Hill in a five-bedroom, four-bathroom colonial set on half an acre of land. Married to a cardiologist, she'd inherited everything, much to her children's dismay, when her husband had plummeted off a small mountain in Canada.

Since Sheila had been the only one with him at the time, and since the marriage had not been a happy one, rumors had immediately begun swirling around town. But that had been fifteen years ago, and those rumors had been largely forgotten by now. It didn't hurt that Sheila contributed lavishly to a number of local philanthropic organizations, something her husband had not done, since he was a well-known cheapskate and general all-around boor. It was generally agreed in Longely that all things being equal, the trade-off of the wife for the husband had been a positive one. After all, as one of Sheila's friends had put it, everyone has to die sometime, and for some people sooner is better than later.

Bernie was thinking, as she pulled up in front of Sheila Goody's house, that despite what people say, money can indeed buy happiness as well as forgetfulness.

"I wonder if she did," Bernie said out loud, as she admired the white lights strung around the crab apple trees fronting Sheila Goody's house and the wreath made out of pinecones and red and pink velvet bows tacked to the door.

"Did what?" Libby asked.

"Push her husband off the mountain," Bernie said.

"I would have if I were her," Libby replied, thinking of a couple of encounters she'd had with him. "But you certainly wouldn't think she was capable of anything like that from looking at her."

"No. You wouldn't," Bernie agreed. Her mother's expression "She looked as if butter would melt in her mouth" leaped to mind. "I think it's the blue eyes and the white hair that does it. She looks like everyone's favorite grandmother. Even fifteen years ago, she just looked sickeningly sweet."

"Which she is so not," Libby said as Bernie parked and she and her sister got out of Mathilda and started for the front door. "I hope we're not too late."

"We'll see," Bernie said, thinking of Alma's reaction to their visit.

They'd taken about ten steps when the front door opened and Sheila stepped out. She was dressed in a pair of dark blue fleece lounging pants and a light blue cashmere hoodie. "I've been waiting for you two," she said. "What took so long?"

"I take it Alma called you," Bernie said.

Sheila smiled. "Who else?"

"What did she say?" Libby asked.

"She said that you were looking for Amber, and that she'd disappeared, and you thought that one of us might have had something to do with it, and that this whole thing was tied up with Millie's accident."

"That about covers it," Bernie said as she took a step inside Sheila's house. "Except for the part about Millie's missing recipes and the fact that her accident really wasn't an accident at all."

"Interesting," Sheila said. "I've been hearing rumors to that effect myself. I just find the whole thing terribly odd."

Libby asked for clarification. "Millie's death? Amber's disappearance?"

Sheila briefly touched her earrings before replying. "The effect that this television show has had on everyone," she elucidated. "You think you know people, then *Baking for Life* comes to town and everyone goes balmy."

"Maybe it's more a question of someone needing the hundred-thousand-dollar prize money," Libby said.

"Or," Bernie added, "wanting to enjoy their fifteen minutes of fame."

"Perhaps," Sheila said. "But I still think some people— mind you, I'm not saying who—have blown this whole thing way out of proportion."

"I think it's easy to pooh-pooh money when you're well off," Bernie said, giving Sheila's earrings a meaningful glance.

Bernie didn't know much about jewelry, but she figured the diamond studs Sheila was wearing had to be at least one carat and possibly two.

"I may not have as much money as you think I do," Sheila told Bernie in a frosty tone. "Not that it's any of your business."

"No. I suppose it's not."

"And these earrings were a gift from my late, lamented husband. They're not to my taste, but I wear them in his memory."

Bernie and Libby were careful not to look at each other. If they had, they would have burst out laughing.

"That's very sweet of you," Bernie said after she'd composed herself.

"I try to be nice to everyone," Sheila said. "I try to follow the Golden Rule."

Libby managed not to roll her eyes. Instead, she decided to bring the conversation back to the matter at hand.

"Did Alma also tell you that she pointed us in your direction?" she asked.

Sheila laughed. "No. She most certainly did not. I suppose I'm your number-one suspect, given what people were saying about Carl's demise."

"She actually didn't mention that," Bernie said.

Sheila made a tsk-tsk noise with her tongue. "How remiss of her. I'm surprised. So what did she say?" Sheila asked.

"She said that Millie tried to steal your boyfriend."

Sheila laughed harder and put her hand to her throat. Bernie could tell that she'd had work done. "Oh dear me. That is too funny. First of all, that was over twelve years ago. Second of all, Mario wasn't my boyfriend; he was my friend. Third of all, he was gay, so the whole thing was completely ridiculous. Talk about being unclear on the concept. However, I am surprised Alma didn't tell you about my BMW."

"What about it?" Bernie asked.

"The fact that Millie ran into it." Sheila threw up her hands in a gesture of disgust. "Honestly, that woman should never have been allowed to get behind the wheel of a car. She was a bad driver when she was younger, and she only got worse as she got older. Then, to top everything off, she refused to pay for what she'd done."

"Surely your insurance covered the damage," Bernie observed.

Sheila frowned. "Of course it did. But that wasn't the point. The point was how she acted and what she said."

"Which was?" Bernie asked.

Sheila shook her head. "Let's just say it was insulting to the memory of my dead husband. And me." She took a look at her watch. Bernie noticed that it was a Cartier.

"Are we keeping you from something?" Bernie asked.

Sheila smiled again. "As a matter of fact, you are. My television program is starting soon. So if you don't mind . . ." Her voice trailed off, and she gestured toward the door.

"So you're not going to answer our questions?" Bernie asked.

"I think I already have," Sheila replied.

"We haven't asked anything yet," Libby pointed out. "You're the one who's been doing all of the talking."

"I was trying to make things easy for you."

"I appreciate that," Bernie said.

"Good," Sheila said. "Since you didn't get it the first time, let me summarize for you."

"I don't think that's what Bernie was saying," Libby told Sheila.

Bernie watched Sheila try to widen her eyes, but she couldn't. Botox, Bernie figured. Sheila was trying to say something when Bernie heard a door open and close in the back of the house.

A moment later, a voice called out, "Yahoo. I'm here."

Bernie and Libby looked at Sheila, and Sheila looked back at them.

"Rose?" Bernie asked, having recognized the voice.

Sheila crossed her arms in front of her chest. "So what if it is?"

"I'm not saying anything," Bernie said.

"But you look as if you want to," Sheila told her as she shifted her weight from her right foot to her left and crossed her arms more tightly over her chest.

"Want to what?" Rose asked as she came bounding around the corner. She was wearing jeans, a black turtleneck sweater, a black motorcycle jacket, and black Uggs on her feet. Even at this hour, her hair was in a perfect French twist. She stopped dead when she saw Libby and Bernie. "Oh dear," she said, putting her hand over her mouth. "Am I interrupting something?"

"It's fine," Sheila told her. "They want to know where Amber is. Evidently, they've misplaced her."

"I wouldn't put it that way," Libby said.

"Then what would you say?" Sheila asked.

"I'd say that she's missing," Libby answered.

"Oh dear," Rose said, putting her hand to her mouth. "How upsetting. What can I do to help?"

"Funny you should say that," Bernie told her. "We stopped at your house to ask you a few questions, but we just missed you."

"In fact," Libby added, "we saw you take off out of your garage. It looked as if you were in a little bit of a hurry. Is everything all right? It looked like some sort of emergency."

"Well, I guess it was, in a manner of speaking," Rose replied. She was standing ramrod straight, with her feet slightly turned out. "I had a brilliant new idea for a cookie. I was so excited. But, unfortunately, I realized after I'd broken the eggs in the mixing bowl that I was out of vanilla and walnuts. So stupid of me. Normally, I'm so well organized."

She leaned forward. "The events of the last couple of days are just so upsetting that half the time I don't know what I'm doing," she confided to Libby and Bernie. "And now this thing with Amber. Of course," she continued, "there is always the chance that Amber is having a fun weekend down in Cancun or someplace like that. I know at that age that's what I would be doing."

"It would be nice to think so," Bernie said.

"You have to be more positive," Rose told her. "You have to send positive messages out into the universe."

Bernie wanted to slap her.

"So, Rose," Libby said, quickly changing the subject, "did you get the walnuts and vanilla?"

"I couldn't," Rose replied. "The store was closed."

"The supermarket in Longely is open twenty-four-seven," Bernie pointed out.

Rose moved her feet into third position and did a demi-plié. "I wasn't going there. I was going to Pierre's."

Pierre's was a shop that specialized in high-end baking supplies. Bernie raised an eyebrow.

"The supermarket doesn't carry Madagascar vanilla and black walnuts," Rose informed Bernie, "as well you know."

"In fact, I do," Libby told Rose, who was now standing on her tiptoes. For a moment, before she turned to Bernie, Libby had a vision of Rose pirouetting around the entryway. "You know," Libby said to her sister, "it's funny, but I thought Rose was heading off to where she'd stashed Amber. It just goes to show."

Bernie nodded. "So did I, Libby. So did I."

"I mean," Libby continued, "I figured that she'd just gotten a phone call from Alma telling her we were on our way to see her, and she decided to get out of the house before we could get there."

"After taking care of a few things," Bernie added.

Libby snapped her fingers. "But wait. Could it be that Rose had Amber hidden in the house and decided to relocate her to a safer place?"

Rose came down on the soles of her feet. "You two are nuts," she cried. She pointed to herself. "Do I look like I'd be capable of forcing Amber to do something she didn't want to do?"

"You're in pretty good shape," Libby told her.

"Yes, I am," Rose told her. "But I'm sixty-eight, and Amber's twenty-two. Youth wins every time."

"Maybe you had help," Bernie suggested.

"Or used drugs on Amber," Libby put in.

Rose shook her head in disgust. "Why would I do something like that? What could I possibly gain?"

"Revenge is always a good motive," Bernie said.

"Revenge?" Rose scoffed. "On Millie? Where are you getting this stuff from?"

"From Alma," Sheila answered.

Rose rolled her eyes. "You're kidding me," she said to Bernie and Libby.

"Not in the slightest," Bernie said. "Alma seemed to think you were a likely candidate," Bernie said to Rose. "She told me to talk to you."

"And me," Sheila said, pointing to herself. "Don't forget me."

"Who could do that?" Bernie said.

"Who indeed," Libby echoed, before continuing her conversation with Rose. "Alma is the reason we went to your house, Rose," Libby told her.

Rose breathed in and out. Then she did another demiplié. "Alma is . . . quite the storyteller," she said when she was through. "She's the one you ought to be questioning. She's the one who threatened to kill Millie, not me. She's the one who was jealous of Millie—pathologically jealous."

"So you weren't upset about what Millie did to your mother's lilac bushes?" Bernie asked Rose, pointedly ignoring Sheila.

"Of course, I was upset," Rose replied. "Why should I deny it? Everyone knows I was upset. Those bushes had been my great-great-grandmother's. They'd been in my family for generations. They were irreplaceable. I'm still mourning their loss." For a moment Rose's eyes flashed, and her mouth formed itself into a sharp line. "The worst of it was that I had asked Millie to park in the street, but she refused. Said it was too far to walk, but she could spend hours traipsing through the mall. Millie was selfish to the core. The only person she cared about was herself."

"And the twenty dollars she owed you?"

Rose stood even straighter, if that were possible. "I believe that debts should be paid off. I believe it is a breach of trust not to do so."

"Fair enough," Libby said. "Just out of curiosity, what would you do if you won the *Bake for Life* contest?"

"That's easy," Rose said. "I would donate the money to the dancer's retirement fund."

"Are we done here?" Sheila inquired before Libby could ask another question. "Because if we are, Rose and I have things to discuss."

"I thought you had a TV program to watch," Bernie said.

"That too," Sheila replied.

Bernie turned to Libby. "So are we done here?"

"Yes," Libby replied. "Except for one question."

"And that is?" Rose demanded.

"What about the car sitting in your garage?"

"You looked in my garage," Rose repeated. "How intrusive."

"Through the window," Libby clarified.

"So now it's a crime to have two cars?" Rose asked.

"Not at all. The reason my sister is asking," Bernie said, "is because someone reported seeing Amber getting into a light-colored sedan similar to the one in your garage, right, Libby?"

"Right, Bernie," Libby said.

"There must be at least five thousand light-colored sedans in this area," Rose observed. "That particular vehicle belongs to my nephew, and it's parked there because it needs a new engine."

"Do you mind if we take a look at it?" Libby asked her.

Rose raised her eyebrows as if to indicate that she couldn't believe what she was hearing. "Of course I mind. You want to see it, get a warrant." She looked at Libby and Bernie and smiled. "Oh wait." She snapped her fingers. "That's right. How silly of me. I forgot. You can't get a warrant because you're not the police and you have no legal standing whatsoever."

"The only reason I haven't called the police on both of you," Sheila informed Bernie and Libby, "is because I'm concerned about Amber too and I want you to find her, which is why you might want to talk to Barbara Lazarus and Pearl Pepperpot."

"Why them?" Bernie asked.

"Ask them and find out," Sheila said. "I'm not doing your work for you. Now I think we are officially concluded here. I wish I could say it's been a pleasure, but it definitely has not been."

"So I guess that seeing the other structures on your property is out of the question?" Bernie asked.

Sheila's property had an old horse barn and a pool house on it. The pool had been filled in by a previous owner, but the pool house had stayed, as had the horse barn.

"What do you think?" Sheila asked Bernie.

"I think that you're going to tell me it'll be fine." Bernie turned to Rose. "See, I'm practicing positive visualization."

"Too bad it's not working," Sheila said. "If I see you on my property I'm going to call the authorities immediately. Are we clear?"

"Totally," Libby said.

"Good," Sheila said.

Bernie gave Sheila her largest, most insincere smile and headed for the door.

"Good luck with those walnuts, Rose," Libby called out as she followed her sister to the door.

She was not in a good mood when she got into the van. As far as she was concerned, she didn't feel she was any closer to finding Amber than she was when she and Bernie had started. The fact that she didn't have any chocolate left didn't help matters either.

Chapter 20

Bernie turned to Libby after they'd cleared Sheila's driveway and said, "You know . . ."

"I agree," Libby said.

"With what?" Bernie asked. "I haven't said anything yet?"

"That I don't buy what Rose was saying about why she left in such a hurry."

"Neither do I," Bernie said. "But that's not what I was going to say . . ."

"Which is?"

"That we should take a look at Sheila's pool house and barn. If we'd been thinking, we would have done that before we spoke to Sheila. Either of those structures is the perfect place to stash Amber."

"It is too bad we didn't think of it before, because now Sheila will be watching for us."

"Mistakes are opportunities in disguise," Bernie chirped.

"I think I'm going to be sick," Libby told her.

"I'm just practicing my positive visualizations," Bernie said.

"Well, practice them somewhere else," Libby informed her.

"The fact that the road to the pool house and the barn go right by Sheila's house will make things a tad more challenging," Bernie observed. "But not impossible."

Libby glanced at Sheila's house. Sheila and Rose were at the window, watching to make sure they left. "How long do you think they're going to stand there?" she asked her sister.

"Quite a long time."

"So how are we going to do this?" Libby asked.

"I figure we'll take the turnoff about a quarter of a mile down and drive along the stone wall. Then we'll park Mathilda and climb over the wall. The pool house can't be more than a quarter of a mile away."

"And if someone sees us?" Libby asked.

"They won't," Bernie assured her. "No one drives on that road. It's not even a road."

"Exactly," Libby said. "It's a dirt path. And it's dark."

"Not that dark," Bernie pointed out. "The moon is out. I used to drive it at night all the time with Benny when I was in high school."

"Yeah, and Dad had to come and pull you out of a ditch," Libby reminded her, remembering the look on her dad's face when he'd gone storming out of the house. She'd been really glad she wasn't the one he'd been going after.

"That's because we were drunk. But we're not drunk now."

"Obviously," Libby answered, although at this point in the evening she wouldn't have minded a shot of brandy, even though some hot chocolate would be better. Her feet were cold, and the prospect of being out and about did not thrill her. "But you do know that Sheila meant it when she said that if she saw us she'd have us arrested."

"She won't see us," Bernie said.

"She'll be able to see the headlights."

"I'm planning on driving with the parking lights on."

"Even better," Libby murmured, visions of broken axles dancing in her head.

"All we're going to do is peek in," Bernie told her sister. "Either we see Amber or we don't. If we see her, we call the police, and if we don't see her we go home. It's a win-win situation all the way around."

"It always seems so simple when you say it," Libby remarked bitterly.

Bernie took her right hand off the steering wheel and patted her sister's knee. "That's because it is."

Libby sat back in her seat and watched the houses twinkling in the darkness. As they went by, she reflected that ordinarily, given the circumstances, she would have had a long, fruitless conversation with her sister about the foolishness of what they were doing. But not now. Now they needed to do everything they could to find Amber.

They drove a quarter of a mile down the road, and then Bernie made a hard left onto a small, unmarked dirt road that ran parallel to a stone wall. The wall went on for seven miles and had been constructed before Sheila's house had been built and the surrounding properties were farms.

At one time, the wall had served as a demarcation line between the fields, but now it was crumbling away. The van swayed and bounced on the rutted road as Bernie picked her way between the potholes, while Libby gripped her seat with both hands to keep her head from hitting the roof. By the time the sisters got to where they were going, Bernie was down to five miles an hour.

"All I can say is that I hope Mathilda forgives us," Libby said when Bernie finally brought the van to a stop.

"She will," Bernie said as she got out of the van. "My kidneys, on the other hand, I'm not so sure about."

Libby could see both the barn and the pool house from where they were standing, and even though the structures were in Sheila's kitchen's line of sight, Libby figured that if she and Bernie went around the back way, Sheila wouldn't be able to see them. If she was looking. Which she probably wasn't. She and Rose had most likely moved into the living room by this time.

"The barn first," Bernie said as she climbed over the wall.

Libby didn't answer because she was trying to get her foot out of the crevice she'd gotten her shoe caught in. How she had managed this she wasn't sure, but she was well and truly stuck.

"Let me help you," Bernie said, trying and not succeeding in smothering a laugh.

"I can do it myself," Libby said, each word coming out through gritted teeth. "It's not funny."

"I'm sorry. You're right. It's not. But you look like a beached starfish," Bernie told her, going off into another gale of laughter.

Libby didn't answer. She was too busy trying to free her foot. Finally, she yielded to the inevitable, untied her laces, and slipped her foot out of her shoe. After that her shoe came out with relative ease.

She rubbed her ankle, then balanced on one foot while she slid her shoe back on. She could feel the bruise. It was swelling up already. By the time she got home she'd probably have a black-and-blue mark. Not to mention the fact that on top of everything else her sock was wet and her foot was cold from touching the snow.

"Come on, Libby, let's go," Bernie said impatiently. Really, she thought. How long does it take to get a shoe back on? They weren't getting any warmer standing here.

"I could have broken my ankle," Libby told her.

"But you didn't," Bernie pointed out.

"Or my nose," Libby said.

"You're fine," Bernie said. "Can you stop whining and start moving? Sheila can see us from here."

"She's probably watching TV by now, and a little compassion would not be amiss here," Libby told her sister while she slipped her shoe on.

"I did say *please*," Bernie told her.

Libby glared at her. "No, you didn't."

"Fine. You're right, I didn't. I'm saying it now. Does that make you happy?"

"Not really," Libby told her. "And for your information, I'm moving as fast as I can." Libby looked at her sister, who was wearing a tight black skirt and boots with four-inch heels. She looked perfect. Bernie hadn't even broken a fingernail, while she, Libby, was wearing sweatpants, hiking boots, and a heavy parka and probably looked as if she'd just gone three rounds with a Sumo wrestler. No matter what she did, Libby reflected, she always ended up with a spot on her clothes or a button missing.

"How come nothing like this ever happens to you?" Libby asked Bernie. "How come you never break a heel or fall or anything?"

Bernie gave a sister a smug smile. "Because I'm not a klutz."

"That is so unfair."

"Life is unfair, Libby. Just be glad I didn't take a picture of you."

"You wouldn't," Libby exclaimed.

"I can't," Bernie said. "It's too dark."

Thank God for small favors, Libby thought as she and her sister headed toward the barn. The ground was uneven, as the field was frozen over with small hillocks and clumps of grass. As Libby walked, she thought about running from the cops out here and decided it would not be a pretty sight. Get arrested or break a leg? Neither alternative was pleasant to contemplate.

"Can't you pick up the pace a little?" Bernie asked

Libby. Somehow she'd managed to get a good couple of yards in front of her.

"I'm going as fast as I can," Libby replied as she leaned down to rub her throbbing ankle.

A moment later Bernie was at the barn, and a moment after that Libby was too.

"The door is open," Libby observed.

"Actually, there is no door," Bernie said.

"I wonder what happened to it."

Bernie pointed to the left. "It must have rotted off and someone dragged it over there."

"Somehow I don't think anyone is being held here," Libby said, indicating the barn with a nod of her head.

"I don't think so either, but I think we should take a look around anyway," Bernie said as she took a step inside. What she didn't say to Libby was that the barn would be a good place to park a body.

But fortunately that wasn't the case. Bernie sighed in relief. The structure was empty, although the animal stalls were still intact, as was the hayloft. The smell of cows lingered in the air, even after all these years. A few tiles had come off the roof, and Bernie and Libby could see the night sky through them.

Bernie looked down at the floor. She could see grease spots. "I guess Sheila must have stored a car here at some point."

"Or a tractor," Libby commented as she gave the interior of the barn a more careful look.

Everything was open. There was no place anyone could hide, but just to make sure, Libby walked in and out of all the stalls. There was nothing in them except a few pieces of paper and little piles of straw and leaves and debris. She imagined that the piles were great places for mice to raise their young.

"Come on, let's go," she said to Bernie after she'd made her circuit.

Bernie nodded. She had been thinking about climbing up to the hayloft and walking around it, but the ladder looked rickety, and she could see holes on the walkway where some of the boards had rotted out. Probably better not to chance it, she decided, especially since she could see from where she was standing that there was nothing there.

"Onward and upward," Bernie said to Libby as she walked out the barn door.

It was a short walk to the pool house, but it was still snowing, only the snow was coming down in sheets now, making it difficult to see. By the time the sisters got to the pool house, their jackets were covered with a thin layer of the white stuff.

"At least it's good camouflage," Bernie said as she blinked some flakes out of her eyes.

Libby just grunted and pointed to the security sign in front of the pool house that was half covered by snow. She was too tired and too cold and wet to talk.

"I saw it," Bernie said as she tried the handle of the pool house door. "It's probably just an old sign. Sheila's house isn't alarmed, so I don't see why this place should be."

With that, Bernie walked around the house and tried the three windows. They were locked as well, which she had expected. She cupped her hands in front of her eyes and tried to see through the glass, but the blinds were closed on the other side of the windows, obscuring her view. She took a step back and studied the building.

From where she was standing, she could see the roof. It was flat and had two skylights on it. Those, she was pretty sure, weren't alarmed. They usually weren't, and this was not what you would call a high-crime area. All she had to do was get up there. A few feet away she saw a metal table. If she put the table next to the wall of the pool house, Bernie was pretty certain she could climb up there and open one of the skylights.

"Help me," she told Libby as she explained what she

was thinking of doing. "I'm not tall enough," she announced after she tried and failed.

"Maybe you should have worn six-inch heels," Libby observed.

"Maybe I should have," Bernie agreed as she gave Libby a speculative look.

"Forget it," Libby said.

"I didn't say anything," Bernie protested.

"You didn't have to," Libby retorted.

"But you're four inches taller than I am," Bernie pointed out.

"It's not happening," Libby told her. "Aside from everything else, my ankle is still killing me."

"Fine," Bernie said. "But I just have one word for you."

"What's that?"

"Amber."

"I hate when you do this," Libby cried.

"Do what?"

"Guilt me into things."

"I'm right and you know it. It's easy," Bernie continued on when her sister didn't say anything. "You saw me. I'll hold the table for you, and all you have to do is climb up on it, grab onto the roof, and pull yourself up. It's only one story. Then when you get to the top, just open the skylight and go down in and let me in. Anyway, as you pointed out before, you're dressed for this and I'm not."

Libby groaned. The phrase "hoisted on her own petard" occurred to her. Although she didn't know what a petard was, she had an idea it was applicable to her situation.

"What if someone's in there?" Libby asked, effectively changing the conversation.

"You mean other than Amber?" Bernie said. "Don't be silly, if there was anyone in there they would have come out already, given all the noise we're making."

Libby sighed. "I just hope Amber appreciates what

we're doing for her," she told Bernie as she climbed up on top of the metal picnic table.

"I'm sure she will when we find her," Bernie answered.

This was something Libby couldn't argue with, so she focused on keeping her balance. Once Libby was on top of the table, she grabbed onto the rim of the roof and tried to hoist herself up. She got halfway before her arms gave up and she came back down.

"I don't know if I can do this," she told Bernie. "I don't think I'm strong enough."

"Try again," Bernie urged.

Libby did, but the results were the same. "I need another couple of inches."

Bernie thought for a moment. She told Libby to wait for a moment as she ran off and got a chair she'd spotted earlier.

"Here," she said as she brushed the snow off and handed it up to Libby. "This should help."

"You want me to stand on this?" Libby asked.

"No. I want you to sit on it."

"I'm going to break my neck. Why can't you do this?"

"Because I'll still be too short. You'll be fine," Bernie told her. "You can do this. It's not as if I'm asking you to do handstands."

"I must be nuts," Libby grumbled as she did what Bernie suggested.

The chair wobbled as Libby stood on it, but Bernie held onto it and it stayed put. The added height was enough, and Libby was able to shimmy her way onto the roof. Once she got there, she walked over to the skylights and brushed the snow away from them. Then she squatted down to get a better look.

Both of the skylights were set flush to the roof, each of them ringed with a rubber thingy—Libby knew they had a name, but she didn't know what it was—that had been designed to keep the elements out. Fortunately, the seals weren't that tight, and Libby managed to get her fingers under the rim of one of them and pull. To her surprise, the skylight came up a little. She pulled harder, and the skylight came up enough so she could wiggle her way in. She looked down. From what she could see, the place was empty.

"I don't see Amber," she called out to Bernie.

"Can you see the whole area?" Bernie asked.

"Not really," Libby admitted, feeling guilty that at this moment all she wanted to do was get off the roof.

"Let's make sure," Bernie called back.

"Easy for you to say. I'd like to see you make this drop in four-inch heels," Libby grumbled under her breath.

"I heard that," Bernie said. "It's not that far."

"It is to me," Libby replied.

Bernie ignored the comment. "I'll meet you at the door," she told Libby, who sighed the sigh of the long-suffering.

Libby tried to give herself a pep talk. "After all, how bad can it be?" she told herself, thinking of all the movies she'd seen where the hero had done this. "Bernie's right. It's not that far down," she said to herself. "If I hang by my hands and let myself drop, it'll be fine."

Only it wasn't.

It might have been if Libby had had the strength to hang by her hands. But not being a gymnast or a stunt double, she didn't. Instead, her fingers slipped, and she tumbled to the ground. Fortunately, she landed on her rump, an area that was well padded. It was the only time in her life that she was grateful for what her mom used to call her big caboose.

"Are you okay?" Libby could hear Bernie calling from the other side of the door.

"No, I'm not," Libby replied as she hauled herself up and dusted herself off.

"It sounded as if you fell. Did you?"

"I could have broken my neck," Libby snapped. Her

ankle was not happy, but at least she hadn't fractured it, she thought, as she made her way to the door to let Bernie in. Thank God for small favors.

"You look fine to me," Bernie told Libby once she'd stepped inside.

Libby scowled. "Well, I don't feel fine." And she didn't. Her rear end was hurting.

"Where'd you land?"

"I'm not telling you," Libby replied. She really didn't want to hear her sister's comments.

Bernie tapped her fingers on her thighs. "Let me think. You're walking around, you didn't break anything so I'm guessing . . ."

"I don't want to talk about it."

"You landed . . ."

Libby held up her hand. "Don't say it."

Bernie closed her mouth. A moment later she opened it again. "On your . . ."

"I mean it," Libby told her sister before Bernie could get the next word out.

Bernie threw up her hands. "I wasn't going to say anything about your you-know-what."

"Yes, you were."

"Fine, Miss Sensitive," Bernie told her sister as she brushed the snow off her jacket. "Then let's talk about this place. Is that okay?"

"There's nothing to talk about," Libby griped. "I told you there was nothing here when I was on the roof."

Bernie extended her hand in a graceful gesture and did a half bow. "As usual you were correct, oh elder sister of mine. But at least we can eliminate the place now."

"I guess you have a point," Libby reluctantly agreed, even though her pride was still injured.

She knew her dad would agree as well. He always said that what you eliminate could be as important as what you find. She thought about that as she looked around.

The pool house was a large, one-room affair with a bath-room off to the left and a galley kitchen off to the right. The main room was furnished with sofas and chairs with dust covers on them, while the coffee table was an em-bossed large, round, metal tray set on wooden legs that looked as if it came from Morocco.

There was no evidence that anyone had been here for quite a while, but just to make sure, Bernie decided to take a quick look through the kitchen, while Libby took the bathroom. Libby was glancing through the medicine cabi-net, which contained, among other things, an old box of Band-Aids, a bottle of peroxide, and a mummified, nearly empty tube of toothpaste, when her sister yelled, "Libby."

"What?" Libby called back.

"Get over here."

"What's going on?" she asked when she reached the kitchen.

"You gotta see this," and Bernie pointed to the inside of the refrigerator.

"What is it? Tell me."

Bernie nodded toward the refrigerator with her chin. "Just take a look."

"Is it gross?"

"You'll see."

Feeling slightly apprehensive, Libby scooted around the open refrigerator door and did as her sister had requested. Her jaw dropped. "Good grief," she whispered.

"Good grief is right," Bernie said.

Chapter 21

"I can't believe it," Libby exclaimed.

"Neither can I," Bernie said.

The two sisters stared at the inside of the refrigerator. It was filled with prepackaged cookie dough, prebaked pie shells, canned frostings, prepackaged rolls, and a couple of cans of Crisco.

"Libby, is this the pool house of the lady who prides herself on baking everything from scratch?" Bernie asked.

"I believe so, Bernie."

"Who scorns prebaked anything?"

"That would be correct, Bernie," Libby said, as she picked up a can of Pillsbury rolls, read the contents, and put them back. It's not that she had anything against prepackaged items—they were perfectly fine in a pinch—but they had listened to Sheila rant and rave about them for all these years!

"God," Bernie said. "Our Sheila is a closet junk eater."

"Amazing," Libby said. "I feel as if we've just discovered that one of our neighbors . . ."

"Is married to three wives," Bernie said, finishing the sentence for her.

"Or," Libby said, "that an Orthodox Jew's favorite

snack is a cheese and bacon hamburger or that a vegan loves a big porterhouse steak."

"Or," Bernie added, "that someone who preaches the virtues of a raw diet actually cooks his meals in a slow cooker or that a nutritionist lives on a diet of Twinkies and Coke."

Libby laughed. "I've got to say I'm feeling really shocked."

"So am I," Bernie said, thinking of all those times Sheila had cross-examined her on the provenance of the ingredients they used at A Little Taste of Heaven.

"And betrayed," Libby said.

Bernie didn't answer. She was too busy rooting around in her bag, looking for her phone. "I'm going to take pictures," she announced.

"Why?" Libby asked.

"Because you never know," Bernie answered.

"You never know what?" Libby asked.

"When the opportunity for blackmail will present itself," Bernie explained as she rooted around in her purse, looking for her phone.

"If you carried something smaller than a trunk, you wouldn't have so much trouble finding things in there," Libby pointed out.

Bernie just grunted. "Got it," she said triumphantly a moment later, and she began clicking away. "I'm done," she said after she'd snapped twenty pictures with her camera phone and closed the refrigerator door. "Now I think it's time to go."

She was in the process of slipping her phone back in her bag when Sheila Goody came barreling through the pool house door.

"Ah ha! I knew I'd find you two here," she said, advancing on Bernie and Libby. "I knew you couldn't leave well enough alone." She shook her finger at them. "I warned you. I told you I was going to call the police on you, even if it does mean postponing the *Baking for Life* contest because they're going to have to find two new judges." She took her phone out of her jacket pocket and brandished it around as if it were a weapon.

"I wouldn't be so hasty with that call if I were you," Libby said.

Sheila put her hands on her hips. "Really?" she said. "Are you not on my property without my permission? Did you not break into my pool house? That's breaking and entering. I will make sure that you are punished to the full extent of the law."

Bernie turned to Libby. "Are you scared?" she asked her sister.

"Terrified," Libby replied. "You?"

"Equally so," Bernie replied.

Sheila raised her phone. "If I were you, given the circumstances, I'd be a little less sarcastic and a little more polite."

"I might be and so would Libby," Bernie told Sheila, "if we hadn't seen the contents of your refrigerator."

Libby watched, fascinated, while the color drained out of Sheila's face. She'd heard the expression, but she didn't know it was for real.

While Sheila tried to rally, Libby put her hand to her heart and told her, "Seeing what was in there made me feel betrayed and shocked."

"That's how I felt too," Bernie added. "And it takes a lot to shock me."

"That's true," Libby said. "It does."

Sheila took a step back. "I don't use that stuff," she stuttered. "I keep it for the men who work here."

Bernie lifted an eyebrow. "You hire bakers?"

"No. No." Sheila sought to clarify. "I'm talking about the men who work on the grounds."

"You mean the undocumented workers to whom you pay a pittance?" Bernie asked sweetly.

"That's not true," Sheila protested. "I pay them the going rate."

Libby laughed. "Surely you can come up with a better story than that?"

"That I pay my workers the going rate or that I bake cookies for them?" Sheila asked.

"Both," Bernie said.

Sheila raised her hand. "I'm telling the truth. I swear I am. Sometimes I bake the men cookies. It's a nice gesture."

"It is, but it would be even nicer if you paid them a living wage," Bernie said. "Even if I believed you," she continued, "which I don't, what you're saying is that you give them dreck and keep the good stuff for yourself."

"No. No. No," Sheila protested. "It's a time thing. I don't have time to bake for them from scratch. And they like these. They do. That's what they eat at home."

"How many people do you employ here anyway?" Libby asked, deciding not to tackle the implications of the last part of Sheila's statement. "You have enough stuff in the refrigerator to feed an army."

"It's because of the way I buy it," Sheila said. By now she was wringing her hands.

"Which is how?" Bernie asked.

"At Sam's Club."

"We don't have a Sam's Club in Longely," Libby pointed out.

"I go to one over in New Jersey," Sheila confessed.

"That makes sense," Libby said. "If I were you, I wouldn't want anyone to see me buying that stuff either."

"It's not like that," Sheila said, even though it was. Her voice had begun to quiver.

"Then what is it like?" Bernie asked. "Tell us. We'd really like to know."

"Yes, we would," Libby added.

"I don't think I want to talk to you two anymore," Sheila said as she folded her arms across her chest.

"I have something that might change your mind," Bernie told her.

"Nothing is going to change my mind," Sheila asserted.

"Nothing?" Bernie asked.

"Nothing," Sheila said firmly.

Bernie drew back the corners of her mouth in a smile. "Are you positive?"

"Absolutely," Sheila replied.

"You might change your mind when you see these," Bernie said to Sheila, at which point she took out her phone and showed her the photos she'd just taken. "What do you think?" Bernie asked her. "Should I post these on my Facebook page? Or maybe I should tweet?"

"Please, don't," Sheila cried.

"I'll tell you what, Sheila," Libby said to her. "You answer our questions and we'll forget about what's in your refrigerator. How's that?"

"Which we can't do if the police are involved," Bernie reminded her. "On the other hand, if you want to call them on us, be my guest."

Sheila waved her hands in the air to silence Bernie. "Don't be ridiculous. No police. Absolutely not. I don't know what I was thinking, making a threat like that. Millie's death must have affected me more deeply than I realized."

"Evidently," Libby said.

"After all," Sheila continued, "I have known the woman for thirty years."

"That's a long time," Libby agreed. "By the way, where's Rose?"

"She went home," Sheila said. "She was tired and upset and wanted to get into bed and go to sleep."

"Fair enough," said Bernie, who was all of those things as well and would give anything to be asleep in her bed at the moment. "Okay. Here's my first question. Did Rose really run out to buy walnuts and vanilla?"

Sheila bit her lip and looked down at the floor.

"I wonder what the other members of the Christmas Cookie Exchange Club would make of the chocolate chip cookie dough I found in your refrigerator or of the pre-made pie shells?" Bernie mused after a minute had gone by and Sheila hadn't said anything.

"Please don't," Sheila said.

"What I do is entirely up to you," Bernie said.

"Let me explain," Sheila pleaded.

"I'd love to hear it," Libby said. "And I hope this explanation is better than the one you just gave us. What were you thinking?"

"I don't know," Sheila said. "I really don't."

"How long does it take to whip up a batch of chocolate-chip cookies, Sheila? Ten minutes? Fifteen at the most."

"I know, Libby. Forgive me. I lost my way."

"You certainly did," Libby told her. "So let me repeat my first question. Did Rose go running out of her house to buy walnuts and vanilla?"

"No," Sheila mumbled.

"Why did she?" Libby asked.

Sheila twirled her diamond studs around, then folded her arms across her chest and tucked her hands into her armpits. "She got a call." Sheila's voice was barely audible.

Bernie leaned forward so she could hear better. "From whom?" she asked.

"From Pearl," Sheila answered, her voice cracking a little.

"What did Pearl want?" Libby asked.

Sheila began wringing her hands again. "It's complicated."

"I bet it is," Libby said.

Sheila remained silent. She began rocking back and forth. Libby looked at her. For a nanosecond, she wondered if she and Bernie weren't being too hard on her. After all, Sheila was in her seventies, but then she thought about Amber and about Millie. Anger took over, and she wanted to slap her. But Libby suppressed the urge and tried for an understanding tone instead. "That's okay," Libby told Sheila. "We have all the time in the world, don't we, Bernie?"

"Absolutely, Libby. Do you want to sit down?" Bernie asked Sheila.

Sheila shook her head and studied a small crack in one of wooden floor slats. After a moment, she lifted her head and began to talk.

"Rose was the one who met Amber at the strip mall," Sheila said in a resigned tone.

"Why did she do that?" Bernie asked.

"Because Amber asked her to, because she'd heard that Rose might have her aunt's recipes."

"Millie's Meltaways?" Libby asked.

"Those and the recipe book," Sheila replied.

"And?"

"I already told you that the recipe for the Meltaways was gone when we got there."

"And Millie's recipe book?"

"That was gone too. But Amber didn't believe Rose. She insisted she was lying. She demanded to speak to Pearl, so Rose took her there."

"Why didn't Amber follow Rose? Why did she get into her car?"

"Because the engine light in Amber's car had come on, and she was afraid it would stall out again. I guess it had been going on for a while."

"True," Libby said. Amber had been having trouble with her car for the last couple of months. It was one of those electrical problems that are extremely difficult to diagnose and fix.

"So Rose took Amber to Pearl's house?" Bernie said.

Sheila nodded.

"Then what happened?" Bernie asked. She was having trouble believing what she was hearing.

"Nothing. She dropped Amber at Pearl's house and went home."

"Just like that?" Libby said.

"Yes. Just like that," Sheila replied.

"So how was Amber going to get home?" Bernie inquired.

"I don't know," Sheila told them.

"Didn't you ask?" Bernie said. "I know in your position I would have asked."

Sheila shrugged. "I've been busy. I haven't had a chance to talk to Rose and find out."

"I'm supposed to believe that?" Bernie said.

"It's true," Sheila insisted.

Bernie studied her, and Sheila returned her look.

"I haven't spoken to her until tonight," Sheila insisted.

"Fine. What did you two talk about?" Bernie said.

"The best kind of cookie sheets to use. Whether cassia or true cinnamon is better as a flavoring. Whether one can substitute waxed paper for parchment paper in a pinch. Things like that."

"I find that difficult to believe."

Sheila shrugged. "Then don't."

"So you didn't talk about Millie?" Libby asked.

"Well, yes, we did," Sheila conceded. "We talked about how sad what had happened to her was. We talked about the fact that she shouldn't have been driving."

"What else?"

"About the TV show and how much it meant to her."

"And Amber," Libby said. "Did you talk about Amber?"

"A little," Sheila conceded.

"What did you say about her?"

"That her aunt's death had affected her."

"In what way?" Bernie asked.

Sheila remained silent.

"In what way?" Bernie repeated.

Sheila threw up her hands. "She just . . . she was obsessed with finding Millie's recipes and her killer."

Bernie and Libby exchanged looks.

"She used those words?" Bernie asked.

"That's what she said to Rose," Sheila told Bernie.

"Why did Rose agree to speak to Amber?" Bernie asked.

"Because Amber threatened her."

"With what?" Libby exclaimed. She couldn't imagine Amber threatening anyone.

"You can't repeat this," Sheila said.

"We won't," Bernie promised. "Right, Libby?"

Libby raised her hand. "Swear."

Sheila leaned forward and lowered her voice a notch. "Amber said that she was going to tell Rose's neighbor's wife that she was having an affair with her husband."

"Dan?" Bernie squeaked.

"How did you know that?" Sheila cried.

"We met him," Libby told her. He wanted to know what we were doing looking in Rose's garage.

"Amazing," Bernie murmured.

"It's not that amazing," Sheila said tartly. "We're not dead yet, you know."

"I meant," Bernie quickly replied, "it's amazing what a small world it is."

"And Rose is an attractive lady," Sheila said, ignoring Bernie's last comment.

"Yes, she is," Bernie agreed. And she was. She couldn't argue with that. "So how did Amber find out?"

"She told Rose she saw her and Dan parked over by Thorden Groves."

Which, Libby thought, was right near where Amber lived.

"I told Rose not to do that," Sheila went on. "I told her that place was too close, but what do I know? Nothing, apparently."

"So what did Pearl want?" Libby asked, changing the subject. "Why did she go out there in such a hurry?"

"Well, Pearl called her and told her it was an emergency and she had to come over immediately, so she hopped in her car and ran right over."

"And?" Libby asked.

"When she got to Pearl's house, Pearl had already left."

"How did she know?" Bernie said.

"Because Pearl's car wasn't there and she didn't answer the door."

"So then what did Rose do?"

"She called me and I told her to come on over."

"Weren't you worried, given what's been going on?" Bernie asked Sheila.

"Honestly? Not really. Pearl tends to get all worked up about things. Frankly, I thought she was just hysterical. She's called one of us when the bottom of her cookies have burned, for heaven's sake, and demanded we come running over. It's ridiculous." Sheila looked from Bernie to Libby and back again. "Are we done here?" she asked. "Because I need to get some sleep."

"Yeah, I think we are," Bernie said as her phone began to ring.

It was her dad. "You have to come home," he told her. "You have to come home now. I have some people here who need to talk to you, people that you're going to want to talk to too."

Chapter 22

When Bernie and Libby walked through the door of their apartment fifteen minutes later, they saw Pearl Pepperpot and Lillian Stein sitting on the sofa across from their dad. Pearl was quivering with indignation, Lillian was making soothing noises, and their dad looked as if he'd give anything to be someplace else.

"See, I told you they'd be here," Sean said to Pearl, who had her hand on her bosom and was taking large, deep breaths. "I told you not to worry."

For a moment, Libby was mesmerized by the sight of the five large, felt roses pinned on Pearl's dress, bobbing up and down as if they were riding the ocean waves. Then she got hold of herself.

"What's the matter?" she asked. "What's going on?"

"What's the matter?" Pearl shrieked. "What's the matter? I've been kidnapped by your counter girl. That's what the matter is."

"You mean Amber?" Libby asked.

"Who else am I talking about? How many other crazy people do you have working for you?" Pearl moved her hand up to her face and fanned herself. "Just hearing her name gives me palpitations."

"She kidnapped you?" repeated a dumbfounded Libby.
"Didn't you hear what I just said?" Pearl shrieked.

"I think the man on the street can hear what you're saying," Sean observed, his patience exhausted. Pearl had always been his least-favorite member of the group, and her
behavior in the last half hour hadn't done anything to
change his opinion.

Pearl threw him a dirty look and went on. "You know
why your counter girl kidnapped me? I'll tell you why,"
she said, without waiting for an answer. "Your counter
girl kidnapped me so I wouldn't win the *Baking for Life*
contest. That's why she did it." Pearl wagged her finger at
Libby and Bernie. "But I foiled her. I escaped."

Lillian patted Pearl's arm. "That might be overstating
what happened a bit, dear."

Pearl's nostrils flared. "You don't know what happened,
Lillian. You weren't there."

"I'm just going by what you told me," Lillian told Pearl,
using the same kind of reasonable tone you would use
with a five-year-old on the verge of a temper tantrum.

"You don't know," Pearl repeated, her voice choked
with emotion. Then she began to fan herself again. "I
don't know if I can go on," she moaned. "This whole
episode is . . . it's that producer lady's fault. All of it. If she
hadn't told Amber she could be on the show, none of this
would have happened." Pearl's voice trailed off and she
looked down at the floor. "Is it hot in here, or is it just
me?" Pearl asked plaintively.

Bernie and Libby exchanged glances. Both were still trying to come to grips with what Pearl had told them.

Pearl cleared her throat. "It's awfully dry in here."

"Can I get you something to drink? A glass of water, or
some tea perhaps?" Bernie asked, taking the hint.

She jumped up. Libby joined her.

"Tea would be nice," Pearl allowed.

"With a drop of bourbon in it?" Lillian suggested to Pearl. "It's perfect on a night like this."

"It sure is," Sean chimed in.

"Well," Pearl said, lifting her head, "I *could* use a drop to steady myself."

Lillian smiled and patted Pearl's knee. "You've had a real shock."

Pearl sat up straighter. "Something to nibble on would be helpful as well. I have low blood sugar," she confided to Libby and Bernie. "It's a terrible curse."

"I'm certain it must be," Bernie said, heading for the stairs. "I'm sure I can rustle up some cookies for you."

"I don't want you to go to any trouble for me," Pearl piously intoned.

"Don't be silly," Bernie said. "You're no trouble at all."

Sean nearly choked when he heard what Bernie had said.

"I'll take some chamomile tea, if possible," Lillian said.

"Why do you insist on drinking that stuff?" Pearl asked her. "It has no taste."

"It does to me," Lillian said firmly. "I find a tisane pleasant at this time of night."

"Well, to me, it's like drinking weeds," Pearl grumped.

Lillian just smiled a saintly smile.

"Now that was interesting," Libby said as soon as they were in the kitchen and out of earshot of Pearl and Lillian. "First Amber is the kidnappee and now she's the kidnapper? Talk about a dizzying turn of events. I don't get it."

"Neither do I," Bernie replied. "But at least we know she's alive. If Pearl is telling the truth."

"There is that," Libby agreed. She started rubbing her eyes, then realized what she was doing and made herself stop. "You think Pearl isn't?"

Bernie refastened her ponytail while she thought over Libby's question. "No," she finally said. "I think she is telling the truth. She really doesn't have any reason to lie. At least none that I can see."

"That's my thought too," said Libby. "Which is good news. Even if Amber has gone over to the dark side."

"We don't know that," Bernie remonstrated, as she put the water for the tea on to boil and took out two teapots, the larger one for the oolong and the smaller one for the chamomile. "Let's not assume anything. We assumed Amber was kidnapped when she wasn't. Now we're assuming Amber's kidnapped someone? On Pearl's word? I think we need more than that to go on."

Libby paused loading a tray up with teacups, plates, cream, sugar, and lemon, as well as a large plate of brownies, chocolate-chip bars, and sugar cookies. "The whole thing makes no sense to me," she declared as she went over to the side cabinet where they kept the liquor, took out a bottle of bourbon, and set it on the tray.

"I guess we'll find out what the story is presently," Bernie said as the water came to a boil.

"I guess we will," Libby said, while she watched her sister fill the two teapots and place them on the tray. "Or try to find out," she amended, thinking of Pearl's penchant for the dramatic.

"We'll just have to separate the wheat from the chaff or is it the chaff from the wheat? I can never remember which it's supposed to be. I wonder what chaff is, anyway," Bernie mused as she and Libby headed back up the stairs, Libby walking slowly and carefully balancing the tray with both hands. "I'm sure, though, that part of what Pearl is going to tell us is true."

"Yeah, but which part?" Libby said.

"That is the question, isn't it?" Bernie replied.

* * *

"It was horrible," Pearl was saying as Libby and Bernie came through the door to their apartment. "Just horrible."

Sean nodded in Pearl's direction with his chin. "Ms. Pepperpot was just telling me about her unspeakable, hair-raising adventures with Amber," he said to his daughters. Libby noticed that the corners of his mouth were twitching as he spoke. "I must admit the story was quite riveting."

"Perhaps she'd like to tell us as well," Libby said to her dad as she set the tray down on the coffee table in front of the sofa. Then she sat in the armchair to the left of the sofa and offered the plate of cookies to Pearl, who took a chocolate-chip cookie and a brownie and began to eat.

"A little bourbon in your tea?" Libby asked Pearl as Bernie sat down in the other chair.

"That would be lovely, dear," Pearl said, brushing cookie crumbs off her bosom. "A little more, if you don't mind," she told Libby when Libby had stopped pouring. "My heart is still pounding," she explained to Sean after she'd finished both cookies and was reaching for a third.

"Nothing like a drop of the hard stuff to help you relax, Pearl," Sean observed. "No tea for me," he said to Libby when she asked him if he wanted two lumps of sugar or one in his. "Just pour me out a shot of the good stuff."

Libby raised an eyebrow. "Really?" she asked because her dad didn't usually drink.

"Really," he replied. "In fact, make that a double. It's been a long night."

"I guess so," Libby said. Obviously the hour he'd spent listening to Pearl had inflicted some damage. "You always were a sensitive soul."

Sean bared his teeth in a grin. "So your mother used to tell me."

"I'll just have my chamomile without anything in it,"

piped up Lillian. "I find sweeteners dull the delicate taste of the flower."

"It's a weed," Pearl repeated. "Every time I see it in my garden I yank it out."

For a second, Lillian looked as if she wanted to strangle Pearl. Then that look was gone and she was her beneficent self again. "It's a flower," she repeated. "People have cultivated chamomile for hundreds of years for its calming properties. Perhaps you'd like a cutting or two, Pearl?"

Pearl snorted at the pointed jibe and took a bite of her sugar cookie, while Lillian smoothed down the front of the flannel shirt she was wearing and flicked a piece of lint off her jeans.

"Unfortunately," she said, continuing the conversation, "I find I don't sleep well if I've had any alcohol or really any kind of stimulant close to bedtime."

"Me either," Bernie lied. Actually, she slept fine after a couple of shots. Really fine. Which is why she wasn't having any bourbon. She was afraid that if she did she'd be passed out in her chair in five minutes or less. Probably less, given how tired she was. "So tell us, what happened with you and Amber?" she asked Pearl after everyone was finally settled down.

Pearl shuddered and put her hand to her breast. "It was horrible. I'm not sure I can talk about it."

"There, there," Lillian said in a tone that Bernie could only describe as patronizing, after which she reached over, took the bottle of bourbon and poured another shot of the stuff into Pearl's teacup.

"I'm just not sure I'm ever going to feel safe living in my home again," Pearl confided as she took a long drink of what Libby figured was now straight liquor.

"Amber broke into your house?" Libby asked.

Pearl waved her hands in the air. "Not exactly."

"Meaning what?" Bernie asked.

Pearl held out her teacup, and Lillian poured in another

shot. At the rate she's going, Bernie thought, we're going to have to carry Pearl down the stairs. Not a good thought, since Pearl must have weighed close to two hundred pounds.

"Meaning," Pearl said after she'd had another sip of liquor, "she was on my doorstep."

"She rang the bell and Pearl let her in," Lillian explained.

"But Amber called first, didn't she, Pearl?" Bernie said, thinking back to what Sheila had said Rose had told her.

Pearl hemmed and hawed.

"Didn't she?" Libby repeated.

"Yes, she made contact," Pearl admitted.

"So her showing up on your doorstep wasn't a complete surprise," Bernie said.

Pearl brought her teacup and saucer up to her mouth, raised the cup, and took a sip of bourbon. "No. Not a complete surprise," she allowed.

Bernie noted that Pearl was talking more slowly now and enunciating each word. Must be the bourbon, Bernie thought, thinking that if she had imbibed that amount she'd be flat on her face by now.

"What did Amber want?" Sean asked, jumping into the fray. "Why did she call you?"

Pearl placed her teacup on its saucer, put both items on the coffee table, clasped her hands together, and rested them on her waist. "Not that it's any of your business," she said primly, "but she wanted to talk to me about Millie's missing recipes. I told her I didn't know anything about them, but she said she was coming over anyway. That she wanted to talk to me face-to-face. I told her not to. I repeated I didn't know anything about them, but she hung up before I could finish the sentence."

Sean took a sip of his bourbon, then put the teacup down. It burned his tongue and left a nice warm feeling going down his throat. He felt his irritation with Pearl for making him miss his favorite TV program melting away. "That was when you called Rose, right?" he asked Pearl.

"I wanted her there to protect me," Pearl said indignantly. "Was that so wrong?"

"Not at all," Lillian murmured. "Absolutely not. I'm glad you did."

As Sean sat in his chair, sipping his bourbon, nibbling on one of Libby's chocolate-chip cookies, and watching the proceedings, he wondered why Lillian was so protective of Pearl, especially in light of the way Pearl was treating her. Watching Lillian lean forward in her chair and rest her forearms on her thighs, he made a mental note to himself to find out.

"What did Amber say that made you think you needed protection?" Libby asked Pearl.

"She said"—and Pearl's breasts heaved in indignation at the memory—"that I was a fat old bat and that I couldn't bake and that I wasn't going to make money off all her aunt's hard work. That none of us were."

Sean snorted in his effort not to laugh, and Bernie hid a smile behind her hand.

"None meaning the members of the Christmas Cookie Exchange Club?" Bernie asked.

Pearl nodded.

"So," Bernie went on, "if she insulted you like that, why'd you let her in when she came to your door? I don't think I would have."

"I was taken aback," Pearl said. "She scared me, banging on the door the way she did."

"Why didn't you call the police if you were scared?" Sean asked. "Or Libby or Bernie, for that matter?"

"I . . . I didn't want to get Amber in trouble."

"Why was that?" Sean asked in disbelief. "You just told us she insulted you."

Pearl bit her lip. "The truth is, I didn't want to because Amber works for your daughters and they like her, and since they're two of the judges on *Baking for Life*, I didn't want to . . ."

"Prejudice them against you?" Sean asked Pearl.

"Exactly," Pearl said, flashing him a grateful smile.

"Then what happened?" Libby asked, taking over the questioning.

Pearl took another sip of bourbon, then extended her arm, cup in hand. "A tad more, if you don't mind," she requested. "My nerves are still in an uproar."

The woman must have a hollow leg, Bernie thought as she obliged and filled the teacup up. Either that or lots of practice.

"She made me go with her," Pearl said after she'd taken another sip.

"Made you?" Bernie asked.

"Yes," Pearl said. She hiccupped. "Made me."

"Did she have a gun or a knife?" Sean asked Pearl.

"Not that I saw," Pearl said. She hiccupped again. "Not that that means anything. She probably had one hidden somewhere in her pants or jacket pocket."

"Did she have a weapon of any kind?" Bernie asked. "A bat? A club? A can of mace?"

"A can of Crisco?" Sean asked. "A pound of butter?"

Libby shot her dad a dirty look, and he clammed up.

"I'm sure she had something somewhere," Pearl countered. "People like that always do."

"What do you mean people like her?" Bernie demanded.

"You know. Crazy people."

"That's an awful thing to say," Bernie told her.

"But it's true," Pearl told her, smiling complacently. She fanned her face with the edge of her hand. "Boy, it's getting hot in here again."

"Why are you saying Amber's crazy?" asked Libby.

"Because who else but a crazy person would have tattoos and pink-and-orange hair and stretch her earlobes out like that?" Pearl replied.

"So," Bernie said, "you just opened the door to this crazy person and went with her?"

"I told you, I was afraid not to," Pearl replied, biting into her fifth cookie.

"Why's that?" Sean asked her.

"Because she had this look in her eyes. I was afraid she was going to burn my house down or do something else if I didn't do what she wanted me to. I mean, for all I know, she could have even been carrying a bomb underneath that coat of hers. It's possible, isn't it?" she asked Sean.

"Anything is possible," Sean said. "But I don't think what you're describing is probable." He raised his hands, clasped his fingers together and put them behind his head. "Tell me what happened next."

"We got into her car . . ."

Bernie interrupted. "Her car?"

"Yes," Pearl said. "Her car."

"Interesting." Bernie murmured. Had Amber recovered it from the tow lot? If so, was it fit to drive? The last she'd heard from Sheila, it hadn't been. "What kind of vehicle was it?"

Pearl waved her hands in the air. "One of those small Japanese thingies."

"Such as?" Libby asked.

Pearl's eyes shut. She snapped them open. "How am I supposed to know? It was light green. Or blue. Something like that. And it had a dent in the fender."

"You're sure about that?" Bernie asked.

"Absolutely," Pearl said. She hiccupped again.

"Was it a two-door or a four-door?" Libby asked.

"Two," Pearl said. "They should make those cars for bigger people instead of midgets. It had a sticker of something that looked like a fish, only it really wasn't."

Bernie and Libby exchanged looks. They both remembered seeing a car that matched that description parked in the driveway of the house Amber lived in.

"She made me drive," Pearl told them. "She told me she knew that I knew where the recipes were hidden and that I had to take her there."

Pearl swayed a little in her seat. Bernie noticed that her eyes looked unfocused.

"Did you?" Sean asked.

"How could I? I have no idea where the stupid things are," Pearl responded. By now she was swaying in her seat.

"So what did you do?"

"I drove her around. What else could I do?" Pearl said. "You know what?" she said abruptly. "I need to go home." She attempted to stand up, and sat right back down.

"I concur," Lillian said.

"Make that two of us," Bernie added.

It took the efforts of all three women to get Pearl out of her seat, down the stairs, and into Lillian's car.

"How's Lillian going to get her out of her car when she gets to Pearl's house?" Sean asked when his daughters came back upstairs.

"She said she could manage," Bernie told him. Even though it was cold outside, she was sweating from the effort of getting Pearl into Lillian's vehicle.

"So what do you think?" Libby asked her dad as she plopped down on the sofa and put her feet up on the coffee table.

"I think this whole thing is giving me a headache." Sean took another sip of bourbon, tasted it on his tongue, and swallowed. "Amber playing vigilante is not what we need right now."

"To say the least," Bernie said. "We have to find her before she does something really bad."

"Agreed," Libby said. She leaned over and took a brownie. "Amber could be back where she's living."

"It's a definite possibility," Bernie allowed. "We could

drive by there and check. If she's not there, we should talk to her roommates."

"Given that she's motoring around in one of their cars, I think they might have something to say," Libby observed.

"Or she could also be staying at Millie's house," Sean said. "After all, she does have a key to the place."

"Also true." Libby sighed. "I can see it's going to be a long night."

"I'll say," Bernie agreed, thoughts of bed vanishing.

"Another thing," Sean said. "I'm wondering why is Lillian being so nice to Pearl?"

"Good question," Bernie said.

"Yes, it is," Sean said. "If I were you, I'd visit Lillian under the guise of finding out whether she needs any help with Pearl and see if you can pry some information out of her." Sean scratched his chin. "I suspect she knows something she's not telling us about Millie's demise. Maybe we can figure out what it is before Amber does." He looked at Bernie and Libby. "Because she's not going to stop until she gets some answers."

"Hopefully, we can convince her to leave that to us," Libby said.

"First, we have to find her," Bernie said.

"True," Libby said. "They're taping tomorrow or the next day. That might bring her out into the open."

"I'd like to see her found before that," Sean said. He studied the lights across the street for a moment. Then he turned and said to his daughters, "Of course, I'd be happy to help"—Libby started to say something, but Sean held up his hand—"but since you won't let me drive, I guess I'm stuck here, sitting in my comfortable armchair, sipping bourbon, and watching my favorite TV shows. It's tough that I can't be out there on this cold, dark, snowy night and I'll have to rely on your reports." And he smiled an angelic smile.

"We never said you couldn't drive," Bernie said as she hoisted herself up off the sofa.

Sean shook a finger at her. "You most certainly did."

"We said you shouldn't drive," Bernie replied. "There's a difference."

Sean snorted. "Talk about nit-picking."

"You never liked driving the van anyway, Dad."

"That doesn't mean that I won't, Bernie," Sean shot back.

"Do you think Dad really wants to go?" Libby asked Bernie once they were outside.

"No," Bernie said, "I think he just wants to give us a hard time in retaliation for us giving him a hard time about driving Marvin's dad's Taurus. That's what I think."

"I don't think I agree," Libby said as she and Bernie got into the van. "If we split things up, we might actually get some sleep tonight."

"This is true," Bernie said.

Libby reached for her phone. "I'm calling Marvin."

"I thought he liked to go to bed early."

"Not this early," Libby said as she got Marvin on the line. "I don't believe it," she told Bernie when she got off.

"Believe what?" Bernie asked.

"When we were helping Lillian with Pearl, Dad called Marvin and asked him to drive him around. He's going to be leaving for our place shortly." Libby clicked off and called her father. "Dad," she said. "When were you going to tell us about Marvin?"

Sean chuckled. "I thought I'd surprise you."

"Seriously, Dad," Libby said.

"Seriously, I was going to tell you once Marvin and I were under way. After all, I can't let you guys have all the fun. I figure Marvin and I will look for Amber while you and Bernie take on Lillian. I think I've had enough of the Christmas Cookie Exchange Club ladies for one night." He hung up.

"I don't know whether to be happy or pissed," Libby said. "Marvin didn't even call and tell me."

Bernie laughed. "It's not like he needs your permission. Anyway, what would be the point? He can't say no to Dad. You should look on the bright side," she said to Libby as she started Mathilda up.

"And that is?"

"That there's a chance we're going to get to bed tonight."

"This is true," Libby conceded. "But I want to be the one to find Amber."

"Why's that?"

"So I can kill her," Libby said.

"Makes sense to me," Bernie replied as they pulled out into the street.

Chapter 23

"What are we going to do if Lillian has left already?" Libby asked her sister as they headed for Pearl's cottage.

"I guess we'll figure that one out when we get there," Bernie said.

But that wasn't necessary because both Pearl and Lillian's cars were parked in Pearl's driveway. Bernie parked behind them, and she and Libby got out of Mathilda. They could hear the sounds of the TV out on the driveway.

"That's a little loud," Bernie observed. "I'm surprised the neighbors don't complain."

"They probably would if it were summer and their windows were open," Libby observed. "You know, I always admired this place."

"Me too," Bernie agreed. "I wouldn't mind living here."

"Ditto," Libby said. It reminded her of a cottage you'd find in some wooded spot.

The house Pearl lived in was a Stanford White three-bedroom cottage that had been built in the 1930s. It had a stone foundation and walls of wood painted brown. Thick pillars supported a snow-dusted, slanting roof, which covered a front porch that was perfect in the summer for sitting out in the cool evening air.

Leaded decorative glass framed the door. Now colored lights twinkled inside the hallway, and a large wreath of woven branches and dried flowers festooned the door. In the summer, beds of old-fashioned roses, daylilies, lilies of the valley, and bleeding hearts lined the walkway to the cottage.

As Bernie walked toward Pearl's house, she brushed some of the snow off the side window of Pearl's car with her hand, then peeked in.

"What are you doing?" Libby whispered.

Bernie grinned. "Being nosy." She pressed her face to the glass.

Libby tugged at her sleeve. "Let's go," she urged. "My feet are freezing."

Bernie straightened up and pointed to the window. "Not until you take a look at this," she said.

"What am I looking at?"

Bernie pointed to a piece of paper lying on the passenger side seat. "That."

Libby pressed her nose to the glass. "It's a piece of paper. So what?"

"Look closer."

"I am."

"Does that look like Millie's handwriting to you?"

Libby squinted. As much as she hated to admit it, her eyesight wasn't as good as Bernie's. The shadow made by the tree next to the street lamp didn't make things any easier. "Now that you mention it, yeah, it does. At least I think it does. It's got that odd *z* in it, and then there's the funny way she crosses her *t*'s."

"Let's see if this baby is locked," Bernie said, and she grabbed the car's door handle and yanked. The door opened. "Tsk. Tsk. Guess someone forgot their due diligence," she said as she brushed the snow that had fallen in from the roof off the seat and onto the ground. Then she reached in and grabbed the piece of paper. "How careless of Pearl. I hear there are lots of thieves walking around Longely this time of year." Bernie proceeded to read what was on the paper.

"What does it say?" Libby asked.

Instead of answering, Bernie passed the paper on to Libby, who scanned it quickly. "This looks like part of a recipe," she said. She corrected herself. "It is part of a recipe."

"Indeed it is, Holmes," Bernie said. "I'm willing to wager that it comes from Millie's recipe book. She used a small three-ring binder, right?"

Libby nodded. Millie had showed it to her a couple of years ago when she was telling Libby she had to be better organized. "It was just like the one I used in Mrs. Sullivan's class in fourth grade. I didn't even know they made those white things anymore." Libby pointed to the white paper rings reinforcing the three holes on the paper. "I used to love putting them on."

"While I hated it," Bernie remarked.

"You didn't do it. Which is why you were always losing your homework. Your pages always fell out."

"Don't remind me," Bernie said. Then she went back to talking about the piece of paper she'd found in Pearl's car. "This is definitely Millie's handwriting." Bernie stamped her feet to keep warm. It had to be below twenty degrees. "I'd say it was a probable match. And"—Bernie raised a finger of her gloved hand—"this is a recipe for a hazelnut torte."

"Millie always bragged about hers," Libby said. "Remember when she told us that hers was better than ours?"

"Just like her cinnamon rolls were better than ours," Bernie scoffed. "Looking at this recipe, I can see why her torte is dry and her icing is oversweet, not to mention the fact that she uses, pardon me, used, too much Kahlua in it. Look at the amount the recipe calls for!" Bernie made a face. "But Millie's baked goods always had to be the best, no matter what she was making. I think," Bernie said after a moment of reflection, "she would have been very unhappy if she'd lost the *Baking for Life* contest."

"So you're saying somebody might have done her a favor by killing her?" Libby asked.

Bernie looked indignant. "Not at all. I'm just saying that it probably never occurred to Millie that she might lose."

"I wish I had that kind of confidence," Libby said wistfully as she handed the paper back to Bernie.

"Overconfidence," Bernie said. "Sometimes that's not such a good thing. Sometimes it makes you enemies."

"Of which Millie seems to have had quite a number," Libby observed. "Except, of course, for Amber."

"Ah yes, Amber. Our errant counter girl. Well, it looks as if Amber was correct about one thing. One of the Christmas Cookie Exchange Club ladies did have Millie's recipe book, after all."

"Or at least a page of it," Bernie replied.

Libby frowned. "But why leave the page on the seat?" she asked. "Given the circumstances, that's a rather odd thing to do."

"Maybe the rings on the binder came apart, and Pearl gathered them back up, but she was in a hurry and didn't see this page. I guess the only way we're going to find out is to ask Pearl," Bernie said.

"If she isn't comatose," Libby observed.

"Yes," Bernie said, remembering the state Pearl was in when she, Bernie, and Lillian helped her down the stairs.

"She's probably sprawled out on the sofa, snoring away," Libby surmised.

Bernie wrinkled her nose at the image.

"Maybe I'm wrong," Libby said.

"I don't think so." Bernie took the piece of paper she'd found in the car, carefully folded it up, and put it in her bag. "For when Pearl wakes up," she explained. "And let's not forget Lillian," Bernie said. "Remember how Dad told us that he thought Lillian was acting too good to be true vis-à-vis Pearl. Maybe he's right. Maybe Lillian will have something to tell us."

"I hope so," Libby said. "At this point I'll take any shred of information I can get."

"Me too," Bernie agreed as she and her sister climbed the three steps that led to the porch and stood in front of the door. The TV sounded even louder now, and as Bernie put her hand up to ring the bell, she noticed that the door was slightly ajar.

"Maybe Lillian was having trouble getting Pearl into her bedroom," Libby guessed, "and forgot to close the door."

"Possibly," Bernie said, picturing Pearl as she stepped into the hallway. "After all, it took three of us to get Pearl into Lillian's car."

"Well, the car *is* small and Pearl *is* large," Libby said.

"Not to state the obvious," Bernie said as she looked around.

The first thing she and Libby saw when they walked through the hallway and into the living room was Pearl, sleeping. She was half on, half off the sofa. Her skirt was riding up around her hips and her mouth was open. She was snoring.

"So much for talking to Pearl," Libby said.

Bernie nodded. "I wonder where Lillian is?" she said.

"The bathroom?" Libby said. "Or maybe the kitchen."

"I'll take one and you take the other," Bernie said.

Libby nodded. Only Lillian wasn't in either place. She was in Pearl's office, going through her drawers, as Libby and Bernie quickly discovered.

"Hi," Libby said. She had her arms crossed and was leaning up against the door frame.

Lillian jumped and spun around.

"So nice to see you're so helpful," Bernie observed. She was leaning up against the other door frame with her arms folded across her chest as well. "I take it you're helping Pearl clean out things."

"As a matter of fact, I am," Lillian said.

"I so don't believe that, Bernie," Libby said to her sister. "Do you?"

"Absolutely not, Libby."

"So what do you think Lillian is doing, Bernie?"

Bernie smirked. "I think she's looking for Millie's recipe book."

"That makes two of us, Bernie," Libby said.

"So what if I am?" Lillian demanded. "I was looking to return it."

Bernie laughed. "Come on now. You can do better than that!"

"It's true," Lillian insisted. She wiped her hands on the front of her flannel shirt.

"Because you always do the right thing," Bernie said, baiting her.

"I try," Lillian said. "Which is more than I can say about you two."

"Really," Libby said. She straightened up, uncrossed her arms, and took a step inside Pearl's office. "What makes you say that?"

"You're allowing Amber to enter the *Baking for Life* contest, aren't you?" Lillian replied. "That's a clear conflict of interest. Amber works for you, and you can't tell me that you're not going to favor her over the rest of us."

"So you've spoken to her?" Libby asked.

Lillian stuck her chin out. "No. I haven't."

"Then why did you say what you just did?"

"I didn't," Lillian said.

"If you didn't, how do you know that Amber's going to be in the contest," Libby insisted.

"The producer lady told me," Lillian said.

Bernie jumped in. "Yes, but that was before Amber went missing."

Lillian laughed.

"What's so funny?" Bernie asked.

"You are," Lillian replied.

"Why's that?" Libby asked.

Lillian smirked. "Because the two of you think you know so much, but you're really running around like chickens without their heads."

"So why don't you help us out?" Bernie said.

"Why should I?" Lillian said.

"Because you're nice," Libby said. "And you really don't want to see anyone getting hurt."

Lillian laughed even louder at that. "I'm not nice, and I don't care if anyone gets hurt. What am I saying?" Lillian threw up her hands in mock horror. "Someone already has."

"Let's not make it anyone else," Libby told her

Lillian's smile grew larger, if that was possible. Looking at it, Libby knew. She didn't know how she did, but she did.

"You know where Amber is, don't you, Lillian?"

Lillian nodded. "Yes, I do. Or I did. But she just doesn't want to talk to you."

Bernie thought there was no mistaking the satisfaction in Lillian's tone. "Amber told you that?"

"No, Sheila did. Amber was at her house trying to find her aunt's recipes when you called."

"Which she didn't succeed in doing because Pearl has them," Bernie said, thinking back to the page she'd found in the car. "Or maybe you have them now, Lillian? What do you think, Libby?"

"I think it's a definite possibility," Libby replied, before turning to Lillian. "You know," she told her, "we could always call the police and tell them we found you rifling through Pearl's things and have them arrest you."

"They'd never believe you," Lillian sneered.

Bernie snapped her fingers. "Sure they would. Shall we see?"

Lillian shrugged. "By all means, make the call if picking on a defenseless old lady will make you feel better."

"You're hardly defenseless," Bernie pointed out.

Lillian laughed. "The police won't see it that way," she assured her.

"You really are conniving, aren't you?" Bernie said.

"Everyone does the best with what they have," Lillian informed Bernie.

"And what do you have?" Bernie demanded.

Libby clapped her hands. *This conversation is getting us nowhere,* she thought. "That's enough," she said as Bernie and Lillian turned toward her. "So did you find Millie's recipe book?" Libby asked Lillian.

"No. No, I didn't," Lillian said. "And if I had, I wouldn't be telling you."

"What were you planning to do with it if you found it?" Bernie asked her, following Libby's lead.

Lillian sniffed. "I wasn't looking for it."

Libby was incredulous. "How can you say that, given the conversation we've just been having?" she asked.

"I can say it because it's true," Lillian said.

"But we . . . ," Libby started when Lillian interrupted.

"I don't remember," Lillian told her in the sweetest tones imaginable. "It must be my dementia kicking in. It's amazing how that works. Sometimes it's an absolute godsend."

Libby's jaw dropped. She was speechless. And it's checkmate, Bernie thought. The game goes to Lillian.

Libby took a deep breath and regrouped. She decided to pursue the line of questioning her father had recommended. After all, she hadn't done so well with hers.

"You must like Pearl a lot," she said to Lillian.

"Why do you say that?" Lillian asked. There was a puzzled look on her face.

"The way you calmed Pearl down back at my house," Libby said. "The way you drove Pearl back here. I'm not sure I would have done that."

"But what else could I do?" Lillian asked, her face a mask of innocence. "No one else was going to get her home."

"Still," Bernie went on, picking up Libby's lead, "she wasn't very nice to you."

"She's stressed," Lillian said. "When she's stressed she says things she doesn't mean."

"She also drinks a lot," Libby noted.

"That's because Pearl's nervous about the contest. She really wants to win it. She needs the money."

"What about you?" Libby asked. "Do you need the money too?"

Lillian's face darkened. "A hundred thousand would be nice," she said. "I'm not going to deny it."

"What would you do with the money if you had it?" Libby inquired.

"Move out to the country and raise alpacas," Lillian said promptly. "Maybe get a few hens so I could have fresh eggs."

"Is that why you were looking for Millie's recipe book?" Libby asked. "So you could win?"

"I told you I wasn't looking for Millie's recipe book," Lillian said.

"Then what were you looking for?" Bernie asked. "Her tax returns?"

"Anyway," Lillian said, hitching up her pants, "I don't need Millie's recipe book to win."

"Then what do you need it for? What were you going to do with it?" Bernie asked.

"You really want to know?" Lillian said.

"Yes, I really want to know," Bernie replied.

"Fine, then. I was going to make sure that Amber didn't find it. I was going to burn the dratted thing in my fireplace. But now I can't, because it's not here. What do you think about that?"

"Why would you do that?" Libby asked.

A red dot appeared on each of Lillian's cheeks. "Amber shouldn't be on the show baking Millie's recipes—immortalizing them, if you will. Because the truth is Millie was a lousy baker. She thought she was so good and she wasn't. No. Amber shouldn't be on the show."

"That's the producer's decision, not yours," Bernie pointed out.

Lillian stamped her foot. "Well, she's wrong."

"You think you're a better baker," Libby asked quietly.

"Yes," Lillian said, "I think I'm a way better baker than Millie. In fact, I'm probably the best of the whole bunch of them. I'm the only one who knows how to make puff pastry, and my chocolate cupcakes are better than anyone's—and that includes the ones you sell at the shop," she said, staring at Libby. "I could have been a professional baker too if I chose."

"What stopped you?" Bernie asked.

"I don't believe in doing things I love for money," Lillian said.

Libby raised an eyebrow. "That's an interesting point of view. Usually people are advised to do what they love and the money will follow."

"That's what I meant," Lillian said. "For instance, I'm not in the contest for the money," Lillian said. "Unlike Pearl. She'll do whatever she can for a buck."

"Like what?" Libby asked Lillian.

"Nothing illegal, if that's what you're getting at," Lillian replied. "I just think it's wrong to do things like work as a secret shopper so you can get people in trouble. That's like being a scab for corporate America. She wouldn't have to do things like that if she'd stop charging stuff. It's a sickness. Pearl thinks that all the stuff she buys is going to make her happy, but it won't. Material things never do."

Bernie nodded. "Absolutely," she lied, thinking of how unhappy she would be without Bloomingdale's or Barney's or Bergdorf's. She guessed she was just shallow.

Libby was silent for another minute. Then she said, "How did you know that Pearl had Millie's book?"

"I didn't," Lillian told Libby. "But when I picked her up to go to your place, I got out of my car to walk up and ring the doorbell and saw a page lying on her car's seat."

"You mean this page?" Bernie asked, taking it out of her bag and showing it to Lillian.

"Yes. That page. I recognized the handwriting. So then I knew."

Bernie stifled a cough. She hoped she wasn't getting sick. That would be, as her mother used to say, the icing on the cake. "So did you ask her about it?"

"Of course, I did," Lillian responded.

"What did Pearl say?"

"She told me she'd sold the binder to Teresa."

Bernie's eyebrows shot up. "Teresa?" Of all the women in the Christmas Cookie Exchange Club, she was, in Bernie's estimation, the most unlikely person to be involved in something like this. "You believed her?" she asked Lillian.

"What do you think?" Lillian sneered.

"I think you didn't," Bernie answered. "Otherwise, why would you be going through Pearl's files? See," Bernie continued when Lillian didn't say anything, "this is why I get the big bucks."

Now it was Libby's turn. "So what were you going to do with the recipe book if you found it?" she asked, jumping to another line of questioning.

"I already told you," Lillian said.

"Tell me again," Libby said.

"I was going to burn it," Lillian said. "Those recipes don't deserve to live."

"That's a pretty strong statement," Bernie said.

"But a true one," Lillian replied.

"Did Millie deserve to live?" Bernie asked softly. If she'd hoped to get a reaction, she was sadly disappointed.

Lillian looked at her blankly and sniffed. "Let's just say that, given her behavior in this life, I can't believe her next one is going to be very pleasant."

"That doesn't answer my sister's question," Libby said.

"I think it does," Lillian said. "If you studied the teachings of the Buddha, you would understand what I am saying."

"What I think you're saying is that you decided to help her out of this life and on to her next one," Bernie said to Lillian.

"Now you're just being stupid," Lillian told Bernie. "Whatever Millie got she brought on herself," she said, and with that she walked out of the office, got her coat, walked outside, and drove home.

"So what do you think?" Bernie asked Libby after Lillian had left.

"I think there was no love lost between her and Millie . . ."

". . . or her and Pearl," Bernie added.

"That's for sure," Libby said. "I definitely would not like to have Lillian for my friend."

"Neither would I," Bernie agreed. "What is it they say about friends not letting friends drive drunk? Lillian was the one who suggested the bourbon. She was the main one who kept on pouring it in Pearl's teacup."

"Well, it is easier to search someone's house if they're passed out," Libby pointed out.

"It certainly is," Bernie agreed. "I can't believe we helped her carry Pearl down the stairs."

"Me either," Libby said indignantly. She was quiet for a minute, then said, "I wonder if Lillian disliked Millie enough to kill her?"

"Or if it's one of the other ladies?" Libby mused.

"Baking as a blood sport," Bernie mused. "It certainly would never have occurred to me."

Chapter 24

The house Amber was renting a room in, 2235, was dark, and there were no cars in the driveway when Marvin and Sean pulled up to it. They were in the hearse because Marvin's car was in the shop.

"The place looks really run-down," Sean observed as he studied the house.

"It looks as if no one is home," Marvin said, coasting into the driveway.

"That's because they're not," Sean said. "Bernie told me Amber's roommates work the night shift at the hospital. If you can call it that," he added. In Sean's mind, *clinic* would be a more accurate term. Still, it was a good place to go if you had a broken bone or a high fever.

"So, then, why are we here?" Marvin asked. "Why don't we go straight to the hospital?"

"Because Amber might be here," Sean told him.

"Whew," Marvin said, the word tumbling out before he could stop it.

"Meaning?" Sean said.

"Nothing, Mr. Simmons," Marvin stammered.

"It sounds like something to me," Sean said.

Marvin pushed his glasses up the bridge of his nose with his thumb.

"You should really get those fixed," Sean told him.

"I know," Marvin said. "I keep forgetting."

"So are you going to tell me what you were going to say?" Sean asked after a short pause.

"I'd rather not," Marvin said.

"Why is that?" Sean asked.

Marvin looked down at the steering wheel. "Because it's stupid, and you might take it the wrong way."

"Tell me anyway," Sean commanded.

Marvin blushed. Even in the dark Sean could see his skin turning darker.

"I just thought you were thinking of breaking in," Marvin confessed.

Sean's eyes widened in mock disbelief. "Me, a former officer of the law?" He laughed. "I'm appalled and shocked that you would think I would consider something like that. No. I leave things like that to my youngest daughter." Then he reached over and gave Marvin a playful punch on his forearm. "Don't worry, kid. The night is still young. We may get to do that yet."

Marvin sighed. One of these days, he would learn to keep his mouth shut. He gestured to the house. "Since no one is home, can we go now?"

"You know what the first requisite of a good investigator is?" Sean asked Marvin.

"No. What?" Marvin said.

"It's patience," Sean said.

Marvin didn't point out that that was a quality Sean had very little of. Instead, he asked what the plan was.

"Amber's roommates get off their shift around six. Now, what I'm figuring is that first we're going to get out of this deathmobile of yours and see if Amber is here. If she's not, we're going to take a walk around the premises and see if we can spot anything of interest."

"Like what?" Marvin said, wishing he'd brought his gloves along, because his hands were cold now and it was chilly out there.

"I don't know. That's why we're looking," Sean told him.

"I'd think it would be helpful if we knew what we were looking for," Marvin said. It was not, in his opinion, an unreasonable thought.

"Yes, it would be." Sean shot Marvin an annoyed glance. "But unfortunately we don't know. If we knew, we could go straight for it." Sean took a cigarette out of the pack in his jacket pocket and lit it.

Marvin coughed and waved the smoke away. "Would you mind opening the window a little?"

"Sorry," Sean said, doing as he was asked. "You know," he said after he'd taken another puff, "when I was head of the LPD . . ."

"LPD?" Marvin asked.

"Longely Police Department. I would have sent four or five guys out on this detail, but now I'm a civilian and there's just us chickens."

"Do you miss it?" Marvin asked.

"Being the chief of police or being a policeman?" Sean asked.

"Both," Marvin said as he watched the wind make the Christmas lights hanging on the eaves of the house next door sway.

Sean thought about his answer for a moment. Then he said, "I miss the sense of excitement and the feeling that I was helping people out. But I don't miss the politics. I don't miss those one single bit. Or the having to do what seemed right instead of what was right."

"Libby said that's why you lost your job, Mr. Simmons."

"Did she?" Sean said, and he grabbed his cane, opened the door, and stepped outside. How he'd lost his job was a

long, complicated story, one that he had no desire to share
with Marvin now. The wind hit him, and he quickly buttoned up his coat.

By the time Marvin had turned the hearse's engine off,
put his collar up, exited the vehicle, jammed his hands into
his pockets, and walked around to the passenger side,
Sean had taken a last puff of his cigarette. He was extin-
guishing what was left of it under the heel of his shoe
while he stood looking up at the second story of the house.

"I don't see any movement in there," Sean said. "Let's
knock on the door and see what happens."

Which is what they did. No one answered. Sean tried
again. There was still no answer.

"Amber could be a heavy sleeper," Marvin suggested as
he ducked his chin into his collar to keep out the wind.

"Not after this," Sean said and he took his fist and
pounded on the door.

There was no response.

"Amber, it's Mr. Simmons," he cried in a loud voice.
"Come out. We need to talk."

Still nothing.

"Well, if she's inside, she's definitely awake now," Marvin said. "As are the neighbors."

Sean looked around. He didn't see anyone stepping out
on their porch. "Maybe Amber just doesn't want to come
down and talk to us. Maybe she's hiding in her bedroom,"
Sean said as he rescanned the inside of Amber's house for
movement.

"At this point, I might be too," Marvin observed.

Sean ignored him and tried the door. It was locked.
"Drats," he said to Marvin, "I left my lock picks at home."

"Do you really have lock picks?" Marvin asked.

"What do you think?" Sean said as he opened the mail-
box and took out its contents.

"Why are you doing that?" Marvin cried.

Sean shrugged. "Curiosity. Just junk mail," he said after

he'd gone through it all. But now he knew the names of the people who lived there.

"You do know that what you just did is a federal crime, don't you?" Marvin informed him.

Sean grinned. "Then I guess you'd better not tell anyone, seeing as you're my accomplice. Come on," he told Marvin. "Let's walk around this dump and see if we can see anything."

"Like what?" Marvin demanded.

"I already told you, Marvin. Anything of interest," Sean responded. "Who knows? Maybe Amber has her vehicle parked in the back. Maybe we'll find the deer target there. Or a length of rope."

"Do you really expect to find something like that?" Marvin asked.

"Well, we won't know till we look, will we?" Sean responded in an exasperated tone.

Then he and Marvin walked around the house and peered in the windows on the first floor. All the lights were off, and they couldn't detect any motion in any of the rooms.

"I just hope none of the neighbors report us to the cops," Marvin muttered as they rounded the corner to the backyard. "Because if anyone looks suspicious, we do."

Sean snorted. "I've said it before and I'll say it again. You worry too much. But if it'll make you feel any better, no one is going to report us, because no one is going to see us. And you want to know why? I'll tell you why," Sean said without waiting for Marvin's answer. "It's because no one looks out their windows these days. No one pays attention to what's happening around them. Everyone is too busy tweeting and texting and watching bad TV reality shows. *Ed Sullivan. I Love Lucy.* Now those were shows. Not the stuff that's on the air now! Look what's happened since *Baking for Life* came to town."

"It hasn't been good," Marvin conceded.

"Not good?" Sean said indignantly. "It's been horrible. And for what? Why did Millie die? Because someone wanted to win some stupid TV show, that's why." Sean poked Marvin in the shoulder with his forefinger for emphasis.

"So you don't think it's about money?" Marvin asked, rubbing his shoulder. For an old guy Sean was surprisingly strong.

"No," Sean replied as he scanned the backyard. "I think it's all about ego." There was nothing of interest that he could see back here, just a coiled garden hose, a couple of chairs, and an old, rusted Weber grill that looked as if it had seen its last summer. "Okay," he said to Marvin. "I think we've done everything we can do here. It's off to the hospital."

Marvin sighed in relief. At least it was warm in the hearse. On the way to the hospital Sean got a phone call from Libby. He was still mulling over the conversation when he and Marvin arrived at their destination.

"How are we going to find out where Amber's roommates are?" Marvin asked as he parked in the almost-empty lot.

"Watch and learn, kiddo," Sean told him. "Watch and learn. You are about to see a master at work."

Marvin started to snicker, caught Sean's look, and managed to stifle it. When they got inside, Sean looked around. The waiting room was empty.

"Slow night," he said to Marvin before he walked over to the woman sitting behind the admitting desk. "Which for us is a good thing."

Marvin noticed that the woman's face lit up when she saw Sean.

"You're not sick, I hope," she asked him as he drew nearer.

"I'm not since I saw you," Sean said, and she blushed. "You haven't aged a bit, Adele."

"Neither have you, Sean," Adele said. She straightened the collar of her nurse's uniform and cocked her head.

"You're too kind, Adele." Sean favored her with a brilliant smile, put his arms on the ledge, and leaned on them. "I was wondering if you could do me a favor."

"If I can," Adele answered.

"Wonderful." Sean leaned in more and told her what he wanted. Marvin could see Adele's head bobbing as she listened to what Sean was saying.

"I know this is a little irregular," Marvin heard Sean say.

"No. No. No." Adele giggled. "Not a problem. Not a problem at all. Especially since nothing's going on here. Why don't you wait over there"—Adele said, indicating some chairs up along the far wall—"while I page them."

"You are my angel," Sean said, and he blew her a kiss and sat down in one of the seats she had indicated.

Marvin followed him, his mouth open in astonishment. Sean looked at Marvin's expression and laughed. "Didn't think the old guy still had it, did you?"

"It's not that," Marvin stuttered. "I just . . ."

"Let me tell you something," Sean said, cutting him off. "Never underestimate the power of charm. It works. It works on the young and the old. It works when other things don't. They didn't call me Sean the Smooth for nothing back in the day."

"Did they really?" Marvin asked.

"No." Sean laughed. "They didn't, thank God. But I was pretty good."

Ten minutes later, two of the three people Adele had paged walked into the waiting room. Sean got up and walked toward them.

"Who's Mike and who's Rudy?" Sean asked them.

"I'm Mike and he's Rudy," Mike said, pointing first to himself and then to Rudy.

"Where's your other roommate?" Sean asked.

Mike shrugged. "She's cleaning now. What do you want with us, anyway?"

"I'm Mr. Simmons, Bernie's and Libby's dad," Sean said, introducing himself.

Mike clapped his hand over his mouth, "Oh my God," he said. "It's about Amber, isn't it?"

"It certainly is," Sean said.

"I told you we shouldn't have done it," Rudy said to Mike. "I told you it was a bad idea."

"Shut up, Rudy," Mike hissed.

"What's a bad idea, Rudy?" Sean asked.

"Don't tell him, Rudy," Mike said.

"Why not?"

"Because we're going to be in trouble."

"You're going to be in more trouble if you don't," Sean said, his voice sounding like the cop he had been.

Rudy looked at Mike, then he looked at Sean and licked his lips.

"Don't," Mike urged.

"Hey, I'm the one who's going to be in trouble here, not you." He turned to Sean. "Okay, Mr. Simmons, I lent her my car," he said.

"Was this before or after my daughters visited you?"

Rudy looked abashed. "After. She showed up and she was really," he hesitated trying to find the word, "really . . . out of it."

"So you lent her your car?" Sean asked. "I think that would be the last thing I would do."

Rudy absentmindedly rubbed the tattoo on his forearm. The movement made the green and yellow snake move. "She wasn't out of it as in being drugged out or anything. She was just very intense. She said she needed to borrow my car so she could find those recipes. She said she had to find them, because if she found the recipes she'd find out who killed her aunt. I felt bad for her. What else could I do? Besides, she'd lent me a couple of hundred bucks last month. I figured I owed her."

"He did," Mike said.

Sean looked from Mike to Rudy and back again. "Can either of you tell me where Amber is now?"

"Don't know," Mike said a little too promptly for Sean's taste.

"I have no idea," Rudy added.

"Seriously," Mike said.

Sean did his cop stare. They both studied the clock on the wall instead of replying.

"So she hasn't called you?" Sean asked after a few moments.

"Nope," Rudy said. He was trying for jaunty, but Sean discerned a catch in his voice.

"She's off with your car, and the fact that she hasn't checked in is okay with you?" Sean asked Rudy, trying to hide his delight. Obviously, he still had it in this sphere as well.

"It definitely is, Mr. . . . ."

"Simmons," Sean told him, resupplying his name. "Because it wouldn't be okay with me."

"She's fine," Mike said.

"You know this how?" Sean asked.

"She's just . . . good at taking care of herself and stuff like that," Mike said.

"I see," Sean said. "May I assume that you've spoken to her, Michael?" Sean asked him. "Is that how you know this?"

Mike didn't say anything.

"Because actually the truth is that Amber's not fine. She's in way over her head, and if you care for her you'll tell me where I can find her," Sean continued, switching to the guilt approach.

"We just told you we don't know, Mr. Simmons," Rudy said. He raised his hand. "Honest injun."

"You may think you're helping her, but you're not," Sean pointed out.

Neither one of the boys said anything.

Sean took a deep breath and shifted his weight from his right leg to his left. He wished he hadn't left his cane in Marvin's vehicle. "Okay, where's the other one?"

Mike frowned. "The other one?"

"The third roommate. Marissa."

"Why?" Mike asked.

"I'd like to speak to her too," Sean told him.

Rudy hemmed and hawed. "She doesn't know any more than we do."

Sean scowled. "I'd like to be the judge of that, if you don't mind," he said.

Mike fingered his earlobes. "She's busy."

"Busy doing what?" Sean asked.

"Ah . . . working," Rudy said.

"So I assumed. What does her work consist of that you guys can come down and she can't?" Sean asked.

Neither Mike or Rudy answered.

"That's what I thought," Sean told them. "You know," he said, "if anything happens to Amber or she causes something to happen to anyone else, you guys are going to bear the responsibility."

Mike looked at Sean and shrugged. "I guess we'll just have to live with that."

Sean turned to Rudy. "Is that how you feel too?"

"Guess so, Mr. Simmons." He looked at the clock. "We have to get back to work now."

"Go ahead," Sean told them.

"That was a waste of time," Marvin said when they were gone.

"Maybe," Sean said. "Maybe not."

"How so?"

"Well, for one thing, we know that they know where

Amber is. Listen," Sean said, catching Marvin's look. "There's no way that Rudy is going to let her go off with his car without being in contact. Would you have done something like that at his age?"

"No," Marvin said after thinking his answer over for a couple of seconds. "Not if it were my only means of transportation."

"Exactly. Two, I'm willing to bet Amber's pretty close by."

"Why do you say that, Mr. Simmons?" Marvin asked.

"Because the crime she's investigating is here, so there's no way she's leaving the area. And three," Sean said as he headed toward the door, "I'm just guessing here, but it wouldn't surprise me if Marissa went off to alert Amber that we were tracking her down. Either that or she's off somewhere getting high."

"But that's bad," Marvin protested.

"Marissa getting stoned?" Sean asked.

"No. Marissa alerting Amber."

"Not if we're quick and she is where I think she might be," Sean said. "Come on," he told Marvin. "Let's get moving."

Chapter 25

Millie's house was dark, and the driveway was empty when Sean and Marvin arrived ten minutes later.

"What do you think?" Marvin asked Sean.

"I think someone was here," he said, pointing to the tire tracks in the snow.

"Amber?"

"Maybe." Sean clicked his tongue against the roof of his mouth, a habit he'd picked up from Bernie. Then he grabbed his cane and hoisted himself out of Marvin's hearse. By the time Marvin caught up with him, Sean was peering through the window into Millie's garage. "No car here," he said.

"I guess Amber's come and gone," Marvin observed.

"So it would seem," Sean said as he continued on to Millie's house.

His legs were bothering him now, and he had to concentrate on getting up the six stairs to the landing. Marvin stayed behind him to catch him in case he stumbled. When Sean got to Millie's front door he rang the bell. No one answered. Not that he had expected anyone to. He was just observing the amenities.

"Now what?" Marvin said as he shook some snow out of the cuff of his pants leg.

"Now we go inside and have a look-see," Sean said.

"But how are we going to do that?" Marvin asked.

"We're going to try the door, and then"—Sean's hand darted into his pocket and pulled out a ring with several thin metal pieces attached to it—"we're going to try these." He turned and jangled them in front of Marvin's face.

"Are those what I think they are?" Marvin asked.

"They most certainly are," Sean told him.

"But you told me you don't have anything like that," Marvin wailed.

Sean grinned. "I lied."

"Where did you get them?" Marvin demanded. I mean, it wasn't as if you could order them on the Internet. Or, for all he knew, maybe you could.

"An old burglar called Fat Hand Freddie gave them to me."

"Gave them?" Marvin asked incredulously. He could see the headlines now: FUNERAL DIRECTOR CAUGHT IN BREAK-IN.

"Yes," Sean said. "He gave them to me in return for a favor I did him. I found a home for his dog when he was going on an extended vacation upstate. The question you should be asking," Sean said to Marvin, "is can I still use them, or have I lost the knack? It's been awhile."

Marvin was smart enough not to say anything. He just stood and watched as Sean struggled with the lock picks. After ten minutes, Sean turned to him and said, "Here. You try."

"Me?" Marvin squeaked. "I wouldn't have the vaguest idea what to do."

"I'll show you," Sean said, and he did. Then he handed the picks to Marvin. "My hands just aren't steady enough anymore.

"Go on," Sean urged, when Marvin just stood there with the lock picks dangling from his hand.

"I don't know if I can," Marvin objected. "This feels wrong."

"Would Amber doing something bad be better?" Sean asked.

"No," Marvin said, looking abashed.

"Then try. We need to get in there sooner rather than later."

Marvin took a look at the expression on Sean's face and knew he wasn't kidding. "Okay," he said. "I'll try. But don't be mad at me if I can't do it."

"I won't," Sean promised, "but you'll do it. It's easy."

Marvin bent over and did what Sean had showed him. He didn't expect to succeed, but to his surprise he did.

"Wow," he said when he felt the tumblers clicking into place. He straightened up and gave the door a push. It opened.

"Good job," Sean said as he stepped inside Millie's house. He turned around. Marvin was still standing on the porch. "Well, just don't stand there like a goofball," Sean told him. "Come inside. It's cold out there, and we don't want the neighbors getting suspicious."

"I can't believe I just did that," Marvin said. He looked stunned.

"It felt good, didn't it?" Sean asked him.

"It kind of did," Marvin admitted.

Sean chuckled as he walked through the entrance hall and into the living room. The place was as neat as Libby had described it as being, except that the sofa pillows were rumpled, a couple of the smaller ones looked as if they'd been used as headrests, and there was a comforter at the foot of the bed. Sean went over and took a look.

"I bet Amber was sleeping here," he said. Then he spied something on the floor and bent down and got it. "Definitely Amber," he said as he held up a Hello Kitty sock. It was the kind of thing that Amber would wear.

"So where do you think she is now?" Marvin asked.

Sean shook his head. "I don't know." He looked at his watch. "But it's late. She probably needs to find someplace to sleep."

"So you think she'll come back here?" Marvin asked.

"She could." Sean thought for a moment. "Or she could go back to her old place. That wouldn't surprise me either."

He was reaching for his phone to call Bernie and Libby when he spied a piece of paper on the coffee table. The paper was a flyer advertising plowing and landscaping services. Around the margin someone had written the initials TR over and over again, and Sean was pretty sure he knew to whom the handwriting belonged to. He should. He'd seen it often enough for the past four years on the order forms in A Little Taste of Heaven when he'd been closing out the register.

"What is it?" Marvin asked, coming up behind him.

Sean picked up the paper and pointed to the letters on the paper. "That's Amber's handwriting."

"And the TR? What's that?"

"I don't know," Sean admitted.

Marvin frowned. "Could it be an initial of some kind?"

Sean laughed. "Very good, Marvin. Very good. Of course. Why didn't I think of that?"

Marvin looked at Sean to make sure Libby's dad wasn't being sarcastic. When he was sure he wasn't, he said, "I'm guessing they don't stand for Theodore Roosevelt."

"I'm guessing you're right," Sean replied. He thought for a minute. His face lit up. He had it. "I bet TR stands for Teresa Ruffino. She's one of the Christmas Cookie Exchange Club ladies brigade."

"I know who she is, Mr. Simmons. We buried her husband and her sister. May I?" Marvin asked, reaching for the paper Sean was holding.

Sean nodded and handed it to him. Marvin studied it for a moment before handing it back to Sean.

"Well," Marvin observed, "I'll say one thing. Amber definitely has this lady on her mind."

"Yes, she does," Sean agreed. He rubbed his thigh to ease the muscle cramp that was beginning to form. "I wonder if Teresa is Amber's next stop?" he mused.

"Don't you think it's a little late for that?" Marvin asked.

"I think so, you think so, but I'm not sure that Amber will think so, given the constraints she's operating under. After all, she's not going to be making a social call."

Sean put the paper back down on the coffee table, took out his cell, and called Amber. It went straight to voice mail. Not a big surprise. But he felt he had to try. Then he called Bernie and Libby and alerted them to what was going on.

"What are we going to do?" Marvin asked Sean, once he'd gotten off the phone.

"We're going to go through the rest of Millie's house and see what else we can find. Then we're going to move your hearse out of sight and settle down and wait for Amber to come back. If she comes back," Sean added. It was a long shot, but he couldn't think of anything else to do.

"For how long?" Marvin asked, a note of panic in his voice. "Because I need to get home. I have a viewing to-morrow."

"Ah," Sean said. "The life of a funeral director is not an easy one." Then Sean looked at the expression on Marvin's face and felt bad at his comment. "We'll stay for an hour and then we'll get out of here."

Chapter 26

"I want to go home," Libby said after Bernie had relayed their dad's message to her. They were on their way back to the apartment, and Libby had been looking forward to a cup of hot chocolate, a bath, and bed—in that order.

Bernie snorted. "Whine. Whine. Whine."

"Like you don't feel that way too," Libby told her.

"I do," Bernie said. "But I'm ignoring it."

"I'm serious, Bernie."

"So am I, Libby. And we will go home. We'll go home after we check out Teresa's house and Amber's place and make sure that Amber isn't at either one," Bernie assured her.

"Amber could be anywhere," Libby pointed out. "This could be a complete waste of time." She was so tired that her bones ached and she was having trouble keeping her eyes open.

"It could be," Bernie said. "But that's not what Dad thinks and . . ."

Libby put up her hand. "I know. I know. He's usually right about this kind of stuff."

"Think of it this way," Bernie told her. "If we find Amber we can catch up on our sleep . . ."

". . . and our work," Libby said, getting into the spirit of the thing.

". . . and get rid of George."

"That would be a blessing devoutly to be wished," Libby conceded.

While George was better than nothing as a counter person, he was only slightly better than nothing. Very slightly better. In fact, he had been getting steadily worse since he'd started at the shop. He still hadn't mastered their credit-card machine for reasons that eluded Libby, and his coffee either tasted like a chicken had walked through it or was so strong it had to be watered down. Most important, there was something wrong with his hearing, so he had a tendency to fill orders with what he thought people would want instead of what they had told him they actually wanted.

"Plus, Penelope will stop calling," Bernie added, interrupting Libby's thoughts.

"Also a good thing," Libby agreed. The producer of *Baking for Life* had been calling every two hours for updates on Amber's whereabouts, or "the Amber situation," as she liked to put it. Okay, that was an exaggeration. It was every three hours. By now Libby was ready to strangle her.

Bernie looked at her watch. "I say we try Teresa's house first. We're nearer. Then we see if Amber's at her place."

"And then we go home," Libby said.

Bernie nodded. "And then we go home."

The streets of Longely were empty at this hour of the night, everyone snugly tucked in their houses, so Bernie and Libby made good time on their way to Teresa's house. While Bernie drove, Libby looked out the window and admired all the Christmas decorations: the white and colored lights wound around the trees and the houses, the candles in the windows, the nodding reindeer on the lawns, and the blow-up Santas with presents spilling out of their sleds. She decided she would like this time of year if she ever had the time to enjoy it. Because she worked in retail, she was usually just glad when it was over.

Next year, Libby decided she'd get an earlier start. That way things wouldn't be so nuts. Because the truth was that despite all her moaning and groaning she really did like making the mince pies with real mincemeat, and the bûches de Noël, and the plum puddings served with hard sauce. She loved doing it, in fact. And she liked decorating the shop window, and she liked handing out Christmas cookies to the kids who came into the shop. It's just that this year, the *Baking for Life* crew coming to town, Millie's death, and Amber's supposed disappearance had put her over the edge.

Libby could feel her heartbeat start to quicken at the thought of what she and Bernie still had to do, and she decided it would be better to think about something else. Like chocolate. Chocolate truffles, to be exact. So far, her chocolate mocha truffles had gotten an extremely good reception, as had her Grand Marnier ones, although Libby decided they had to cut down on the liquor a bit. Maybe A Little Taste of Heaven should add truffles and French macaroons to the shop's offerings next year. They could package them in fancy cellophane wrappers, six to a roll, and market them as stocking stuffers. Libby was thinking about the kind of packaging she would like, maybe something with green and gold in the design, when she became aware that Bernie was talking to her.

"So what do you think?" Bernie was saying.

"Think about what?" Libby asked her.

"About what Amber knows about Teresa."

"Aside from the fact that she thinks that Teresa has Millie's recipes."

"Yeah," Bernie said. "And . . ."

"Does she think that means that Teresa killed Millie?"

"I'm guessing it does," Bernie said. "What about you?"

Libby half unzipped her jacket and unwrapped her scarf from around her neck. The heat in the van had finally kicked in. "No, I don't," she said when she was done. "Absolutely not. I'm sorry, but no matter how much I try, I can't see Teresa lugging that deer target out into the middle of the road."

"Neither can I," Bernie admitted. "Unless, of course, she had help."

"Like who?" Libby challenged.

Bernie shook her head. "You got me."

"In fact," Libby went on, "I don't see her even coming up with an idea like that—I mean what does she know about deer targets . . ."

". . . Maybe one of her neighbors hunts," Bernie said, interrupting.

". . . much less implementing a plan like that," said Libby, finally finishing her sentence.

Bernie glanced at her. "Implementing," she said. "Are you doing one of those word-a-day thingies again?"

"Don't start, Bernie," Libby warned. "I'm not in the mood."

"I'm not starting anything," Bernie told her. "I was just asking a question. I think learning new vocabulary is a positive. Why do you always take things I say in a negative fashion?"

"Because I'm a negative person," Libby promptly answered. "As you never tire of telling me."

By now Bernie and Libby were five miles from Teresa's house.

"You're never at your best when you're tired," Bernie observed.

"Oh, and I suppose you are?" Libby shot back as the van went over a bump.

Bernie was about to make a snotty comeback when she spotted the headlights of a car zooming down West Road. She leaned forward to get a better look at the vehicle because it was hard to see it in the dark on a road with no streetlights. She was just about to point it out to Libby when Libby gestured at it.

"Look," she cried. Suddenly she wasn't tired anymore.

"I see it too," Bernie told Libby.

"It's the same model car Amber borrowed."

"I know."

"Do you think Amber's driving it?" Libby asked Bernie. "Could we be that lucky?"

"Boy, I hope so."

"Well, speed up and let's find out," Libby said. She was so excited she was practically bouncing up and down in her seat.

Bernie shook her head. "No can do. If I speed up, whoever is driving will see us."

"I wish it were daytime," Libby complained. "Then we could get a look and see what color hair the driver has."

"Yeah," Bernie said. "If it's brown or blond, we would know it's not our girl."

Libby sighed. Then she brightened. "On the other hand, if the car turns into Coville Lane, then there's a chance that it's Amber on her way to Teresa's house."

"Which means we'll know very soon," Bernie said.

"In a minute, to be exact," Libby said.

At which point the car in front of them made the turn.

"Ah-ha," Bernie said as she slowed down even more and turned in too. "The plot thickens."

She just hoped that Amber—because she was pretty sure that's who it was—didn't notice them and take off. One thing was for sure, though. It was hard to follow anyone when it was nighttime and there were only two cars on a two-lane road. Bernie supposed she could always kill her lights, but Coville Lane was bumpy and full of curves and potholes. It wasn't worth the risk to the van, so she hung back as far as she could.

"She's definitely going to Teresa's," Libby announced as she watched the car in front of them hang a left onto Westcott.

Bernie grunted her agreement. She was too busy driving to talk. A moment later the car in front of them made a sharp right onto Maiden Lane and pulled into the driveway of the third house on the left.

"Definitely Teresa's," Bernie said as she put her foot down on the accelerator. The van made a grinding noise and sprang forward.

By the time they got to Teresa's house, Amber was out of her vehicle.

Bernie rolled down the van's window. "Amber," she cried as she braked. "Hold up a minute."

Amber spun around and faced the van. "You," she gasped.

"We want to talk to you," Bernie said.

"But I don't want to talk to you," Amber yelled.

"You're not helping matters," Bernie said as she got out of the van. "You're making them worse."

"Explain how," Amber challenged, standing with her legs apart and her hands planted on her hips.

"We told you we would take care of things," Libby said to Amber after she got out of the van too. "Let us."

"Well, you're doing a lousy job," Amber cried. Her hair was even more a mess than usual, and she looked as if she hadn't slept for days.

"That's because we've been busy looking for you," Bernie said.

Amber turned on her. "Now you're saying this is all my fault," she yelled, advancing on her.

"No, she's not," Libby said, in a soothing tone of voice.

"Yes, I am," Bernie said. "We've been so worried about you that we haven't been able to think clearly about anything else."

Libby nodded. "It is true. We've been going down one path when perhaps we should have been going down another."

"Meaning?" Amber said. It had started to snow again, and she brushed a few snowflakes off her face.

Libby was about to explain, when the door to Teresa's house flew open and Teresa came stomping out. She was wearing big, fuzzy kitten slippers, a flannel nightgown dotted with roses, a black parka, and curlers in her hair.

"What is going on out here?" she demanded.

"Well," Libby began, but before she could finish her sentence Amber jumped in.

"I want my aunt's recipes and I want them now," Amber said.

"Are you crazy?" Teresa asked her. "Because you look like you are."

"No, you're the one that's crazy if you think you can get away with killing my aunt," Amber cried, balling up her hands into fists and taking a step toward her.

Teresa clutched her parka to her chest and took a step back. "How can you say anything like that?" she cried. "Millie was my best friend."

"Not according to her, you weren't," Amber replied. "You want to know what my aunt called you? She called you a snake in the grass."

"That's not true," Teresa said.

"Oh yes it is," Amber said. She raised one of her hands. "I swear it."

Teresa's eyes narrowed. "If anything she was the snake in the grass. She was the one who spread rumors, hateful ones," she blurted out. "Your aunt was a mean, mean woman. There. I've said it, and I'm glad I did."

"See," Amber said, shaking a finger at her. "My aunt was right. You *are* a liar. All this time you were pretending you liked her and you hated her." Amber stamped her foot. "I want my aunt's recipes, and I want them now, or else, trust me on this, you're going to be very, very sorry."

Teresa straightened up and glared at Amber. "Are you threatening me?"

"You threatened my aunt," Amber shot back.

Teresa's jowls quivered. "I refuse to stand here and be insulted and bulldozed on my own property. I'm calling the police." She turned and started toward the front door.

"Oh no, you're not," Amber cried, taking a step toward her.

Bernie took two quick steps and put herself between Teresa and Amber. "Let it go," Bernie said to Amber. "Libby and I will take care of this."

"You haven't so far," Amber pointed out.

"Please, Amber. Give us a chance," Libby begged.

"No. I'm not going anywhere," Amber told her as she tried to step around Bernie to get to Teresa. "I'm staying right here until she"—she pointed to Teresa—"gives me back my aunt's recipes and confesses to what she's done. Do you hear that, Mrs. Ruffino?"

Teresa spun around and faced Amber. "You should be ashamed of yourself, speaking to a woman of my age like that."

"Just because you're old doesn't mean you're worthy of respect," Amber shot back.

"She doesn't know what she's talking about," Libby said to Teresa, thoughts of lost customers and having to bail Amber out of jail dancing in her head.

"I most certainly do," Amber insisted.

"No, you don't," Bernie said. "It's the drugs she's taking," she explained to Teresa. "She's having a bad reaction."

"I'm not on anything," Amber cried.

Bernie grabbed one of Amber's arms and began dragging her to her car. "My mistake," she told Teresa. "She's just crazed with grief."

"I am not," Amber yelled.

"You most certainly are," Libby said.

Amber tried to wrest her arm away, but Bernie held on. Then Libby came around and grabbed Amber's free arm.

"Calm down," Libby told her as she held on for all she was worth.

"Let go of me," Amber shouted.

"Absolutely not," Bernie told her through gritted teeth. "Not until you come to your senses."

Amber gave one more yank, and when that didn't work, all the fight seemed to go out of her. She went limp, which Bernie decided was a good thing because she didn't know how much longer she and Libby could have held on to her.

"Amber, give Libby your keys," Bernie ordered.

"Why?" Amber demanded sullenly.

"Because she's going to drive your car and you're coming in the van with me," Bernie told her. She was still holding on to Amber's arm. Just in case.

"But I don't want to, Bernie. Why do I have to?"

"Because my sister says so," Libby told her, channeling her mother.

"Where are we going?" Amber asked in a small voice.

Bernie decided Amber looked about ten. "We're going to see if we can figure things out," Bernie said. And she turned and waved at Teresa, who was standing in her doorway, watching the whole scene unfold. "Go back to sleep," Bernie yelled in as cheerful a voice as she could muster. "Tomorrow is going to be a big day."

"I'm still going to call the police," Teresa said.

"Go ahead," Bernie said. "But we'll deny everything."

"You wouldn't dare," Teresa said.

Bernie laughed. "Watch me."

In the end, Teresa contented herself with slamming the door on them and waking up Alma to tell her about the outrage that had just been perpetrated on her.

Chapter 27

The ride back to Libby and Bernie's apartment was silent. No one said a word. Now everyone was sitting in the living room, drinking hot chocolate made with 72 percent dark chocolate, cream, and a touch of brandy, and eating slices of cinnamon toast, and still no one was talking. Amber was on the sofa, flanked by Bernie and Libby, while Sean was ensconced in his armchair with his leg resting on a footstool. The only audible sounds were the ticking of the clock on the wall and the sounds of everyone eating. Finally, Libby couldn't stand it anymore.

"What were you thinking?" Libby demanded of Amber as she watched her gobble down a piece of cinnamon toast.

"I guess I wasn't," Amber confessed as she reached for another piece of toast.

It was her fourth by Libby's count. "When was the last time you ate?" Libby asked her.

Amber stopped to think. "Well, I had a couple of handfuls of Cheerios last night."

"And?" Bernie said.

"A package of M&Ms this morning," Amber said.

"That's all?" Libby asked.

"Yeah." Amber shrugged her shoulders. "I've been so upset, I guess I just forgot to eat."

"That should only happen to me," Bernie observed. She never forgot about food. She spent half her day thinking about what she was going to eat at her next meal.

"Amber, no wonder you've been acting the way you have," Libby said. "You have low blood sugar." In Libby's world, as it had been in her mother's, low blood sugar explained everything. "I'm going to get you some soup," she announced, and she got up and went downstairs to fetch it. Five minutes later, she was back with a tray on which rested a bowl of lentil soup, four slices of buttered French bread, and a dish of freshly grated Parmesan cheese. "Here," she said, putting the bowl down in front of Amber. "Eat."

Amber attacked the food as if she hadn't had a decent meal for weeks. No one said anything until she was done.

"I guess I didn't realize how hungry I was," Amber said when she was through.

Sean nodded. "Few of us do," he commented.

"I'm sorry, but I don't know what that means," Amber told him.

Sean laughed. "I guess what I'm saying is that few of us realize how angry or hungry or happy we are at the time we're feeling those emotions. Forget it," he said, seeing Amber's blank look.

She frowned and started twirling one of her pigtails around her finger. "I really messed up, didn't I?" Amber said.

"That's one way of putting it," Bernie said.

"Are you going to fire me?" Amber asked.

Libby answered. "Fire you? No. Kill you? Yes. . . . I'm kidding," she said when she saw the panic in Amber's eyes.

"I understand if you would want to," Amber said, looking from Bernie to Libby and back again.

"Kill you?" Bernie asked sweetly.

"Fire me," Amber replied.

"We're not firing you," Bernie said. "For one thing if we did, we'd be stuck with George."

"We don't want to think about that," Libby told her.

Amber was silent for a minute. Then she said, "What if Teresa calls the cops on me like she told me she was going to do?"

"So what if she does?" Libby said. "The worst that would happen is that you'd get a restraining order slapped on you."

Amber's eyes blazed. "I should get one against her. She killed my aunt."

"You have no proof of that," Sean pointed out. "None at all."

Amber glared at him. "I would have had if your daughters hadn't dragged me away,"

"No," Bernie said. "You would have been arrested if I hadn't dragged you away."

Amber slouched down in her seat. "This just sucks," she said.

"Yes, it does," Sean agreed.

"So you're telling me there's nothing I . . ."

"We," Bernie corrected.

"Fine. Nothing we can do about this?" Amber demanded of Sean.

"No. I'm not telling you that at all," Sean told her.

"Then what are you saying?" Amber asked him.

"Why don't you tell us what you've found out," Sean replied, "and then I'll tell you what I think we should do. Note the pronoun *we*. The *we* refers to Bernie, Libby, and myself."

"I get it," Amber said.

"I just want to make sure we're all on the same page," Sean said.

"We are," Amber said. And she began to talk.

She started with her meeting with Rose in the parking lot and ended with her drive to Teresa's. Sean, Bernie, and Libby listened attentively to what Amber had to say. She talked for fifteen minutes and no one interrupted. Finally, when Amber was done, Bernie asked her why she was so sure that Teresa had her aunt's recipes.

"Because," Amber spluttered, "Lillian told me that she had them. That she had bought them from Pearl. That's why."

"She could have been lying, you know," Bernie pointed out.

"Why would she do that?" Amber asked.

"Tell me you're kidding me," Bernie told her.

"Several reasons," Libby responded when Amber didn't answer, and she began ticking them off on her fingers. "She could be covering for herself. She could be covering for someone else. She could be getting even with someone else."

"Oh, God." Amber dropped her head in her hands. "I don't know what to think anymore," she moaned. "I feel as if I'm going around and around in circles. Everyone tells me something different."

"I know the feeling," Libby said gloomily.

Sean took a last sip of hot chocolate and gently set his cup down on his saucer. "Maybe we need to think about this in a different way," he suggested.

Amber raised her head. "How?" she challenged.

"Okay," Sean began. "Let's start by reviewing what we know. Correct me if I'm wrong, but so far none of us have come up with anything substantial. The only thing we've learned is that all of the women who belong to the Christmas Cookie Exchange Club had grievances against Millie, grievances that have been simmering under the surface for a long time. Then the circus comes to town—aka *Baking for Life*—and all hell breaks loose. Agreed?" Sean said, looking around the room.

"Agreed," Bernie, Libby, and Amber echoed.

"Now," Sean continued, "it's also important to remember that what happened to Millie may not have started out that way. It may have started off as a way to delay Millie, maybe rattle her a little so she wasn't at her best at the bake-off."

"Or a way to steal her cookies," Amber said.

"That too," Sean agreed. "Here's the way I see it. As of right now we have a crime that's not officially a crime and seven ladies who categorically deny they had anything to do with Millie's death and the stealing of her recipes." He looked around at the three women. "Am I right?" he asked.

"You know you are," Libby responded.

"That was a rhetorical question," Sean told her.

"Sorry," Libby murmured and drank a little more of her hot chocolate.

"All of these women have motives of one kind or another, and to make things even more difficult," Sean continued, "we have no means to compel any one of those ladies to talk. We can't arrest them, and we can't break into their houses and see if they have Millie's recipes hidden somewhere."

"We could," Bernie said, a dreamy look coming into her eyes.

"I guess you could," Sean responded. "However, you're not going to."

Bernie brushed a crumb of cinnamon toast off her lip. "I never said I was going to. I was talking theoretically."

"Good," Sean said. "Because aside from everything else, we don't know that those recipes are in their houses. Whoever has them might have buried them someplace or trashed them, for all you know. In fact, we don't even know that the person who has the recipes—if anyone does—is the person who set up the deer target and engineered Millie's death. The two things might be completely separate events."

"So what are you suggesting, Mr. Simmons?" Amber said, leaning forward. "That we give up?"

"Not at all," Sean replied. "I'm suggesting that we go about this a different way."

Amber leaned back on the sofa and folded her arms across her chest. "Like how?"

"Well, I find that when you get into a fix like this, it's always good to go back to the beginning."

"Meaning?" Libby asked.

"Meaning," Sean said, "that we need to know why *Baking for Life* came to this town and chose these women to be contestants."

"You think that's relevant?" Bernie asked.

"At this point, I think everything is relevant," Sean said. "The unexplored avenue is the avenue that might point us in the right direction."

"You may be right," Bernie conceded. "So I guess we should talk to Penelope and see what we can find out. Anything else?"

"Yes," Sean said. "Now we come to the manner of Millie's death and the mysterious vanishing deer target."

"Sounds like a bad Victorian novel," Bernie quipped.

Her dad shot her a look, and she became quiet. "Why do I say mysterious?" he pontificated. "I say mysterious because this is something that most ladies of a certain age, at least these ladies, don't have lying around in their garages. It would be a very uncommon item unless their husbands hunted. But they don't have husbands, and the ones that did have spouses had spouses that didn't hunt.

"So did someone borrow the target? Where did it come from? There are four stores in the area that sell sporting goods. It might be instructive if one of us visited them and asked if anyone remembered selling a deer target to one of our ladies."

"Makes sense to me," Amber said.

"Definitely worth a shot," Libby agreed.

"There's something else," Sean said, pausing to take another bite of cinnamon toast. "How did whoever did this set the target up? That thing weighs a fair amount and is awkward to carry, and yet we're talking about someone setting it up, tying it off, and coming back and removing it. I just can't see one of the Christmas Cookie Exchange Club brigade doing that," Sean said. "They're too old."

"How ageist," Bernie said, smiling.

"But true," Sean said. "Listen, if I can't be ageist, who can?"

"Okay, but Rose is still in pretty good shape," Bernie countered. "I bet she could do it."

"And Pearl and Sheila definitely have the heft," Libby added.

"Heft does not equal muscle," Sean pointed out. "As for Rose, she's limber, I'll grant you that. But strong enough for this? Probably not."

"So what are you saying?" Amber asked Sean.

"I'm saying that this was probably a two-person job," Sean answered. "The question is which two ladies did it?"

No one said anything, because no one had an answer.

"Anything else?" Libby asked.

"Yes, there is," Sean replied. "Did anyone check out the story of the person who reported the accident?"

Libby and Bernie looked at each other.

"Ah, no," Bernie said.

"Well, if I were you I'd get over to the Minces and talk to them tomorrow."

"But Matt already told us what happened," Libby said.

"This is called double-checking," Sean told her.

Libby sighed. "Fine," she said.

"Hey," Sean told her, "far be it from me to . . ."

Libby interrupted. "No. You're right, Dad," she said.

"As per usual," Sean couldn't resist saying. He turned and directed his gaze at Amber. "Now we come to the last and, to my mind, the most interesting question." He paused for dramatic effect, then said, "Amber, perhaps you would be kind enough to tell us where the recipe for Millie's Majestic Meltaways is?"

Amber reacted as if she'd been punched. "You're looking at me as if you think I have it," she cried, sticking her jaw out.

"That's because I think you do," Sean replied in a pleasantly conversational tone.

Bernie and Libby looked startled.

"Is that for real?" Bernie said.

"I think so," Sean said.

"Think!" Libby exclaimed.

"Yes, think," Sean replied. "Actually, I'm fairly sure."

"How can you say that?" Amber demanded.

Sean smiled. "I can say it, my dear, because I believe it's the truth. The reason I'm saying that is because you haven't mentioned Millie's Majestic Meltaways at all recently, whereas before that was practically all you talked about. Now you keep talking about Millie's recipe book. From what I can make out, none of the ladies of the Christmas Cookie Exchange Club are talking about it either, a fact that leads me to conclude that they think it's off the table, to coin a modern-day expression."

"That's right," Libby said, jumping into the conversational fray. "Now that you mention it, Dad, I haven't heard Amber or anyone else say anything about it."

Then Bernie spoke. "That means you either don't care or you have it. Which is it, Amber?" When Amber didn't say anything, she continued. "I don't buy that you don't care. You certainly thought that recipe was important enough when you had us go running off to Millie's house to find it." Bernie stopped talking when another thought occurred to her. "Did you take the recipe for your aunt's Meltaways?" she asked Amber. "Did you stage that scene in Millie's kitchen to make it look as if a robbery had taken place?"

Amber narrowed her eyes. "Don't be ridiculous," she snapped at Bernie. "Why would I do that?"

"Why indeed," Bernie said. "I don't know. That's why I'm asking."

Sean leaned forward. "Tell us," he urged Amber. "You won't get into trouble."

Amber looked at Sean, Bernie, and Libby and then studied the seam on the arm of the sofa she was sitting on. "Everyone will be mad at me," she murmured.

"Everyone will be madder at you if you don't," Sean told her.

Amber chewed on one of her fingernails for a moment. "I have most of the recipe," she finally said, mumbling into her hand.

"I don't understand," Libby said.

"I talked to Penelope and . . ."

"You talked to Penelope," Bernie exclaimed. "She's been calling us every half hour demanding to know if we'd heard from you."

Amber hunched her shoulders and leaned forward. "Well, I wouldn't tell her where I was, so I guess she was trying to find out if you knew anything," she said.

"What does all this have to do with Penelope?" Sean asked.

"Well, she wanted me to be on the show and . . ." Amber stopped.

"We know that. Go on," Bernie urged.

"She wanted me to bake Millie's Meltaways." Amber stopped talking again.

"Tell us," Sean repeated, nodding encouragingly.

"I told her I didn't know where the recipe was, and she told me she had overheard someone saying that Millie had hid an extra copy in her composting bin. Only they had looked and it wasn't there."

"Did Penelope remember who said it?" Libby asked.

"She mentioned Alma," Amber said.

"So if it wasn't there, how did you find it?" Sean asked.

Amber looked up, allowing herself a self-satisfied grin. "I remembered that Millie had two composting bins. One was in the garage, and the other one was out in the garden. Alma must have looked in the garage. If you didn't already know that there was a composting bin in the garden, you would never have seen it. It was covered with a tarp, and there was snow on top of the tarp."

"So you have most of the recipe?" Libby asked.

"Yes. Some animal nibbled part of the bottom half of the paper away, but I think I can recreate the last couple of steps and the baking time," Amber said. She touched her nose ring.

"So why didn't you tell us?" Libby asked Amber.

Amber twisted her hands together, then touched her nose ring again. "Penelope didn't want me to tell you. She didn't want me to tell anyone. She wanted it to be a surprise. She said it would be really cool if I just walked on the show and told everyone that I was taking my aunt's place. That that would be good theater and would help the show's ratings. She was going to pay me. How cool is that?" She asked Libby and Bernie.

"Pretty cool, I guess," Bernie conceded.

"She said that maybe someone would notice me and I could get on some more TV shows because I had presence. She even said she'd ask the person who was responsible for what happened to Aunt Millie to come forward. That she thought she knew who she was. But that it had to be a secret because she didn't want this person to know. She wanted to catch the expression on their face when she named them."

Bernie's face grew dark. "I really am going to kill Penelope," she muttered.

"But then," Amber continued explaining, "I wasn't sure that I believed her."

"Good call," Sean interjected.

Amber flashed him a brief smile. "Especially about knowing who killed Aunt Millie. So I decided to do some investigating on my own. I just figured if I could find my aunt's recipes, that would lead me to who killed her." She slumped down in the sofa and ran a finger along its arm. "Guess I should have talked to you guys, huh?"

"Guess you should have," Bernie said. She stifled a yawn. She was suddenly exhausted. The relief at finding Amber was making her crash, she thought. She hadn't realized just how tense she'd been. "So you've figured out the recipe?" Bernie asked Amber.

"Yeah," Amber replied, sounding more definite than she had a moment ago. "At least, I think I have. I'm pretty sure I know what brand of chocolate Millie was using."

"That's a big step," Bernie said, "especially when you consider what's on the market these days."

"And I think I know what kind of shortening she was going to use."

"Butter?" asked Bernie.

"Nope," said Amber.

"Oil?" guessed Libby.

Amber shook her head.

"Crisco?" Bernie asked.

Amber shook her head. "Not even close."

"Not lard, I hope," Libby said.

Amber laughed. "Hardly."

"Then what?" Libby asked, and then she amended herself. "No. Don't tell us," she said, "if you're going to be in the show."

Amber flashed her a sheepish smile. "I'd like to be, if it's okay with you. I don't want to cost you guys any more hassle."

"It's okay with me," Libby said.

"And me," said Bernie. "As long as you leave the investigating to us."

Amber didn't say anything.

"Deal?" Bernie prodded.

Amber thought for another minute. "Deal," she finally said.

"Good," Libby said, and she handed Amber the keys to Mike's car and told her to go home.

"So what do you think?" Bernie asked her dad and sister after Amber had left. "Do you think she's telling the truth?"

Sean nodded. "Mostly, I think she is."

Bernie got up and began clearing off the table. "Well, I know one of the things I'm doing tomorrow."

"Make the meringue mushrooms for the bûches de Noël?" Libby asked.

"Besides that," Bernie said. "I'm going to have a little chat with Penelope. That's what I'm going to do."

"This," Libby said, "I want to see."

Chapter 28

The morning came too quickly for Bernie and Libby. Before they knew it, their alarms had gone off and they had dragged themselves out of bed.

"I don't do well on three hours of sleep," Bernie groused to Libby. She had poured boiling water over some freshly ground French roast coffee and was waiting to push the plunger down.

"Tell me about it," Libby replied as she made herself and her sister two fried eggs each.

The eggs came from a friend of hers who raised Araucana chickens. The shells were pastel-hued, and the yolks were marigold yellow. As Libby put a dollop of olive oil in the pan and waited for it to heat up, she thought about how much she loved these eggs. How pretty they were. Then she broke four eggs into the oil and smiled as she listened to the popping and hissing sounds the oil made. When the eggs were done, she gently lifted them out with her spatula, put them on plates, and slid a couple of pieces of slightly stale French bread left over from the day before into the oil.

"We need the sustenance," she explained to Bernie

when she saw her sister looking askance at what she was making.

"No one needs that much sustenance," Bernie replied, pushing down the plunger on the French press.

"I do," Libby said as she took the bread out of the pan, put the eggs on the bread, and covered them with the salsa she'd made yesterday. Then she handed the plate to Bernie, who in turn handed Libby a cup of coffee.

"This will look great on my hips," Bernie complained, digging in.

"Just be thankful you don't have my hips," Libby replied as she sprinkled some crumbly white cheese over everything.

Bernie was wise enough not to say anything. By her third bite, Bernie had to admit that Libby was right. She did feel better. She did have a long day in front of her. Egg whites and arugula just weren't going to do it. To hell with her hips. She'd start on her diet after Christmas, when her life was calmer. When she was done eating, she loaded the plates into the dishwasher, then she and her sister got down to work. At seven o'clock, Amber came in, looking more than a little worse for wear, took her place behind the counter, and started stocking for the morning rush. At nine o'clock, Bernie took breakfast up to her dad, then went back to filling the orders for cakes and pies and cookies that were on the list for the day.

By one in the afternoon, the lunch rush had died down, and Bernie and Libby decided that things were in pretty good shape at the shop. They were free to canvass the sporting goods stores in the area, after which they would try to track down Penelope. Bernie had been attempting to call her, but so far she hadn't answered Bernie's calls. Or Amber's, for that matter. The lady Bernie had spoken to at the production company Penelope worked for said she often got that way before a shoot.

"What can I say?" she'd ended with. "She's a diva."

"No kidding," Bernie had said before she'd hung up.

"Maybe Brandon knows where she's staying," Libby said as she and Libby walked out of the shop.

Bernie gave her a sharp look. "Why do you say that?" she asked.

Libby shrugged. "Because he knows everything."

"That's what being a bartender means," Bernie said.

"Did you think I meant something else?" Libby asked as she climbed into the van and started her up. Today was her turn to drive.

"Like what?" Bernie demanded.

Instead of answering, Libby reached over and turned on the radio. It seemed like a better course of action.

Bernie looked at her sister for a moment, decided not to pursue the conversation, and made herself busy fastening her seat belt. "At least Amber is back," she observed, holding out a conversational olive branch.

"And George isn't," Libby said. "So that's a double blessing."

Bernie shook her head. "People just get blinded by the media," she said, thinking of Amber's conduct. "Dad is right. We have this group of little old ladies—who never cause any trouble . . ."

"That we know of," Libby said.

"Fine. That we know of," Bernie repeated. "But the point is that a television show comes to town and all hell breaks loose. It's bizarre."

"You're right," Libby said.

She didn't say anything else. The roads were slippery, and she had to concentrate on her driving. Twenty minutes later, they arrived at Frontsmith Mall, where the first of the sports stores was located. They didn't have any luck there. The clerk didn't recall a woman of any age buying a deer target recently.

"If you remember, call us," Bernie said, writing out her name and phone number on a scrap piece of paper for the clerk.

"I will," the clerk promised.

He was wearing a bemused expression on his face, and Bernie was positive he was going to tear up the paper with their names and phone numbers and throw it in the trash as soon as they left the store.

"We should have business cards," Libby observed as they left the mall. "We'd look more professional that way."

"We do have business cards," Bernie said. "They just have the store name on them."

"We should get other ones printed up," Libby replied as they headed toward their van.

"What should they say?" Bernie asked. "Amateur detectives at work? Nancy Drew, Inc.?"

"Okay, I get it," Libby told her sister as they climbed into Mathilda.

It went the same way at the next three places they stopped. None of the clerks remembered a woman buying a deer target.

"Well, that was a waste of time," Libby was saying when Bernie's phone rang.

She fished it out of her bag and looked at it. "It's Penelope," she told Libby and took the call.

Libby watched her sister nod her head as she listened to what Penelope was saying.

"We'll be right over," Bernie finally replied. "It'll take us just a minute. We're right around the corner," she lied. "No, I insist," she added and clicked off.

Libby raised an eyebrow. "What was that all about?"

Bernie grinned. "Nothing, really. I said we'd be right over, and Penelope said that wasn't necessary, and I said that it was. I really want to speak to her in person," Bernie said with a vehemence she usually reserved for commenting on Spandex and plastic shoes. Then she added, "By the way, they've changed the location of the show. It's going to be at the high school auditorium now."

"Nice of Penelope to tell us," Libby said.

"Yes. Isn't it, though? Anyway, she's over at the high school checking sound and camera angles for tomorrow night, so let's saddle up and get going."

"This is going to be interesting," Libby murmured as she started Mathilda, backed up, and drove over there.

It was a little after three, and the high school halls were empty by the time Libby and Bernie arrived. The first person they saw when they entered the auditorium was Penelope's assistant. Bernie had figured her for her early twenties when she'd seen her at RJ's, and she decided she was correct in her assessment. She was tall and thin, with copper-colored, ear-length, curly hair, heavy black eyebrows, and a sharply defined chin.

She was wearing your standard TV crew garb, jeans, a black T-shirt, and a plaid flannel shirt, and as Bernie watched the woman testing the speakers she couldn't help feeling as if she'd seen her in another context, but she didn't know what that was.

"Hi," Bernie said, approaching the woman. "Is Penelope around?"

"Yeah," the assistant said, glancing up. "She's here somewhere."

Bernie studied her face for a minute and said, "I have the feeling I know you from somewhere."

The woman laughed. "Everyone always says that. I guess I have a common face."

"I guess you do," Bernie conceded. "Although not in a bad way," she hurriedly added.

Penelope's assistant laughed again. "It's okay. I know what you meant."

"Did you go to school here?" Bernie asked, still trying to place the woman.

The woman shook her head. "Sorry. Do you shop in New York?"

Bernie nodded. "I do. Why do you ask?"

"I used to work as a salesgirl in Barney's, and you look like someone who shops there. Maybe that's where you saw me."

"Maybe," Bernie agreed to be polite, although she didn't think that was the case.

The woman wiped her right hand on her jeans and extended it. "By the way, I'm Terri," she said. "That's Terri with an *i*, not a *y*. My family moved around a lot, and when I started school they'd see my name and assume I was a boy."

Bernie smiled. "That must have been annoying,"

"A little," Terri allowed. "I always wanted to have a name like Sue or Nicole. Something definite gender-wise."

"Well, my name is Bernie, and this is my sister, Libby," Bernie said, introducing themselves.

Terri nodded and ran her hair through her curls. "You're two of the judges, right?"

"Right," Libby said. She was just about to say something else when Penelope came through the auditorium side door. She looked, Libby decided, as if she hadn't slept for a week. Her hair was sticking straight out, she wasn't wearing any makeup, and her skinny jeans and black turtleneck made her look even thinner than she already was, which was saying a lot.

"Oh, there you are," Penelope said, advancing toward them. "Can you two be here an hour early? We'd like to do a little press conference thingy."

"Press conference?" Libby squeaked. She hadn't counted on this.

"Yeah." Penelope said. "Not a big deal." Then she looked Libby up and down. "I assume you'll be wearing something a little . . . nicer tomorrow night."

"She will," Bernie told Penelope before Libby could say anything. "I'll see to it."

Penelope checked her phone. "I can't believe how much I have to do before tomorrow."

As if on cue, Terri bobbed her head at Bernie and Libby. "I'm checking the lighting," she told Penelope. Then she scurried away.

Penelope pursed her lips as she looked at Terri retreating. "That one," she reflected, "has been nothing but trouble. Of course," she added, "this whole show has been nothing but trouble. From the moment we came to town, all we've had has been bad luck. It's just been one thing after another."

"Why did you come to Longely?" Libby asked.

"Why indeed?" Penelope said. She checked her phone again. "Because I was told to."

"By whom?" Libby inquired.

"By the head of this production company, if you must know. He's friends with some local lady, and I guess she suggested it, and he thought it was a good idea. You appeal to the older crowd, you get the holiday thing in there, you get the Northeast. We haven't done anything in this neck of the woods for a while."

Bernie took a step forward. "Why did you do what you did with Amber?" she asked Penelope without any preamble.

"Do what?" Penelope inquired.

"Have her disappear like that."

Penelope's eyes widened. "So you found her?"

"No thanks to you," Bernie told her.

Penelope glanced at her watch. "I didn't have her do anything. She took off on her own. In fact, I've been trying to get hold of her too."

"My sister and I have been worried sick," Bernie said. "We thought that Amber had been kidnapped."

"By whom?" Penelope sniggered. "A bunch of old ladies? Get a grip." Penelope looked at her watch again. "Anyway, I merely suggested the idea to her. She was the one who took the suggestion and ran with it."

"But why did you suggest it?" Libby asked, genuinely puzzled.

Penelope looked at her as if she had an IQ of fifty. "Drama."

"Drama?" Libby repeated.

"Yes, drama," Penelope said impatiently. "We've already got that going with Millie's death. Amber's appearance was going to amp things up another notch."

"I still don't get it," Libby declared.

Penelope snorted. "What's not to get? Amber would have come out on the stage, and you would've gasped and yelled and cried, and we would have used it. And now, as I said, I'm going to have to think of something else, because let's face it, watching seven old ladies competing to see who gets the prize for baking the best cookie is snoozeville."

"Well, it certainly would have boosted your ratings to reveal Millie's killer on your show," Bernie observed.

Penelope made a dismissive sound. "I assume that Amber told you that?"

"Indeed she did," Bernie said.

"That's not what I said to her," Penelope replied.

"Then what did you tell her?" Libby asked.

"I told her it would be cool if that happened. I didn't say it would happen." Penelope looked at her watch again. "I am seriously running out of time here. Terri!" she yelled.

Terri came running out on the auditorium stage. "Yes?"

"Take these two," Penelope said, gesturing to Bernie and Libby, "and show them where they're sitting." She turned back to Libby and Bernie. "Got to go," she told them.

"I'm late, I'm late for a very important date," Bernie

chanted softly as she watched Penelope practically run out the door.

Libby turned and looked at her sister. "Huh?"

"She reminds me of the White Rabbit in *Alice in Wonderland*. You know, always running?"

"I wonder," Libby murmured.

Now it was Bernie's turn to look at her.

"I wonder if she engineered Millie's accident as a publicity stunt," Libby mused.

"I don't think even she's capable of something like that," Bernie said. "She's a self-absorbed nit, but that would indicate a depth of self-absorption that's just plain scary."

"Pathological," Libby said.

Bernie nodded. She thought about whether what Libby was postulating could be true as Terri showed them where she and Libby would be sitting. She was still thinking about it when she and Libby walked out the door and Bernie spotted the production company van parked in the driveway. And that's when it hit her.

"Jeez," she said to Libby. "I'm a total moron."

Libby grinned. "Ah ha. Self-realization at last."

Bernie playfully punched her sister in the arm. "No. That."

"What's that?" Libby asked, rubbing her forearm. For someone who weighed one hundred and ten pounds her sister packed a pretty mean wallop.

"The truck," Bernie said.

Chapter 29

"I don't get it," Libby said to her.

Bernie let out an exasperated sigh. "The truck, Libby. Look at the truck."

Libby looked. "So?" she said after a moment had gone by. All she saw was an equipment truck. There was nothing out of the ordinary about it that she could see.

"Look at the production company logo," Bernie instructed.

"I'm looking," Libby said, and she was. "But I still don't see anything."

By now Bernie was practically jumping up and down with excitement. "Look at the picture on the truck."

Libby looked. It was a picture of two German shepherds standing side by side.

"What is that a picture of?" Bernie demanded.

"Two dogs, obviously," Libby replied, wondering where this was going.

"Obviously. And what is the name of the company printed on the truck?" Bernie asked.

"Buddy and Muddy Productions. So?" Libby said. And then she got it. She clapped her hands over her mouth. "Oh my God, that's Stanley Buckle's company."

Bernie beamed. "Exactly. He has two shepherds called Muddy and Buddy, remember?"

"How could I forget?" Libby shuddered. "I thought they were going to eat me."

Bernie laughed. Her sister was not a dog lover. "They were just jumping up on you to say hello."

"And steal the rolls."

"No. You threw the rolls at them. Naturally they grabbed them and ran away."

"Be that as it may," Libby said with as much dignity as she could manage. The memory still rankled. "Buckle has been here, what?"

"Almost a year," Bernie replied, thinking of the house he'd bought.

It had been one of those tear-down-and-rebuild jobbies. She and Bernie had been up there to cater a dinner party right after the new house had been completed, even though in Bernie's estimation the old one had been perfectly fine. The new house was huge. Aside from eight bedrooms and eight bathrooms, it contained a screening room and a bowling alley.

"And we know who sold him his house," Bernie said, thinking out loud.

Libby nodded again. "Had to be Bree Nottingham. She's the only one around here who would handle that kind of sale."

"Well, they don't call her real estate agent extraordinaire for nothing."

"That's for sure," Libby said as she zipped up her parka.

"I bet she was the one who suggested using the Christmas Cookie Exchange Club ladies on the show," Bernie said, continuing with her line of thought. "She must have thought it would be good publicity for Longely."

"I bet you're right," Libby said. "But . . ."

"I know," Bernie said, interrupting her, "but I can't see how that helps us with Millie's death."

"Me either," Bernie admitted, picturing Bree Nottingham in her signature pink Chanel suit and Manolos. "But at the very least we should call and find out if we're right about this."

"Because," Bernie and Libby chorused together, repeating their dad's mantra, " 'You never know what's going to turn out to be important and what's not.' "

As luck would have it, Bree happened to have half an hour free and was willing to meet with them at the Unicorn Nail Salon, where she was getting a pedicure. The salon was located near the strip mall where Amber had left her car.

The place was usually jammed on the weekends and after four o'clock on the weekdays, but today it was strangely empty. Given all the Christmas parties this time of year, Bernie had expected the place would be packed, but maybe everyone was out doing their Christmas shopping.

Bree was the only person in the place, except for the manicurists, two ladies who were getting manicures at the far end of the room, and a Korean woman who was reading a magazine at the front desk.

"What you want?" the woman asked, barely looking up. "Pedicure? Manicure? Both?"

Bernie shook her head and pointed to Bree. "I'm here to talk to her."

The woman shrugged and went back to reading.

"Hi," Bree called, beckoning Bernie and Libby over.

She put her *People* magazine down and took a sip of her coffee, which was sitting on the table by her side. Her Chanel bag was carefully placed on the far end of the table, out of harm's way. Bernie spied Bree's bright pink suit jacket on the coatrack by the door. The color made her smile. It was like a slap in the face to their dreary Northeastern winters.

Bree held up a bottle of mint-green nail polish. "What do you think?" she asked Bernie and Libby. "Too young? Too weird?"

"Not at all," Bernie said. "I love the color. Maybe even get your mani in that color with French tips?"

Bree smiled. "Why not? What about you, Libby?"

"It's great," she said, with as much enthusiasm as she could muster, since she never got her nails done.

The manicurist gestured for Bree to put her feet into the water bath, then took out the left one, put some lotion on it, and began to massage Bree's leg and foot.

"Tom gives the best foot massage," Bree trilled.

"Nice," Libby said. The idea of a stranger touching her feet was not an idea she was prepared to entertain.

"So," Bree said, giving Tom her second foot. "I gather from the conversation we had that you want to know if I was the person who suggested the Christmas Cookie Exchange Club brigade to Stanley?"

"We do," Bernie said.

Bree took another sip of her coffee. "Guilty as charged."

"May I ask why?" Libby inquired.

"You may," Bree told her. "The question is: will I tell you?" Then she smiled to show she was making a joke. She looked down at her hands for a moment before going on. "I knew Stanley was looking for a new group of contestants, so I suggested the Christmas Cookie Exchange Club ladies.

"I thought it would be nice for Stanley, because the filming would be convenient for him, it would be nice for Longely, because the town would get a little bit of publicity, and it would be nice for the ladies to get some recognition at this late date in their lives, not to mention giving them something to be excited about. I know that Millie was especially excited. I thought I was doing a good thing."

"You were. It's too bad it didn't work out," Libby observed.

"One never knows, does one?" Bree said reflectively. She sighed. "If there's one thing I've learned, it's that accidents happen and there's precious little we can do to prevent them. Ask your father. I'm sure he'll agree with me."

"Possibly," Bernie told her. "Only this wasn't an accident."

Bree studied her diamond ring, then moved it up and down on her finger before speaking. "The police said it was," she observed.

"Amber said it wasn't," Bernie pointed out.

"So I heard," Bree said as she watched Tom wipe the lotion off her legs, then reach for the bottle of clear polish for her undercoat. "And you believe her," she asked Bernie.

"Yes, I do," Bernie replied.

"So do I," Libby said.

"Why am I not surprised?" Bree said dryly. "After all, both of you would be biased in her favor."

"No. We have evidence," Bernie declared.

"Evidence that the police must feel is not worth pursuing," Bree pointed out. "Otherwise they'd have been out investigating."

"We're hoping to change their mind," Bernie remarked.

"Interesting," Bree said. She took another sip of coffee, then carefully put the cup down. "You know," she said, "accidents happen—it's a fact of life, and these ladies are old, and some of them don't have that much time left. Sometimes it's better to let things go, especially when you can't change anything back. Remember, our souls and those of others are what we make them."

"I don't think I can let go of this," Libby said.

"That's too bad," Bree said as she watched Tom working.

He had finished applying the first coat of mint green nail polish and was just beginning the second coat.

"Bree, what do you know?" Libby demanded.

"What makes you think I know anything?" Bree asked, finally looking up at her.

"Because I can see it in your face," Libby told her.

"Then you're seeing something that's not there," Bree told her. "The only things I know about are houses and real estate."

"I don't believe you," Bernie told her. "You know everything that goes on in Longely."

Bree smiled at Bernie, revealing a set of dazzlingly white teeth. "You flatter me, but that's simply not true."

Bernie studied Bree's face for a moment. "You know who did it, don't you?" Bernie guessed, the words tumbling out of her mouth before she realized what she was saying.

A shadow passed over Bree's face. It was there for just a second, but it was there, and when Bernie saw it, she knew what she'd said was true.

"Don't be silly," Bree said. She gave a nervous little laugh. "How could I possibly know something like that?" Then her cell phone rang, and she reached over and looked at the screen. "I have to take this," she announced to Bernie and Libby, after which she began to talk.

"She knows," Bernie said to Libby once they were outside. "She definitely knows who killed Millie."

"She suspects," Libby said.

"Strongly suspects," said Bernie, amending her last statement.

"Either way, she's definitely not going to tell us," Libby said.

"On this we can agree," Bernie replied. "And we can't make her. But then think about it," Bernie continued. "Why should she? She has everything to lose and nothing to gain by sharing her suspicions with us."

"Still," Libby said, "I had the feeling that she wanted to tell us."

"Why do you say that?" Bernie asked.

"I don't really know," Libby said. "I wish I did, but I don't." She sighed and decided to call the Minces. Hopefully they'd have better luck with them, because at this rate, she and Bernie were getting nowhere fast, and she really wanted to have something positive to tell Amber when they went back to the shop.

Unfortunately, that didn't turn out to be the case.

Chapter 30

Libby got off her cell phone and turned to Bernie. "So?" Bernie said.

"So we're going to the ice rink," she announced.

"Why?" Bernie asked.

"Because according to Selma Mince's babysitter that's where Selma Mince is. She's watching her daughter practice."

"Figure skating?" Bernie asked.

"Ice hockey," Libby said.

Bernie raised an eyebrow. "Times have certainly changed." She used to play ice hockey informally with the boys when she was a kid. But on a team? Never.

"That's for sure." Libby looked at her watch. "Evidently, Selma will be there for another half to three-quarters of an hour."

"Let's go," Bernie said as she climbed into the driver's seat. Libby's driving was just too slow, especially at a time like this. Once Libby was inside, Bernie threw the van into reverse and eased her way out of the parking lot. A moment later they were on the road.

The ice rink was located one town over from Longely.

Situated in a cheap commercial district, dotted with buildings made of cinder blocks, it was flanked by a bowling alley on one side and a diner on the other.

"I haven't been here in, what?" Bernie paused to silently count. "Fifteen years?"

"Maybe even more," Libby said. Their dad used to bring them here every Saturday to skate when they were kids.

"It doesn't look as if it's changed," Bernie said, nodding in the direction of the blinking neon sign that read WELCOME SKATERS.

Once they went inside, Bernie and Libby felt as if they'd gone back in time. There was the same hurdy-gurdy music playing, the same bleachers, the same skate shop, the same refreshment stand where they sold greasy hot dogs and microwaved pizza, only now there were girls in uniform on the ice and parents in the bleachers.

"God, I loved those hot dogs," Libby reminisced.

Bernie laughed. "So did I. But I bet we wouldn't like them now."

"I don't know. I still like Ho Hos," Libby confided.

"Me too," Bernie said. "And those fried apple pies. I loved those. They were so good. Do you know what Selma Mince looks like?" she asked Libby, changing the subject.

"She came into the shop once," Libby said, scanning the bleachers. She never forgot a customer's face, even if they'd been in A Little Taste of Heaven only once. "There she is," Libby said, pointing to a plump, dark-haired lady in the fourth row, who was bundled up in a blue parka, a white velour hoodie, and mom jeans, and was pouring herself what looked like a cup of hot chocolate from the thermos she was holding in her gloved hand.

"Yes?" she said when Bernie and Libby approached her. "Are you Lexi's mom and aunt?"

Bernie laughed and shook her head. "No."

"Do I know you?" Selma asked.

"Probably not," Bernie said. "My sister and I run a shop called A Little Taste of Heaven."

"I was in there once. You guys have great cinnamon rolls." Selma took a sip of her hot chocolate. "So do you two have someone playing on one of the teams?" she asked, gesturing with her cup.

"No, we don't," Libby said. "We have a question about a recent accident."

Selma looked blank. "What accident?"

"It happened a few days ago. An elderly lady named Millie Piedmont ran into a tree and died," Bernie said. "You might have seen it on TV."

Selma bobbed her head. "I remember reading about that. That was terrible. Just terrible. They should put a sign up there."

"Yes, they should," Libby agreed.

Selma looked from Libby to Bernie and back again. "But I don't understand what that has to do with me?" Selma said as she put her cup down and recapped her thermos.

"We're hoping you can answer a question for us," Bernie told her.

"About the accident?" Selma asked.

"Yes," Bernie said.

"I don't see what I can tell you," Selma answered, her eyes straying to the rink. "Good assist," she yelled out to a skinny girl decked out in a blue shirt with stitching that read "The Bobcats." "My daughter," she explained.

"I figured," Bernie said.

"But what does this have to do with me?" Selma asked as she kept her eyes on her daughter, who was battling a larger girl for the puck.

Libby began. "Well, the person who reported the accident had just left your house and we . . ."

Selma frowned and interrupted. "You must have the wrong person."

"No. She gave the police your name," Libby told her, "and you guys are the only Minces in the phone book."

"Then the policeman heard wrong," Selma declared.

"I'm pretty sure he didn't," Libby said.

"Listen," Selma said to them. "I think I can tell you with one hundred percent certainty we did not have any visitors to our house then. I would have known. I was home making dinner." Selma put her hand up to her mouth. "It's okay, honey," she yelled. "You'll be fine."

Bernie and Libby both followed her gaze and saw Selma's daughter sprawled on the ice.

"Now, if you'll excuse me," Selma said to them as she started down the bleachers. "My daughter needs me."

Bernie and Libby looked at each other.

"Well, this certainly puts things in a whole different light," Libby said as she watched Selma descend to the rink.

"So the Good Samaritan turns out not to be so good, after all," Bernie commented. "I wonder what Matt's going to say?"

"Let's call him up and find out," Libby suggested.

Chapter 31

"So you're telling me that the woman lied to me," Matt said. He'd been on his way to sign out when Libby and Bernie flagged him down. "And that she was the one who caused the accident?"

"Do you have another explanation?" Libby inquired in turn.

Instead of answering, Matt took a sip of his coffee. "How did you find me, anyway?" he asked Libby.

"Denise," Libby replied.

"I'm going to have to give her a good talking to," Matt said.

"It's not her fault," Libby said. "Bernie told her it was an emergency."

Matt scowled. "If she's going to marry a cop, she's going to have to learn to be a little more closed-mouthed."

"So," Bernie said, "we were wondering . . ."

"The answer is no," Matt said.

"To what?" Bernie asked, interrupting. "I haven't asked you anything."

"Yet. *Yet* being the operative word here. I'm saving you the trouble. I'm being proactive. I'm not giving you the driver's name."

Bernie put her hand to her chest. "I would never ask you to do that. That's confidential information. You could get in trouble for telling me that."

"Exactly," Matt said.

"*If* anyone found out. But they won't," Bernie said.

"You know this how?" Matt demanded.

"Because we won't tell anyone, will we, Libby?"

"Cross my heart and hope to die," Libby said.

"Absolutely not," Matt said.

"Don't you want to right a wrong?" Libby asked.

"No. I want to get home, change, and go bowling."

"Millie really was killed, you know," Bernie said. "Maybe on purpose, maybe not. But the event that caused the accident was engineered."

"We've been over this before. You have not one shred of proof to support your allegations," Matt replied.

"What about the woman who called in the accident not being where she said she was?"

"What about it?" Matt retorted. "Maybe she was having an assignation with someone. Maybe she'd gone to buy dope. Maybe she was running away from home. There are lots of reasons she could have lied to me."

"You don't actually believe that, do you?" Bernie asked.

"Yes. As it happens, I do," Matt replied.

"I'll give you three pies," Bernie cooed.

Matt snorted. "You think I can be bought for a pie?"

"Okay," Libby said, upping the ante. "Then how about I cater a dinner for you and Denise?" She could see Matt was weakening. "A romantic dinner. She loves our chocolate mousse."

"So you're bribing me?" Matt said. "I want to be clear about this."

"I like to think of it as a mutually beneficial exchange of services," Bernie said. "And," she added, "what if Bernie and I are right? What if this person did have something to do with Millie's death?"

Matt thought that over for a moment. Maybe Bernie *was* right. "Fine," he said.

"Fine, what?" Bernie asked.

"You win." The moment Matt said those words he regretted them, but it was too late to take them back. *What have I done*, he thought as he gave Bernie and Libby the witness's name, address, and phone number. "But this information didn't come from me," he warned.

"Absolutely not," Bernie said.

"Never," Libby said.

"Because if this comes out, I'll have you arrested," Matt told them.

"For what?" Bernie demanded.

"I don't know," Matt said. "But trust me, I'll think of something."

"Roberta T. Hall," Bernie said, repeating the name Matt had given them. "Does it ring any bells?"

Libby shook her head. "Not with me."

"Me either. Well, let's see what Ms. Roberta T. Hall has to say," Bernie said as she pulled out onto the road and drove in the direction of the address Matt had given her.

Five Weatherford Lane was located close to the Thruway, two miles outside of Longely.

"I feel like I'm back in San Francisco," Bernie commented, looking at the row of Victorian mansions nestled together. "They look like Painted Ladies."

The houses all had wreaths on their doors and candles in their windows, and the block blazed with light in the gray afternoon. Bernie parked in front of 5 Weatherford, and she and Libby got out, walked up the carefully shoveled walk, and rang the bell. A few minutes later, a pleasant-looking lady dressed in an obviously hand-knitted sweater answered the door.

"Yes?" the woman said, over the strains of Handel's *Messiah*.

Bernie smiled at her. "We're sorry to bother you, but we're looking for a Roberta T. Hall."

The lady looked confused. "Who?"

"Roberta T. Hall. We were told she lived here," Libby said.

The woman shook her head. "Sorry, but you must have made a mistake. There's no one here by that name."

"Are you sure?" Bernie said. "We need to talk to her about a family matter. It's important."

The woman smiled. "I'm positive. The only person who's lived here recently was a boarder, and he moved out five months ago."

"Is it possible that you took in the woman we need to speak to before that?"

The woman shook her head. "Oh no," she said. "You see, I never take in girls. They're just too much trouble. These days they're wilder than the boys. Now, if there isn't anything else . . ."

Bernie shook her head, and the woman closed the door. "What do you bet that the cell number that Matt gave us doesn't work either," she said to Libby while they walked back down the porch steps.

"I'm not betting," Libby said as she watched her sister dialing the number.

"It's been disconnected," Bernie announced.

"Now there's a surprise," Libby said as they reached the van. "What now?" she said as she got in.

"Good question," Bernie replied. She sighed. She didn't want to face Amber.

"What are we going to tell Amber?" Libby said, echoing her sister's thoughts.

Bernie sighed. "I wish I knew." Then she had an idea. "This woman's last name is Hall, right?"

"So?" Libby said.

"Maybe she and Alma Hall are related."

"Bernie, do you know how many Halls there are around here?"

"A lot, Libby. But do you have a better idea?"

Libby admitted that she didn't.

"I mean," Bernie continued, "maybe she knows who this woman is."

"I guess it's worth a try," Libby said doubtfully.

"It's better than calling all the Halls in the phone book," Bernie commented as she drove off to Alma's house. "Which we can't even do anymore since most people don't have home phones," she added.

Chapter 32

Bernie and Libby pulled up to Alma's house twenty minutes later, parked, and knocked on her door.

"We're just about to eat," Alma said when she answered.

"I just have a quick question for you," Bernie said.

Alma glared at her. "Haven't you done enough damage already?"

"Damage?" Bernie asked.

"Yes, damage. Going about highlighting all these issues that people have forgotten about."

"I'm sorry," Libby said. She didn't want to stand here and debate the issue. "Do you know a Roberta T. Hall by any chance?"

"No," Alma said. "I don't."

"Are you sure?" Bernie asked.

Alma snorted. "Of course, I'm sure."

"Maybe she's a second or third cousin?" Libby asked. "A distant relative?"

"The only relative I have is my nephew."

"Is he here?" Bernie asked.

"Yes, he is," Alma answered. "As a matter of fact, he lives over the garage."

Bernie was just about to ask Alma if she could speak to him when she heard a door slam. The noise sounded as if it had come from the back of the house.

Alma spun around. "Robert," she cried. "Did you just go out? Dinner's going to be on the table in a second."

Bernie and Libby looked at each other. The same idea occurred to both of them. Robert. Roberta. This was too much of a coincidence, and like their father, neither of them believed in coincidences.

"Your nephew must have heard us talking," Bernie said. "Guess he doesn't want to meet us."

"I certainly can't fault him for that," Alma told them stiffly.

"What's your nephew's middle name?" Libby asked Alma.

"Terry," Alma replied. "Why? What's that got to do with anything?"

"Terry Hall," Bernie said. "He went to Longely Central, didn't he?"

"For a while. And then he moved down to Charlotte with my sister," Alma said. "Why?"

Bernie held up her hand. "Bear with me for a second. Does he have a twin sister by any chance?"

"No," Alma told her.

"Are you sure?" Libby asked.

"Of course, I'm sure," Alma told them.

Bernie looked at Libby. "Are you thinking what I'm thinking?" she asked.

"I certainly am," her sister replied. She turned to Alma. "We need to speak to your nephew."

Alma looked totally bewildered. "What are you talking about?" Alma said to Libby. "I was just about to put dinner on the table."

"That might have to wait," Bernie said to her. Then she turned to Libby. "I bet he's heading toward the garage," she said.

"I think so too." She and Bernie turned and sprinted toward it.

They arrived just as the garage door was going up. From where they were standing they could see that the vehicle lights were on and the engine was running. *God, I hope he doesn't run over me,* Bernie thought as she ran around the car and yanked the driver's side door open.

The man who was sitting behind the driver's wheel bore a remarkable resemblance to Penelope's assistant, Terri.

Except for the sex and the fact that his head was shaved, that is.

"Get out of the car," Bernie ordered.

He hesitated. Bernie could see from the action of his hand that he was about to shift into reverse. So could Libby.

"Don't do it," she cautioned. "You'll just make things worse."

Alma's nephew laughed harshly. "How can things be worse?"

"Believe me, they can be. We know you didn't mean to cause Millie's death."

"I didn't," Alma's nephew said.

"That's why you came back, isn't it?" Bernie said, handing him a way out.

He nodded. "I didn't mean for things to come out the way they did. I really didn't. But at least I called the police. That should count for something."

"It will," Bernie said encouragingly.

"Penelope says I shouldn't have done that. She says I was a fool."

Alma came up behind them. "What's going on here?" she asked after she'd paused to catch her breath. "I don't understand."

"Perhaps Terry will explain," Libby said. "That's Terry with a *y* instead of an *i*, correct?"

"What do you mean, 'Terry'? His name is Robert. Terry

is his middle name. I already told you that," Alma said. Her voice had begun to quaver.

"I go by Terri with an *i*, Auntie," Terri said gently.

"But that's a girl's name," Alma objected.

"I know," Terri replied. He took a deep breath and let it out. "I wanted to tell you before, but I didn't know how, so I'm saying it now."

Alma clutched at her cardigan. "What are you saying now?"

Terri closed his eyes. "I'm a transvestite," he said, the words coming out in a rush.

"Oh, dear," Alma said before she fainted dead away.

Chapter 33

"I don't get it," Amber said.

It was the afternoon after the *Baking for Life* contest had taped, and she, Bernie, Bree Nottingham, Libby, and Sean were sitting in the apartment above the shop, nibbling on Millie's Majestic Meltaways.

"These really are good," Sean said as he helped himself to another one. "Millie would have been proud of you," he told Amber.

Amber brightened. "You think so?"

"Definitely," Libby said. "Using one hundred percent virgin coconut oil for the shortening is brilliant."

"They were the best cookies in the contest," Bernie said. "You won fair and square."

"But Rose is contesting the results. She says that she should have won, and that this whole thing was rigged," Amber cried.

"Well, in a sense it was," Sean said as he added a little more cream to his coffee. "But it doesn't matter because your cookies were still the best."

"I don't understand what you mean," Amber told him. "I don't understand anything," she added plaintively.

"What's there not to get?" Bernie said. "The whole thing is perfectly straightforward. Not."

Libby put her hands on the small of her back and pushed. She'd been rolling out pie dough for the last four hours, and her lower back ached.

"From what's come out, the whole thing was Penelope's idea," Libby said. "Like she told us. She wanted to increase ratings, and she figured this would be the ticket."

"But why pick my aunt?" Amber asked.

"Ah," Bernie said. "That's where things begin to get tricky. Evidently, Terri told her boss the story about Alma trying to get Millie to stop driving, and that gave Penelope the idea."

"No good deed goes unpunished," Sean murmured.

"Exactly," Bernie said.

Amber wrinkled her nose. "It gave her the idea for the deer target? She doesn't strike me as the kind of person who would know about that sort of thing."

"Ordinarily you would be right," Libby said. "But she'd just finished shooting a program about bow hunters, and the production company had a couple of extra ones lying around. So Penelope told her idea to Terri and he, being the ambitious, favor-currying person that he is, figured out where to put it. After all, before he got a job with the production company, he lived here."

"At 5 Weatherford Lane," Bernie interjected, taking up the narrative. "Terri was the detail man. He knew from his aunt that Millie got easily rattled. Maybe she'd withdraw from the competition and his aunt would win. From his point of view, it was a win-win situation all the way around. He'd get props from Penelope, maybe even a promotion, his aunt would have a better chance at winning the contest, and Millie would get paid back a little of what she deserved."

"Only things didn't work out that way," Sean observed.

"No, they didn't," Bernie said. "Terri called Millie earlier and told her her cookies didn't have a chance of winning—he was just letting her know on the QT, as it were. Naturally, that got Millie really upset. Then Penelope called and said she was just making sure that Millie was leaving because she didn't want her to be late. Which infuriated Millie. And then Terri went out and set up the deer target and pulled off to the side of the road and waited.

"He heard the crash," Libby continued as Bernie paused to eat a small piece of the lemon bar that Alma had baked. "According to him, he waited and he waited and when he didn't hear anything, he went to check on Millie. She was passed out."

"So he took the cookies," Amber said.

"And hid the deer target in the woods," Bernie added.

"Why didn't he take it home with him?" Amber asked.

"It was quicker for him to drag it into the woods than to take it apart and load it in his trunk."

"Then he called 911?" Amber asked.

Libby nodded. "And waited for the police to come. He told me he didn't want anything like this to happen, and I believe him," Libby said to Amber. "The fact that he stuck around and waited for the cops to come proves it. He said he just wanted to make sure that Millie was all right."

"It really is a pity, and so unnecessary too," Bree said, breaking her silence. She took a sip of her coffee and delicately replaced the cup on its saucer.

"I'm not sure I'd use that word," Libby said.

"Unnecessary in the sense that Stanley told Penelope this was the last season of this show unless the ratings picked up," Bree explained. "She could have come up with a different strategy. This one was just nuts."

"To say the least," Sean said dryly.

"Why didn't you tell us?" Bernie asked Bree.

"Tell you what?" Bree inquired.

"What was going on," Libby replied.

"But I did," Bree protested. "At least I hinted."

Libby gave her a puzzled glance. "If you did, I didn't hear it."

"Well," Bree explained, "I didn't tell you because I wasn't sure. I surmised what happened from a conversation with Stanley. But like I said, I did throw you a hint."

"Which was what?" Bernie demanded.

Bree sat up straighter. "There's no reason to take that tone with me. I was trying to help."

Bernie apologized. "Sorry," she said. "Go on."

"I did try and tell you," Bree insisted. "I mentioned the word *soul*, and *alma* is the word for *soul* in Spanish. I was trying to point you in the right direction."

Bernie shook her head. She didn't think she would have gotten that one in a thousand years. Maybe two thousand.

"So what's going to happen to everyone?" Amber asked, interrupting Bernie's thoughts.

"My guess," Sean said, "is that Penelope will be tried on reckless endangerment charges, and Terri will be allowed to plead to a lesser charge since he gave Penelope up. He'll probably end up with probation."

Everyone was silent for a moment. Then Amber said, "What's going to happen to Terri?"

"My dad just told you," Libby said

"With his aunt," Amber explained. "About the whole . . . cross-dressing thing."

"Well, she bailed him out," Sean said, "so she obviously got over her shock."

"But you told me she fainted when he told her that he was a transvestite," Amber said.

"That's true," Bernie said. "But evidently Alma's gotten over that."

"Why do you say that?" Amber asked Bernie.

"Because she told me last night that she was taking Terri down to New York on a shopping trip. Evidently he likes my style, so she wanted to know where I buy my stuff. After all," Bernie continued, "he is her only nephew. I guess," Bernie said, looking at Bree, who was decked out in a black-and-white tweed Chanel suit, "clothes really do make the man. Or, in this case, the woman."

Amber laughed. "I've always thought so." She pointed to Millie's recipe book. It had been lying on the doorstep of the shop when Libby had opened that morning. "I'm just really glad I got this back." She turned to Sean. "Who do you think returned it?"

"Don't know," Sean said. "I suppose it could be any of the Christmas Cookie Exchange Club ladies. Does it matter? Because if it does I . . ."

Amber interrupted. "No. No. It's fine. Having the recipe book back is all I care about. Not that all of Millie's recipes are that great, but they're hers and that's what counts. It's a sentimental thing."

"Amen to that," Sean said as he ate another Meltaway.

Recipes

The following recipes are fun to both make and eat.

Christmas Mice

This recipe is from Betsy Scheu, who told me she used to make these with her goddaughter at Christmas. When you look at the recipe you'll see why kids would love these at any time of the year.

1 jar maraschino cherries with stems
1 package Hershey's chocolate kisses
1 package slivered almonds
Same number of chocolate kisses as cherries
1 small tube white cake-decorating icing
1 small tube red cake-decorating icing

Unwrap the kisses and set them aside. Remove the cherries from their juice, rinse, and set them aside.

Melt chocolate in a double boiler or in a glass bowl over a pan of hot water; when melted, take off heat. Dip 4 to 6 cherries in chocolate until they are completely coated except for their stems. Set them on wax paper with the stems positioned horizontally.

Attach a chocolate kiss to the side of the cherry that's opposite the "tail." (The chocolate kiss is the head, the cherry is the body, and the stem is the tail.) Place two slivered almond "ears" between the kiss and the cherry. Continue to dip cherries (body) and attach kisses (heads) and almonds (ears) until you've used all the cherries.

Place two small dots of white icing on the kisses where the mouse's eyes would be. Place a small dot of red icing on the end of the chocolate kiss for the nose, and add a red dot on top of each eyeball. Put the mice aside to let the chocolate harden, or place them in the refrigerator if time is short.

Cookie-Cutter Ornaments

This recipe and the one for Almond Crescents, below, come from Sheryl Madlin. This one is another fun project to do with a child around holiday time.

1 cup cornstarch
2 cups baking soda
1½ cups water

Put the ingredients in a pot, stir until smooth, cover the pot, and cook until thick, so that the mixture looks like dry mashed potatoes. Take the pot off the heat, roll the dough out onto a surface, and cover with a cloth until cool. Use cookie cutters to stamp out shapes. Bake at 250 degrees until hard. Decorate.

Almond Crescents

These are your classic Christmas cookie.

1½ cups soft butter
½ cup sugar
½ cup ground almonds
1 cup flour
½ tsp salt
1 tsp vanilla or almond extract
Confectioners' sugar

Cream butter. Slowly add sugar, beating well until light and fluffy. Add nuts, flour, salt, and extract until dough forms. Break off pieces of dough and roll into crescent shapes. Bake at 300 degrees for 10 minutes. Take out of the oven and dredge in confectioners' sugar.

Christmas Fruit Drops

The following recipes are from Carmel Ruffo, an excellent and prolific baker. Like my grandmother, she cooks by eye, taste, and smell. But luckily for us, unlike my grandmother, she also writes things down.

1 cup shortening
2 cups brown sugar
2 eggs
⅔ cup buttermilk
3⅔ cups flour
1 tsp baking soda
1 tsp salt
1⅓ cups broken pecans
2 cups candied cherries, halved
2 cups dates, cut into very small pieces
Pecan halves

Mix shortening, sugar, and eggs. Stir in buttermilk. Blend together all dry ingredients. Add to wet ones. Stir in pecans, cherries, and dates. Chill dough for at least an hour.

Heat oven to 400 degrees. Drop rounded teaspoonfuls of dough 2 inches apart on a lightly greased baking sheet. Place a pecan half on top of each cookie. Bake 8 to 10 minutes. Makes 8 dozen cookies.

Carm's Chocolate Christmas Cookies

8 cups flour
2 cups sugar
½ cup cocoa
1½ cup shortening
2 tsp baking powder
½ tsp salt
1 tsp cinnamon
1½ tsp cloves
3 shots whiskey
1 tsp vanilla extract
2 cups milk

Mocha Glaze

1½ cups confectioners' sugar
2½ tbsp melted butter
2 tbsp unsweetened cocoa
2½ tbsp unsweetened brewed coffee
½ tbsp salt

To prepare the glaze, combine sugar, butter, cocoa, coffee, and salt; stir until well blended. Add a little more hot coffee or hot water to get the desired consistency.

For the cookies, mix all dry ingredients in a bowl. Stir in milk, whiskey, and vanilla and mix with your hands into a giant ball. Wrap dough in wax paper and chill in refrigerator for 1 hour. Remove dough, and roll with hands into 1½-inch balls. Place on a greased baking sheet and bake at 375 degrees for 10 minutes or until a tester comes out clean. Dip cookies in glaze immediately after removing from the oven. Let cookies stand on a rack until cool. Makes about 5 dozen cookies.

Filled Cookies

6 cups flour
3 eggs
1 cup milk
2 cups sugar
1 cup shortening
5 tsp baking powder
1 tsp salt
1½ tsp vanilla

Filling

1 lb dates
1 lb figs
1 lb raisins
1 cup white wine

Simmer the filling ingredients together for 10 minutes and put aside to cool.

To make the dough, combine all the dry ingredients, cut in shortening, then add eggs, followed by other ingredients. Form dough into a ball, cover with wax paper, and refrigerate for an hour.

When dough is ready, roll it out into a rectangle and cut it into three even strips. Put a line of filling down the center of each strip and pinch the cut ends of the dough together to hold in the filling. Bake at 400 degrees for 10 minutes. Remove and cut strips into 1-inch slices.

Italian Christmas Cookies

2½ cups all-purpose flour
1 cup granulated sugar
¼ cup soft butter
½ cup whipping cream
2 tsp baking powder
1 tsp almond extract
½ tsp salt
1 egg, separated
1¾ cups confectioners' sugar
½ tsp almond extract
½ cup chopped almonds
½ cup chopped red and green cherries

Mix together flour, granulated sugar, butter, whipping cream, baking powder, 1 teaspoon almond extract, salt, and egg yolk. Work well with hands to blend. Cover and refrigerate for an hour or more. Heat oven to 375 degrees. Divide dough in half. Roll each half into an 8-by-6-inch rectangle on a floured board. Square off corners. Place on greased cookie sheet.

Beat egg white until foamy. Gradually add confectioners' sugar and 1/2 teaspoon almond extract. Beat until stiff and glossy; spread onto rectangles. Sprinkle nuts and cherries on top. Cut into 1-by-1-inch rectangles. Bake for 10 minutes. Cut again.